The  over the seated members of TALON Force, then relayed the desperate situation.

"The president of Zimbabwe has just ordered the arrest of every white farmer in the country. If there is another attack on cattle anywhere in the world, then those farmers and their families are going to be put into holding camps. And that's not all. . . ."

Stan and Jack shifted uncomfortably in their seats. What did a bunch of dead cows have to do with them?

The president continued. "The Indian government has stated that if any cattle in India are attacked, they will nuke a major city in Zimbabwe, while the Pakistanis have stated that if India attacks Zimbabwe, Pakistan will attack India. And to top it all off, the white militia groups in South Africa have threatened civil war, and I quote, 'For every white farmer arrested by the government, we will attack and destroy one of the Black Townships.' Now, is there anyone left who still doubts the severity of the situation?"

No one moved.

TALON FORCE

SLAUGHTERHOUSE

Cliff Garnett

A SIGNET BOOK

SIGNET
Published by New American Library, a division of
Penguin Putnam Inc., 375 Hudson Street,
New York, New York 10014, U.S.A.
Penguin Books Ltd, 27 Wrights Lane,
London W8 5TZ, England
Penguin Books Australia Ltd, Ringwood,
Victoria, Australia
Penguin Books Canada Ltd, 10 Alcorn Avenue,
Toronto, Ontario, Canada M4V 3B2
Penguin Books (N.Z.) Ltd, 182–190 Wairau Road,
Auckland 10, New Zealand

Penguin Books Ltd, Registered Offices:
Harmondsworth, Middlesex, England

First published by Signet, an imprint of New American Library,
a division of Penguin Putnam Inc.

First Printing, November 2000
10 9 8 7 6 5 4 3 2 1

People sleep peacefully in their beds at night
only because rough men stand ready
to do violence on their behalf.

—George Orwell

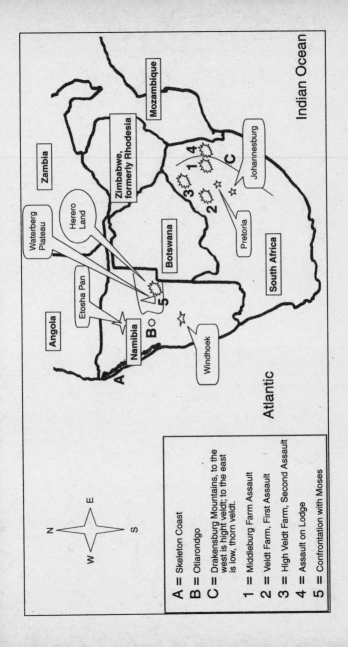

Prologue

A cow stood near a water tank, streams of saliva dangling from its chin. Every few seconds the muscles in the cow's neck and body convulsed and her head jerked back and to one side—as if trying to see something behind her. The old Hereford raised her nose into the air and snorted. The spray of saliva, sticky and airborne, landed on the stiff carcass of a second cow. Flies launched into the air in protest. With a sudden bellow of great pain, the cow hunched her back and fell violently onto her side, feet thrust straight out and quivering. Slowly, as if the air was being let out of a balloon, she relaxed and died, her legs still trembling in the final spasms of death. Next to the dead cow's body was her yearling calf, already fallen victim to death's rigors.

Crows hopped from one body to another, quarreling raucously, in a pasture littered with bloated, lifeless bodies.

May 27, 6 p.m.
Macintosh Dairy, Tiverton, England

Algie Macintosh noticed the wild-eyed rush of Clover into the milking parlor. She'd always been an easy milker—

never a problem in the stanchions. Now he couldn't get her to stand still. She had no interest in her feed although she'd rushed to her stall in the milk line. The cow bellowed, rushing forward only to back out of her stall in a rhythmic display of irritation.

"What's the matter then, ye bloody bugger?" He slipped into the small milking stall next to the agitated Jersey. He caught the milk cow's halter and pulled her head around. The last thing he would see was the raw terror in the normally gentle milk cow's eyes as she yanked her head away and swung into him, knocking him into the wall.

May 28, 4 a.m.
train station, Yonezawa, Japan

The glass felt cool and smooth against his work-roughened fingertips. Wilhelm Von Heich lovingly fingered the vial concealed in his pocket as he walked through the crowded train station. Towering a foot above the local Japanese, the powerfully built, blond Boer was oblivious to their sidelong looks of open curiosity. He refused to think of what would happen to the well-tended cattle of the Japanese farmer. Von Heich knew his own cattle were safe at home. He focused only on his mission and waded through the throng of people. He didn't hear the native, melodic language when he rented his car. Rather, he was hearing the jubilant cries of his compatriots—cheering for the New Rhodesia.

May 28, 0900 hours
Pentagon subbasement, Washington, D.C.

The scene pulled away and merged into the lifeless bodies of cows. Hundreds of cattle, most of them dead, a few still standing but dying on their feet and toppling over. The next scene was an overhead view of a feedlot, the pictures being taken from a light plane. Carcasses of dead cattle covered the entire feedlot and spread into the pastures beyond.

"The total dead is just over three thousand head," said presidential aide Jane Whaite-Worthington. "The toll in Japan isn't as high but is more frightening."

The image on the television flickered and steadied into a single image of a dead cow. The camera panned across the cow, then pulled away to show another dozen dead, gruesomely bloated bodies. "This was at one farm, the next scene is a farm three miles away," Whaite-Worthington said. "These cows all died within an hour of each other. The Japanese have cordoned off the entire area and haven't reported any new deaths in the last twelve hours. The next scene is from a dairy near Tiverton in England."

The image changed again. This time it was of a steady stream of milk draining from a huge, stainless steel collection tank into the sewage system. "The attack hit the region's largest dairy farm," she said. "Just to be safe, all the milk collected from the cows before they started dying has been dumped."

"Did anyone test the milk before dumping it?" General Jack Krauss asked.

"Yes, it was clean but no one wanted to take any chances and put the public at risk."

"Okay, what is it? What's killing a bunch of cows?"

"A virus, specifically the Anita virus, General," she said. "We want you to prepare to dispatch one of your TALON Force teams to the location of the virus and return it to this country before there are more deaths."

General Krauss leaned forward and focused on her. "Your boss wants me to send the finest group of fighting men and women in the country on a wild-goose chase to, as I heard you say it, *return* a virus to this country."

The look on Krauss's face pulled into a tight sneer. "That implies it has been stolen *from* this country and if it has been, I would think that it would be a job for the FBI or some other group. *Not* TALON."

"Sir, it is a job for TALON Force."

"Ma'am," Krauss said, his voice starting to break with tension. "That's a hell of a waste of our resources. TALON Force was created to function as a surgical tool to ensure our national security. I'm not sure that a bunch of dead cows is a threat to national security. A few years ago there was a problem with mad cows in England. Maybe it's the same thing."

"This isn't the same thing," she said.

"How do you know?"

"The cattle deaths all occurred at nearly the same time, although in different parts of the world. But, there's more . . ."

"I'm listening," Krauss said.

"Just before the first cows died, the owners of each operation—the Wyoming feedlot, the Japanese cattle farm, and the English dairy—all received a phone call. A female voice told them that their cows were dying."

General Krauss leaned back in his chair. "Animal rights fanatics?"

"We don't think so."

"Who?"

"Are you familiar with the political history of southern Africa?"

Krauss nodded.

"We believe that a group of South Africans, probably a splinter group of the Boer Nationalist Movement—pre-Mandela—have managed to obtain a bovine virus from the University of Northern Colorado."

"How is this a national security crisis?" Krauss asked.

"We think this was a demonstration of what the group is capable of doing with the virus. Just an example. If our hunch is right, they want the old Rhodesia restored."

"What do you base your hunch on?"

"The date and timing."

The general waited for more information.

"Do you know what the thirty-first of May is?'

Krauss wrinkled his forehead. "The Pretoria resolution?"

"Exactly. One hundred years ago the Boers accepted the British peace terms ending the Boer War."

Krauss didn't reply.

"We think they are going to start killing more cattle."

"I still don't see the security crisis."

Whaite-Worthington's voice climbed a half an octave. "Do you have any concept of exactly how important cattle are in the world?"

"I like a good steak."

"General, cattle are not just for food. By-products are used in medicine. The nation's agricultural industry is tied heavily to cattle production. If the cattle industry is destroyed, our agricultural economy would be devastated. That's just a scratch on the surface of what's at stake here."

Krauss rubbed his chin with his prosthetic hand, the real one having been blown off in combat, so the story goes. NSA computer expert Sam Wong watched him. He knew the general was always reluctant to commit TALON teams. They were too valuable and there were so few of them. Out of the hundreds who'd been tested and trained, less than fifty troopers had made it. The loss of even one member was a constant worry to the general. Without turning around, Krauss said, "Wong, what do you think?"

"We don't know who to stop, yet."

"We've got some leads," Whaite-Worthington said. "As soon as we know who we're up against and where they are, the president wants a TALON team to respond."

"Having a team waiting for an operation is dangerous," Krauss said.

"If our hunch is right about the date, and they do issue
a formal set of demands, the zero hour for those demands can be expected to be Friday afternoon, Pretoria
time—probably the exact moment of the anniversary of
the meeting at Vereeniging. That leaves us approximately fifty hours to find the terrorists and recover the
virus. This crisis demands more resolution and determination than you normally find in third-world neighbor-
hood cops, General."

Sam didn't answer. Silence filled the room. The president could order the team to go. He hadn't. Yet. He
could still send the order down and then Krauss would
lose control of the operation. Experience had taught the
general to keep the politicians out of the operational
phase as much as possible.

"Wong."

"Yes, sir."

"Put Eagle Team on call. Give them twenty-four hours'
training time on the mission."

"Where?"

"Denver. We'll use Buckley."

"Yes, sir." Sam started to stand up.

"One more thing." Krauss directed his comment to
Jane Whaite-Worthington.

"Yes, General Krauss?"

"Mrs. Worthington," Krauss said. "Give Sam everything you have, including the history of this virus."

"Of course, General."

"Ma'am," Krauss said, his voice low and menacing, "I
don't want *anything* kept from my team. I don't want
any surprises."

She nodded her acquiescence.

Sam turned for the door and overheard Krauss telling
Jane Whaite-Worthington that he hoped he wasn't sending his team out unnecessarily. "I don't think your boss

understands that these people are not Boy Scouts but the best this nation has to offer."

"He understands that, General. I don't think you understand how serious this could become."

Sam closed the door before he heard the general's response. General Krauss's pretty secretary looked up at Sam.

"You going?"

Sam nodded.

"Good luck."

Sam nodded again and hurried toward his own office. He'd send the phone calls from his computer terminal. Each team member would receive the call on their pager and would know that it was a summons. The numeric display was a code telling which airline would be holding tickets for an impending mission. As each member of TALON Force Eagle Team deplaned at Denver International Airport, an MP in plainclothes would meet them and drive them to Buckley Air National Guard Base in the Denver suburb of Aurora, Colorado. Sam planned to brief the team himself.

Chapter 1

Sam watched the team arrive, one by one, at Buckley. The Denver skyline dominated the western horizon and to the east was the high prairie of Colorado. The casual visitor to the airbase would never guess that it is one of the nation's most secure, unless they wandered off the beaten path. Those adventurous souls would eventually find one of the numerous chain-link fences surrounding one of the several special-operations centers built on the base. There, they would encounter Buckley's security and if they questioned the MPs, they could meet their god. Few civilians realized the sensitive nature of the airbase and its shoot-to-kill policy for intruders.

That's why TALON Force was meeting here. Security was guaranteed—no questions asked. If the team needed anything, their special requirements were easily filled— be it weapons, information, or other specialized equipment. With DIA minutes away, it was easy to leave Buckley for any place in the world. The near proximity to the Denver Federal Center afforded TALON ready access to as much of the Federal government's intelligence as they had in Washington.

The team, however, wasn't meeting in one of the secure compounds. Instead they found themselves in a long, single-story brick building that belonged to a Ma-

rine Air Group. Within the building's walls, a Marine
reservist and a handful of active-duty Marines studied
satellite photos that had been taken around the world.
The building was secure and had all the equipment the
team would need to plan for what General Krauss was
calling "Operation Bovine."

Sam sighed heavily and opened the door of his rented
car. He walked to the brick building. After the briefing,
Major Travis Barrett would take over the operation. Sam
pushed the door open and went into the foyer and then
passed through a long hallway. He walked slowly past
the doors to various offices before he finally stopped in
front of the briefing room and pushed the door open.
His six fellow members of TALON Force Eagle Team
were waiting for him. He knew that when he told the
team what this mission was, they would stare at him in-
credulously. Why, they would rightfully wonder, would
the most sophisticated and lethal team of specialists in
the United States be sent halfway around the world to
stop a bunch of crazies from killing cattle?

Because, Sam had practiced explaining, if TALON
Force doesn't stop it, in less than four days there will be
civil war in southern Africa and the European Common
Market will collapse.

Would that, Sam wondered, get the team's attention?

Inside the briefing room, Sam again realized the seriousness of their situation. A tall Marine sergeant in dress
blues stood at parade rest. His 9mm Baretta was hol-
stered in the pistol belt at his waist, but the flap wasn't
snapped. The sergeant held a leather briefcase in front
of him, secured to his wrist with a locked chain. Sam
walked to the Marine and handed him his ID. The Marine studied it then looked at Sam.

"You have the key, sir?"

Sam nodded and handed it to the Marine. He took the
key and inserted it in the lock on the handcuffs, turned
it, then put the key in his pocket. From his left breast

pocket the Marine took another key, one that looked almost identical, and inserted it in the same lock and turned it again. The lock popped open. The sergeant handed the key to Sam, snapped to attention, and marched toward the door. Sam knew that until he opened the door, the Marine would be standing in the hallway. No one would get inside, nor would anyone leave without Sam's permission.

Once the door was closed and locked, Sam turned to the members of the team. He smiled and said, "Our mission code name is 'Bovine.' The mission is to stop a group of fanatics from killing cattle." Sam watched the six other members of Eagle Team stir uncomfortably in their seats. Travis Barrett cleared his throat and looked at Lt. Commander Stan Powczuk, his second in command.

"You're kidding, right?" Jack DuBois guffawed. "You dragged us up here to chase cattle rustlers?" The big Marine captain had flown to Denver from his duty station in New Orleans at the 12th Naval District headquarters.

"Not cattle rustlers, Jack," Sam said to his closest friend. "We've got someone killing cows, thousands of cows, and not in one place."

Sam opened the briefcase and removed a stack of folders and a CD-ROM. He passed the folders out to everyone at the table. No one opened his or her folder until Sam put the CD in the computer under the podium and clicked on the PowerPoint program. The closed-circuit television screen jumped into life and Sam followed on the TV screen and his own folder by explaining what was appearing and how it all tied together.

"The photos on top," Sam began, "are of dead cattle in Wyoming. As you can see from the aerial shots, there were several thousand head killed. They all died within an hour after the first one. The next two photos are from England. This was a dairy. The shot of the man crushed by the cow shows you just how quickly they died. The last two photos were received just two hours ago from Japan. These cattle were in individual pens; each one was being carefully raised for the Japanese beef market. These cattle died in less than twenty minutes."

"How many cattle were killed?" Jennifer Olsen, the team's spook from Naval Intelligence, asked.

"We don't have a total count," Sam said.

"Why? I mean gawd damn, who in the hell wants to kill a bunch of cattle?"

Sam heard the anger in Travis Barrett's voice. He figured that it was because Travis was a Texan, and like to all good Texans, cattle were important.

"We'll get to that," Sam said. "If you'll turn to the briefing page, you'll get what we know to one hour ago."

Sam waited until everyone was looking at the same paper then started going down the list. "All of the cattle began dying at about the same time, which was eighteen hundred hours, Greenwich Mean time. That means this was a coordinated attack. All of the cattle died within one hour of the first death. The owners of the cattle each received a warning via telephone five minutes before the first cow died. The female caller's voice was in thick English, similar to British but different. We now suspect it was a tape recording originally made in South Africa."

Sam waited for questions. When none came he continued. "In about twelve hours the Japanese National Security Police will be arresting a South African. His name is Wilhelm Von Heich. Von Heich is from a cattle farm near Kopies, South Africa. He is of Boer extraction and his great-grandfather, during the Boer War, was hanged by the British. To this point, he's led a rather mundane life. As far as we can tell he's never been in serious trouble with the law. He arrived in Japan two days ago and took the train to Yonezawa. He then rented a Toyota and drove on to Takano. He is believed to have released a virus upwind of the farm where the cattle were killed. Since then, he's been driving aimlessly around the countryside. He holds a ticket for the ten-twenty p.m. train from Yonezawa to Tokyo. The Japanese police believe he will probably take a room at one of the *ryokans* near the train station and wait for the train."

"Why don't they just pick him up?" Stan Powczuk, Eagle Team's Navy SEAL, asked.

"The Japanese don't want an international incident if it can be avoided. All they have is circumstantial evidence—with one exception. Please remove the sealed envelope in your folder."

Sam waited. When the rustling of paper had stopped he looked at the team. "This next bit of information is what must be kept from the public, at all cost. Please open your envelope." There are times, Sam knew, when keeping something from the public was the only way to avoid panic. If the world knew the scope of the damage that was being done, no one could predict the outcome or the reaction of people.

Captain Sarah Greene, the team's biowarfare specialist, gasped loudly. "They've got to be insane!"

"Who?" Sam asked.

"The people who made this crap. What are they trying to do? I thought the Anita virus was to be destroyed."

"It was sent to Plum Island by the scientists at the University of Northern Colorado who developed it."

"Why?" Sarah demanded.

"Do you remember the way the Indians were defeated in this country?" Sam said.

"Firepower?" Travis said.

Sam shook his head slowly. "They were starved into submission. The government had an 'official-but-unofficial' policy of killing off the buffalo. Without the buffalo the tribes couldn't survive. Several years ago, about the same time as the mad cow scare in England, our government got the idea that in a future war it might be easier to beat an enemy if they didn't have any livestock for food. You know, an army travels on its stomach."

"That's not good enough, Sam," Sarah said.

Sam looked uncomfortable under Sarah's intense gaze. She suspected the truth. He stopped the computer program and looked at the team. "Somehow, either not all the virus got to Plum Island or some of it got off."

Sarah studied her folder then looked around the room and said, "According to this report, ten cc's of Anita mixed with a quart of common tap water can be sprayed into the air with a household atomizer and release enough virus to kill every cow exposed to it for the next six to eight hours."

"Uh-huh," Sam said.

Sarah shook her head and continued reading, then gasped again. "How did someone steal it?" she demanded.

"We're not sure," Sam said. "The FBI is working on that right now, but we've got an idea."

"Sam," Sarah said, leaning forward. "I know what this virus is and what it can do. Even if it was on Plum Island and the scientists there saved some, how did it get off the island?"

"There is an international student at the University of Northern Colorado who is missing. He's from South Africa. Our suspect in Japan lives and works on a South African ranch that is owned by our missing student's father. There's more information coming in now—scrambled but we'll get hard copy when it's in."

"So, if we know all that, then what are we doing here?" Travis asked.

"Eagle Team," Sam said slowly, "has been assigned two tasks. First, two of you will accompany me to Japan where we will collect our suspect to bring him here. With luck the FBI will also have the missing student in custody by then. From them, we hope to learn where the rest of the virus is located. Then we go get it."

"Doesn't sound like a team mission, yet," Travis said.

"There's more," Sam said. "As you can see, the FBI now believes twelve vials of the virus are missing. Each one contains one hundred cc's of the virus compound. Each vial can be reduced ten times, so the virus, without growing any more of it, can be spread liberally around the globe. You already know what it is capable of doing. If you would please return the information on the virus to the envelope and give them to me, that information will be destroyed."

Once Sam had the envelopes, he asked them to remove the last sheet of paper. Everyone read it and when each had finished, looked up at Sam. He returned to the PowerPoint screen. "One hundred years ago this Friday, the fate of most of southern Africa was sealed when the Boer War ended. It's a bitter day in the hearts of most Boers." Sam flipped to a screen showing the single demand of the terrorists.

"That's all they want? Their own country?" Jack said. "That's really not any of our business. The Boers already fought their own revolution and lost, first a hundred years ago, then in the nineteen eighties when they lost again. And why do they want Zimbabwe? Wasn't Rhodes on the side of the British?"

"Yes, he was. But, he founded Rhodesia and its fall from white minority to black rule in the early eighties and the name change from Rhodesia to Zimbabwe hasn't been forgotten. Some people don't ever stop fighting their war," Sam said. "They want Zimbabwe turned over to them by Friday, 1400 hours, Pretoria time, as a new Rhodesia, which is a slap to the British, or they will release the virus in two hundred locations around the globe. Between now and their deadline, they will produce one demonstration each day. Each demonstration will be in a different part of the world."

"That's a tall order for any terrorist group," Travis said. "What do we know about them?"

Sam smiled at Travis. "You get the operation folder, Travis."

Travis nodded and stood up. He walked to the front of the room, took a folder from Sam and sat back down to study it. Sam turned back to the group. "We have a planning and organization window of less than twenty hours. General Krauss has ordered that during that time, Jack, Jennifer, and I are going to Japan to escort our suspected terrorist back here."

"When do we leave?" Jack asked.

"Now," Sam said. "We've got three F-18 Bs waiting to fly us to Vandenburg in California. From there we're taking the X-37 to an air base near Tokyo. That'll put us on the ground in about six hours. With the date line, we're going to be jumping ahead a day so for now, the operation stays on Washington time."

"We picking the guy up?" Jack asked.

"The Japanese will make the arrest," Sam said. "Then they will turn him over to us at the gate of an air base to be specified later. Our job is to bring him back, but arrangements have been made for us to observe the arrest."

"Let's go," Jack said, and stood up.

The rest of the team, those not going to Japan, crowded around Travis. In a few hours they had to have a plan that included equipment lists, travel arrangements—every detail needed to be planned out. They would need to devise a way to stop an unknown group of South African extremists who were demanding their own country from killing off the world's bovine population. No one now had to tell them what was at stake.

May 29, 1600 hours
Yonezawa, Japan

Sam, Jen, and Jack were tired of traveling. The flight from L.A. to Tokyo had been rough. The L-1011 carrier plane had bounced and skipped through the air until reaching altitude. It then dropped the X-37 and its two rockets and ignited, pushing the plane into a sub-orbital flight. Unfortunately the air wasn't any better over Japan and the sweeping descent into Japanese airspace was equally rough. The small plane, landing like a glider, tossed in the sky like a giant leaf, leaving the team with jangled nerves.

"Next time I'm jumping in," Jen said, following Sam to a waiting car. Within minutes they were on their way to Yonezawa to meet their local contact, Toshi Kyoda, a member of the Japanese National Security Force in a *ryokan*, or hostel.

Sam smiled at Jack as he dropped his bag on the floor of their room. The paper-thin walls that separated them from Jen were not enough to impede conversation. "Hey, Jen," Sam said.

"Yeah?"

"Look how thin these futons are. They must not get many Western travelers here."

Jennifer chuckled. "If we were spending the night, Jack couldn't complain about the bed being too soft."

A strange voice from the hallway said, "We can arrange for softer mattress if you prefer."

"Excuse me?" Jen said questioningly.

As she spoke, Sam could hear the gentle swish of a weapon being drawn. He wondered what it was and how she'd managed to get it past the Japanese officials in customs. When he looked at Jack he was surprised to see the big Marine holding a deadly looking dagger made from some sort of nylon.

"I think," Sam said, "that is the voice of Mr. Kyoda."

"Correct," the voice said. "And I will refrain from future movement until those weapons are returned to rightful places."

"Can't be too careful," Jack said.

"I agree," Kyoda said. "But it is very unlikely that foreign man we are seeking would be kind enough to meet us here."

"Why haven't you picked him up?" Jack asked.

"When it is safe for me to enter, and keep my head, I will explain."

The sound of weapons being sheathed was clearly heard in the hall and Kyoda slid the door past the *shoji* screen of Sam and Jack's room. Sam bowed deeply as Kyoda stepped into the room. In his peripheral vision Sam watched Jack bow slightly, the big black man's eyes never leaving Kyoda. Sam wondered if it was Jack's defensive nature or maybe a lack of cultural knowledge. After formal introductions and greetings, they waited silently for Jen, who also bowed in a Jacklike manner to Kyoda. Sam decided it must be a combination of American defiance, cultural misunderstanding, and defensive wariness that kept the round-eyed Americans from indulging in the rigid Asian formality.

When everyone was settled on comfortable cushions, Kyoda smiled at the Americans. "I understand that I am to be your team's liaison in Japan—and other places if necessary."

"Then you should know what's next," Jack said.

"I do." When a new contact was made there was a short but foolproof identification system used by the team. He looked at Jack, who nodded for Jen to begin. She took a palm-sized reader from her handbag and placed it on the floor. Jennifer then pulled a small screen from the side of the reader and held it firmly in place. She looked at Jack and nodded. He pressed his thumb onto the screen and Jen pressed a key on the reader.

The connection to Washington's database was instant. A green light glowed momentarily and then the screen was blank. Jack removed his hand.

"Your turn," she said to Kyoda.

He leaned forward and pressed his thumb onto the screen. Once again the green light glowed and faded. Kyoda sat back and Jennifer watched the screen. After a few seconds of silence she smiled at Kyoda. "Welcome to TALON Force, Mr. Kyoda."

"Thank you," he said smiling, then asked, "If my prints had not matched, would I have left alive?"

"No," Jack said.

"I believe you," he said. "Your fame precedes you Captain DuBois. Japanese Intelligence has you listed as one of the most lethal men alive."

"I only do what I need to do," Jack said.

"For your government?" Kyoda asked.

"For my country."

"Those are two very different entities, Captain DuBois. Your government or your country?"

Jack looked at him without answering.

Sam looked at his friend's stockinged feet. They were massive, yet he'd seen the big man move as lightly as a cat. Amazing, Sam thought. He looks like he should be a bear but he's the most graceful and gentle man I know. He unconsciously leaned toward his massive black friend.

"What additional information do you have for us?" Jen asked.

Sam shifted his gaze to Jennifer. She'd neatly deflected what had threatened to become an ideological knife between the two men. Whether Kyoda intentionally challenged Jack's blackness or his loyalty, Sam wasn't sure. Kyoda, Sam realized, was deft with words. He wondered how Jack had taken the verbal thrust.

"Nothing has changed since your last briefing. We should all rest for next few hours," Kyoda said. "We will be picking up our terrorist just before he boards the ten-twenty."

Jack nodded. "How do we take him?"

"We will have security forces surround him at the station. When he is in the open they will place him under arrest and then escort him to your Air Force base in Yokohama."

"And then?"

"We have agreed to allow you and your companions to escort Mr. Von Heich to the United States where he will be detained, questioned, and I am sure, given a fair trial."

"Why aren't you keeping him?"

"Because we have an agreement with your president."

Sam knew there wasn't any need to pursue the issue. As for travel back, General Krauss would arrange it. All they had to do was check in using the satellite phone and they would have the drill. Sam waited to see what was next.

"What time's kick-off?" Jack asked.

Kyoda looked blankly at Jack. "I do not understand."

Jack smiled. "When do we get Von Heich?"

"The manager will bring you tea at nine p.m., if that is sufficient."

"It'll do," Jack said, standing. "Now, if there isn't anything else, I think I'll take advantage of that hot bath down the hall and then hit the hay."

Kyoda stood. "It will be a perfect exercise, DuBois-*san*."

"You ever hear of a dude named Murphy?" Jack asked.

"No, who is he?"

"Call him a philosopher," Jack said. "He once said that if anything can wrong, it will."

"You are saying?"

"I'm saying that since I get to take this guy back to the States and that I am supposed to observe this perfect exercise at that station, I want you to make sure there's a back-up plan."

"There is always back-up plan," Kyoda said. "I will return for you at nine p.m. Please rest until then." He bowed to the team, who returned the bow, and turned to leave.

The three stood silently until they were sure Kyoda was gone, although each of them was positive that whatever they said would be overheard by his people at the hostel.

"What do you think or our newest contact?" Jennifer asked.

"He seems sharp enough," Sam said.

Jack was quiet for a moment and then growled, "He reads too many fuckin' comic books." He turned for the door and the baths.

May 29, 2100 hours
Yonezawa, Japan

The team was discussing the soon-to-come action when the inn manager delivered a tray of hot tea and rice cakes to their room. A few minutes later Kyoda tapped on the screen and asked to enter. After formal greetings he told the team that a Western meal had been prepared for them.

"Steak and spuds?" Jack asked.

"Not quite," Kyoda said. "Crepes filled with sautéed shiitake mushrooms and covered in a light cream sauce." He waited for the team to finish preparing themselves for work. Sam knew he couldn't see a single weapon, but Kyoda must have known the team, at least Jack and Jen, were armed. He wondered if Kyoda thought of asking, then realized that the Japanese agent probably knew better. They couldn't be sure whether or not Kyoda was armed—Sam figured no one really wanted to know. It was a professional thing.

It didn't take long before the team was ready to leave the room and follow Kyoda to the waiting meal. Sam noticed that the well-dressed Japanese man was wearing a flesh-colored, nearly invisible wire to an earphone. When they'd all sat down on carefully arranged cushions, Sam tried to see the microphone for the two-way radio. Wherever it was, the tiny device was carefully hidden.

"I've arranged for you to watch the apprehension of Mr. Von Heich from an office at one end of the station," Kyoda said. "The blinds will be set so you can see out but it will be very difficult for anyone to see in."

"How far will we be from the action?" Jack asked.

"That depends on Von Heich. If he does not try to get in the lead car, but instead, boards at the middle of the train, we will be about twenty-five meters from him."

"I just want to make sure we don't lose this guy," Jack said.

"I understand. However, you will not take custody of him until we reach the Air Force base at Yokohama."

They fell into silence until the crepes were finished and Kyoda pushed himself to his feet. "We should go," he said. "We are going to walk to the station and it would be better if we were inside before he leaves his *ryokan.*"

"You know where he is?" Jack said.

"Of course."

"Then why don't you take him now?"

"We want to give him every opportunity to make any contact, whether it is local or by telephone, before he leaves this area. If he had local help, we want to know who."

Jack nodded, then followed Kyoda to the door. After everyone was once again wearing shoes, in the team's case black combat boots with steel toes, they walked casually down the street toward the station. The small city of Yonezawa was alive with those people who were scheduled for the night shift. Sam could smell the different foods and hear the clash of day's end. He enjoyed the walk and was disappointed when they reached the station. Once the team was settled into the office they relaxed and waited. Kyoda stood near the door.

"How many of those people are yours?" Jack asked.

"Most of them," Kyoda said. "We do not want civilians getting in the way."

Jack grunted and looked out the covered window. When Kyoda announced that Von Heich had left the inn, Jack stood straighter. Sam turned his attention to Jennifer. She moved to a vantage point where she could watch out the window, but had a clear shot at the door. When the big, beefy, South African Boer farmer strolled onto the platform Jack commented on the man's size.

"He's friggin' huge," Jack said. "He looks like a human tank next to all those little guys."

"Our agents are trained to handle people of his stature," Kyoda said.

"Yeah. Okay," Jack said. "When are they gonna take him?"

"The train will be slow opening its doors, so that escape route will be blocked and it will make it easier," Kyoda said.

Jack, Jennifer, and Sam waited. The train's whistle sounded in the distance and the throng of people began to tighten. Sam watched as the crowd seemed to surround the Boer, like an amoeba taking in its prey. As the electric train entered the station then slowed and stopped, there was a surge in the crowd. But the doors didn't open.

"Now," Kyoda said, "they will take him."

"Yeah, looks like they're trying to do that," Jack said, "but I don't think he's cooperating."

Kyoda didn't answer. He was listening to his earphone.

Sam watched the unfolding scuffle. It was obvious that the huge Boer hadn't planned on being arrested and wasn't going without a fight. He shoved the Japanese agents out of his way, trying to break free of the crowd. The Japanese struggled to maintain control of the situation and not allow it to deteriorate into an ugly incident, but Von Heich was determined to escape. When one of the agents stepped in front of the pushing and shoving South African, the big man seemed startled for a second then renewed his shoving match. When the agent took a swing at the thrashing Boer, the change in the South African was swift and unexpected. He deftly deflected the blow and grabbed the agent by the back of the neck, shaking him like an errant dog on his farm. The agent was obviously stunned by the response of Von Heich and the viselike grip around his neck, millimeters away from a painful and crushing death. The South African turned the hapless agent around and grabbed the man's crotch. Like a sack of potatoes, he picked the small man up, holding him over his head. All motion ceased while the agents and their quarry studied each other. Suddenly the Boer threw his victim at the crowd of antagonists, taking down a half-dozen men and one woman. He scrambled through the opening left by fallen agents and right toward the office where the team was watching the perfectly planned arrest disintegrating into a medieval melee.

"Did you see that!" Jack said. "That son-of-a-bitch is one hell of a street fighter. I bet he grew up fighting with the black kids who lived on his farm."

Kyoda didn't answer but cupped his hand over the earphone. Sam watched the South African break free of the cluster of agents and reach down for a large box. The big Boer picked it up with some effort, and heaved it at the agents. Two operatives ducked the box and closed in on him, but were knocked to the pavement with staggering and bloody blows to their faces. Jack suddenly pushed Sam out of his way.

"Enough of this shit!" Jack shouted and picked up the chair at the desk. He threw it through the window at the small swarm of agents and the lone South African. Jack followed the chair through the window, shouting, "Banzai, you little fuckers!"

All action seemed to stop as the huge black American, made blacker yet by his clothes, burst from the window, following the airborne chair and shards of glass. Jack didn't slow as he cleared the window, but stepped over the chair, swinging a hammerlike fist as he moved. The blow, with enough force to shatter a four-by-four, landed on the Boer's jaw and turned his face. Jack expected the man to go down and was surprised when he didn't. Instead the Boer shouted, "Bloody kaffir, where'd you come from?"

Jack was on the balls of his feet, fully recovered and anticipating the Boer's next move. When his opponent returned his charge, pound for furious pound, Jack pirouetted lightly out of the man's reach. As he spun out of Von Heich's way, Jack slammed his doubled fist down on the back of the charging Boer, between his shoulder blades, hoping to knock the air out of the South African and force him down. Sam shouted, "¡Olé!"

But, the blow didn't take the Boer down. Instead he stumbled and was fighting to regain his balance when Jack pivoted again. This time, he planted his right foot solidly in the Boer's crotch. The kick sent Von Heich reeling toward the shattered window. The South African caught himself on the frame and turned around, readying himself for another charge. Sam saw a flash of motion. Jen had a grip on the South African's chin and hair. A thin trickle of blood stained his neck.

"Move again, asshole," Jen said into the man's ear, "and I'll open you up from ear to ear."

The big man went limp and allowed the agents to swarm over him, snapping him in leg irons and cuffs.

"Good move," Jack said.

"Yeah, well you were having too much fun and Sam was turning into a cheering section."

Jack laughed, then began rubbing his hand. Kyoda stepped through the window. "That was quite a performance, DuBois-*san*."

Jack shrugged.

"Your Mr. Murphy seems to be quite a fortune-teller."

"Yeah, well, you learn to trust him."

Kyoda nodded and looked back at the shattered window. A crowd had gathered to watch as the big South African was hustled away. "What about the damage?" Kyoda asked.

"Charge it to international relations," Jack said.

May 30, 0030 hours
USAF base, Yokohama, Japan

That night Kyoda watched Jack help the prisoner into a U.S. Air Force military police vehicle for the short ride across the Yokohama Air Force Base tarmac parking apron to the waiting Air Force C-141 Starlifter cargo plane. The big loading ramp was down, waiting for the passengers.

"I suppose there will come a time when we will once again work together," Kyoda said to the team.

"It will," Jennifer said. "There always seems to be something."

Kyoda shook hands and bowed, first to Jen, then to Sam, and finally to Jack. When he straightened, Jack was smiling. "You remember that question you asked me last night?"

"About which one, yes," Kyoda said.

"The answer's on paper, it's the Constitution," Jack said, then turned for the plane.

Sam could see the confusion on Kyoda's face. "The Constitution is what gives our government a country to govern. That's where Jack would ultimately place his loyalty."

May 30, 0035 hours
USAF base, Yokohama, Japan

"Just sit down and relax," Jack said. He pushed the big Afrikaner into the seat. "We don't have any attendants on these flights so you'll just have to listen to me."

Von Heich glared at Jack, who returned the stare coldly. Sam and Jennifer sat down and pulled the seat and shoulder belts over their arms and buckled themselves into the canvas-webbed seats of the Lockheed C-141. "You don't think you could have gotten us one of those fancy jets the brass use to scuttle around in do you?"

Sam shook his head. "I wish. Not with him. And the X-37 was called for TALON Force Cobra Team," he said and sighed. Sam was still amazed that Jack had been able to manhandle the big Afrikaner without leaving a mark on him. After the brief train station scuffle, the man had been reasonably quiet and cooperative. Mostly he kept repeating that it was a free flight to the States and from there to his new home. Once, in the military police car, he had turned to Jack and snarled that he didn't want any kaffir touching him, but Jack had applied a bit of pressure and that ended the conversation. In a few more minutes they would be airborne, refuel in Anchorage, then continue on to Colorado Springs and Peterson Air Force Base. "We'll have a van waiting for us at Pete Field," Sam said.

Jennifer nodded. The engines were winding up and the noise was deafening. Before it became painful, a black air crewmember walked through the cargo hold of the plane and handed out ear protectors. When he got to the Afrikaner, the Boer slapped them away.

"I don't need anything from an American kaffir," he said.

Jack picked up the ear protectors and looked at his hostage. "Wear 'em, sir. It'll make it easier for the right people to ask questions."

"Fuck off, nigger."

Jack smiled and held the ear protectors apart over his prisoner's head. He let go and they snapped back together. "Wear 'em or I'll glue 'em to your head. And strap yourself into the seat, or I'll do it for you."

The prisoner slumped in his seat and began fastening his five-point harness. Jack made sure the shoulder and seat belts were tight, careful not to touch the Boer. When he was satisfied, he cuffed Von Heich's hands together. In a few minutes the plane began moving and once on the runway, didn't waste any time but went to full throttle. They were airborne minutes later. Everyone seemed to relax once the plane was in the air. After it leveled off at 40,000 feet Jen leaned back and drifted off to sleep. The last few hours, although not as harrowing as past missions, had still been strenuous and Sam could see the weariness around her eyes.

The first two hours of the flight were uneventful and their prisoner even slept some. He began fumbling with the buckle of his seat belt and Jack put his hand on his arm.

"I've got to piss, you bloody ape," he snarled. "You want to hold it for me?"

Jack removed the handcuffs then nodded in the direction of the head. "Don't play with it."

The Afrikaner stood up and walked toward the small bathroom in the plane. Jack's eyes followed him. Von Heich stopped and looked at the sandwiches and drinks that were in a basket on the deck. He looked back at Jack and pointed to the lunches. Jack nodded and the

Afrikaner bent over and studied the contents. Jack watched him pick up several and put them back, studying each to see which he wanted, if any. After handling a half dozen, the Boer stood up and turned back to the head, pulled the door open, and stepped inside.

Sam knew that Jack had thoroughly searched the prisoner. There was no way he could be carrying anything. Still, it made him nervous that the belligerent Afrikaner was out of their sight in the bathroom. Jack was the ex facto team leader but Sam asked if there was any way that he could have missed something in the search.

"No, but I'll search him when he comes out."

Sam nodded.

When the door opened, the Afrikaner's face registered the surprise of seeing Jack waiting for him.

"Spread 'em . . . sir."

Sam listened to the exchange and watched.

"You've searched me, kaffir."

"I'll search you again . . . sir."

"It should be *boss*-sir."

Jack turned the Afrikaner around so he faced the wall. When the prisoner didn't move, Jack pushed his hands up so they were on the bulkhead. "Spread 'em."

"You bloody black bastards are through, you know. Mandela, Mbeki, and the rest of you are going back to the stinking bush where you belong. Live like animals and pigs. That's what you are. Animals . . ."

Jack put his hand on the Afrikaner's neck and gently squeezed. "I'd like to snap it."

"Can't stand the truth, kaffir?"

Jack felt Von Heich shift his position and, anticipating his intent to fight, the Marine stepped back to get more leverage. He felt the big man's hands move. Jack snapped the man's head to one side and pinned his wrist back, almost to the breaking point. "Still care to argue, sir?"

"Let me go, you black bastard."

"Say please."

"Fuck off, kaffir."

Jack leaned into the Boer, applying more pressure. Sam watched. Jack's anger was apparent and Sam became uneasy. The big Marine could kill the Afrikaner with a flick of his hands. They couldn't let that happen and he stood up. Jen watched from her seat.

Sam said, "Maybe he'd like to go a few rounds in the ring with you after this is over?"

Jack smiled and twisted Von Heich's hand. "Yeah, mouth. How 'bout that? We finish up whatever this is all about and then the two of us step into the ring. Let me kill you with gloves on."

"I never box kaffirs," the prisoner answered. "Their skulls are too thick and you can't hurt the fuckin' bastards."

Jack gave the arm one more twist and let the prisoner go. The Afrikaner was rubbing his wrist while he walked back to his seat. Jack picked up a sandwich and said, "Hey, Billy." Von Heich turned around and Jack tossed the sandwich toward him. The Afrikaner looked at the sandwich on the deck then put his foot on it and ground it into the metal. "Stupid kaffir," he said.

"Sam," Jack said. "I have never wanted to kill anyone as much as I want to break that man's neck."

"Forget it," Sam said. "He's just pushing your buttons." The flight resumed its quiet drone and everyone seemed content to relax. After an hour of inactivity, Von Heich asked if he could stand up and stretch. Jack nodded and stood near his prisoner. The Boer looked at Jack and turned around, walking toward the tail of the aircraft. Sam looked back and forth from Jack to the pacing Boer. The tension level began to climb. Sam's mind began to flip through a mental database of events and places. He knew the man was doing something.

Jack must have guessed it as well because he began to move closer to the prisoner. The Boer lunged at the tail end and pulled a cable with a large black box from the wall. There were three buttons: one red, one yellow, one green.

"Stop him, Jack!" Sam shouted. "It's the cargo door. He'll blow the plane out of the sky!"

Jack growled and started for his nemesis. "This time I am gonna kill that crazy son of a bitch!"

"No, you black ape," the Afrikaner shouted. "I'm going to kill you, and everyone on this plane."

Jack looked back at Sam and Jen. "Fasten your belts!" He dove for the Afrikaner at the same instant Von Heich pressed the red button. There was an explosion of noise and air as the plane's pressure collapsed and Jack was hurled toward the widening crack of the loading ramp. The Afrikaner cackled hysterically and held on to the cable as the suction of air pulled him toward the increasing gap. Papers, sandwiches, and cargo were sucked out the door. The black crew chief hurled past, slammed into the bulkhead, then disappeared into the void. Jack tangled his feet in the cargo webbing and then worked them loose to begin inching toward the prisoner. With one hand, Jack reached out and grabbed the man's hand and held onto him. He felt the rushing air winning. The plane was now nosed over and pitched down, the pilots fighting for control. The ramp was still going down, but it was vibrating wildly. Jack hauled his struggling prisoner back into the plane, a murderous rage gripping at his bowels. The plane was still dropping, the angle so steep they could hear the scream of the wind and the roar of the engines trying to force the plane back under control.

Slowly, like some lumbering beast of the past, the plane's descent slowed and control was restored. But the ramp was still down and the roar of air was deafening. One of the flight deck crew stumbled into the cargo compartment, a 9mm in his hand.

"You crazy bastards," he shouted, then he saw Jack and the prisoner facing each other. The Afrikaner still held the box. The crewman looked at Sam.

"Disagreement about politics," Sam shouted above the roar.

Jack yelled, telling Von Heich to step off the ramp and get inside the plane.

"Why, kaffir?"

"You don't want to die."

"I'll be the first to die in the revenge."

"What revenge?" Jack asked.

"Rhodes," the man said. The plane began to lurch and bounce. The drag of the cargo ramp and the damage from the fall was tearing the plane apart.

The crewman handed the pistol to Sam and said, "Shoot someone," then hurried back to the flight deck.

The bouncing worsened and the ramp bucked. The Afrikaner fell to his knees, still holding the control box. The plane angled upward and he began to slide toward the edge, the bouncing making it difficult to hold on. Jack reached for his hand. Sam saw the Afrikaner mouth something to Jack, and then he turned loose of the control box and slid off the ramp, disappearing behind and below the plane. Jack pulled the control box back inside and tried to raise the ramp electronically but it wouldn't budge. Then he tried the manual crank but the ramp was jammed. He went back to Sam and told him he was going to talk to the pilot. A few minutes later he was back and strapping himself into a canvas seat.

"What'd he say?" Sam asked.

"Said it's going to be rough but we'll make Alaska."

"No, not the pilot, that crazy African."

Jack looked at him. "Nothing." He shook his head slowly. "It's not worth it."

Sam looked at his friend. He felt a shudder of helplessness. Whatever the Boer had said to Jack had shaken the big Marine. It was dangerous to the team but as long as Jack did his job Sam wouldn't be forced to say anything other than what he had to put in his report.

Chapter 2

Jan Steiner looked over his shoulder. With nothing but the deep black of night surrounding him, he pushed the accelerator of his rental car to the floor and roared into the darkness. He liked Wyoming, the vast expanses of nothing but wilderness reminded him of home. Instead of impala and springbok, pronghorn and mule deer roamed the American grasslands. Down to the small hamlets of the countryside, Wyoming reminded him of the Transvaal.

He turned the radio on. Strains from a favorite classical piece—Wagner—thundered through the speakers and he turned the volume up. The emotional swell of cymbals and the boom of the bass drum matched his mood. With flair befitting the music, he pressed a button and the side windows rolled down. The wind rushed through the car, screaming madly with the concerto. Jan felt a steady calm, his mind and body at peace with the power pouring over him. He squirmed in the shoulder harness of his seat belt until it rested over his chest comfortably, and then he roared on into the night.

Black miles disappeared beneath the speeding car as the young South African sped east through the rural countryside. Lost in the glamour and glory of his imagination, he swept through several small sleeping towns. The "William Tell" overture was blasting over the radio when he glanced in the rearview mirror. Out of the night, lights flashing red, yellow, and blue were gaining on him. For a second Jan thought that maybe the trooper would be speeding to an accident, then he checked his speedometer. The orange hand rested comfortably at ninety.

Jan's breath caught momentarily in his throat and his stomach lurched. He debated as to whether he should pull over or to try and outmaneuver the trooper. The lights whirled in a rhythmic pattern and he watched, mesmerized, as the patrol car closed the distance between them. Suddenly, the music faded into dry static and he felt a wave of heat wash over his body. His hands trembled on the steering wheel and the sweat from his palms made it slick. The flashing lights filled his rearview mirror and the patrol car's headlights cast eerie shadows on his dash. Jan sucked in a great gulp of breath and jammed his foot to the floor.

The rental car slowly pulled away but by the time Jan had put 250 yards between himself and the lights, the other car crept forward, again closing the gap. He knew he wouldn't be able to outrun the patrol car although he might be able to out-drive the officer at the wheel. With one eye on the rearview mirror and the other on the yellow lines of the highway, Steiner began looking for small county roads in which to ditch the patrolman. He knew fortune was on his side when he rounded a mild curve. A small dirt road appeared in the swath of his headlights. Jan braked hard and cranked the wheel counterclockwise, sliding the car to the left and onto the road. The sedan drifted onto the gravel in a cloud of dust. He dropped the car into second gear, gunned the engine, and blazed off into the dark depths of the country road. He shifted to third and again, the patrol car gained ground. Now he saw the lights of a second patrol car flashing down the highway.

"Damn!" He slapped at the steering wheel with the palm of his hand and tried to concentrate on the winding road. The car slid in the loose stones and threatened to leave the road as he rounded a particularly sharp curve.

By the time Jan corrected his slide the state patrolman had caught up to him. The wail of the siren pierced the dark as a high-pitched shriek. For the first time, real fear gripped his bowels. Fighting a sense of impending doom and panic, he stomped on the brake and forced the car into a hard right turn, bouncing and sliding onto a short approach. He floored the sedan and crossed a cattle guard. The noise of the tires over the metal guard growled a brief, loud explosion and the rental jerked heavily into the pasture. Steiner glanced back. The trooper had overshot the approach. He grinned with his small victory and set off over open prairie before the patrol car had recouped the lost ground. The car bopped and jolted over the uneven terrain and Steiner weaved in the seat with the bumps.

He tore through the pasture narrowly avoiding a group of jagged boulders. Startled cattle fled from the thundering car. Jan looked in his rearview mirror. The second patrol car had caught up to the first and together they launched into the pasture after him. Great puffs of dust illuminated by the various lights cast a ghostly haze over the prairie. Steiner shifted to fourth and pointed the car south. The ground looked even and open. He figured he could make it to the other side of the pasture and find a gate—losing the troopers in the process—maybe he would even cross the state line. He crested a small hill and pushed the accelerator to the floor, letting gravity propel him faster through the pasture and down the hill away from his pursuers. He glanced in the mirror again, hoping to see nothing but darkness behind him. Jan noticed the brief hollow scream of the engine as the car's tires momentarily left the ground. Too late to correct the car's course, he braced himself—legs and arms locked. The nose of the sedan plunged violently into a dry wash. With a painful groan the car's momentum pushed its rear end over before it came to a sickening, crunching halt. Steiner faded into oblivion as he saw the colorful flashing lights spread over the ground.

May 29, 0330 hours
Fort Collins General Hospital, Colorado

"Excuse me! Excuse me, sir. You can't go in there." Jan thought he could hear the agitated voice of a woman outside his door. The gash across his forehead stung and each time he drew a breath, his chest protested in agony.

The woman followed two men into his room. Each man wore a dark, loosely tailored sport jacket and pants. They also wore dark glasses although Jan was sure it was still dark outside.

"Good morning, Mr. Steiner." The man smiled.

"I'm sorry, but this man needs his rest. You'll have to leave," a short blonde woman with a florid face said sternly. The nurse circled around the man and stood with her hands on her hips between the men and Jan.

The man who had spoken smiled down at her—he was a full foot taller than she. "I'm sure Mr. Steiner appreciates your concern. He'll be fine." He opened the door of a small wardrobe that stood next to the bed and pulled Jan's tattered clothes from a hanger and tossed them onto the bed. "Get dressed."

The nurse scrambled for the clothes but the tall man stepped in front of her.

She glared at the man and then turned away and hurried out the door. Jan could hear the quick shuffle of her footsteps. She presumably went in search of a doctor. He lay there unsure of what to do. Every time he moved, his body cried out in pain. He gingerly sat up. "Who are you?" His tongue felt thick when he spoke.

"We're from the FBI," said the first man as he flipped

open his credentials and then tucked them neatly away in the breast pocket of his jacket. "We're taking you into custody and to do that, we need to take a little ride. Now, get dressed."

Blinking in disbelief and pain, Jan tried to take a deep breath. "I've cracked three ribs. I can't go anywhere."

"Buddy, your ribs are only cracked, you're not bleeding—not even close to dying. Now get your pants on or we're taking you out of here in what you're wearing." The tall man folded his arms across his chest and waited. "Oh, wait. Let me help you with that." He reached for Jan. He placed two fingers over the IV needle imbedded in the young South African's hand. In one swift movement, he tore the tape off and removed the needle from its vein.

Steiner howled. Blood oozed out of the puncture wound and ran between his fingers. He blanched and gasped. Eyes round with shock, he stared in drug-laced confusion at the men in his hospital room.

"Judd?" The first agent turned to his partner. "Better get a wheelchair. I think our boy isn't going to be able to walk out."

Jan watched Judd disappear through the door. He nearly collided with the doctor who had burst into the room at the same time, the blonde nurse on his heels like an indignant terrier.

The doctor spun away from Judd. "What the hell is going on here?" he snarled at the agent still waiting for Jan to dress.

"Mr. Steiner is needed for questioning. We're taking him into custody."

"This man isn't going anywhere. Can't you see he's been injured?" The doctor produced Steiner's chart and thumped it angrily.

"Yes, Doctor. We're aware of Mr. Steiner's injuries. I assure you, we will provide him with the best possible care." The agent smiled.

The sarcastic tone in his voice wasn't lost on the doctor. "If you think you're taking this man out of my care, I want to see some identification." The doctor's eyes bulged with fury. "And I want to know the name of your superior!"

Wordlessly, the agent again produced his identification and handed it to the doctor.

The doctor snatched the small leather folder out of the agent's hand and began reading it. He held it in his hand for a several minutes and then turned to the nurse. "Get Mr. Steiner a wheelchair, please."

Before the nurse could react to the doctor's instructions, the second agent bumped the door open. He pushed a wheelchair up to the bed.

"At least let me give him some medication for the pain," the doctor said as he returned the agent's identification.

"Sorry, Doc. Mr. Steiner needs to be alert but if you want to help him into that chair, I'd be much obliged." The agent smirked.

Minutes later, the agents escorted Jan Steiner, white-faced, in a wheelchair, to a waiting limousine. In ominous silence, they drove off. Jan saw that Fort Collins's nightlife was shut down.

May 29, 0830 hours
Buckley ANG Base, Denver, Colorado

Travis Barrett paced, walking slowly around the classroom where the members of Eagle Team listened to current news of their forthcoming mission. An information brief had been delivered via special courier. He tapped his leg with the brief as he walked. "Okay, team, we've got some real problems here. We're working on a short fuse—no time for games. We need to get this information and then we need to move." Barrett's voice deepened before he continued. "Von Heich, before his untimely demise"—the major smiled wryly—"had been employed by a Boer farmer in South Africa's Transvaal. His name—Eric Steiner." He paused and looked at the team members gathered around the table. No one spoke; all were listening intently.

"This farmer is well connected, he's financially secure, and his son has attended the University of Northern Colorado for the past two years—the virus originated there. Jan, Steiner's son, has been picked up for questioning and will be arriving shortly. Any questions so far?" Travis stopped and studied the faces of his teammates. He noticed the look exchanged between Hunter Blake and Sarah but neither said anything. "Jan Steiner is twenty-three. He's been studying biology and agriculture at UNC. He has access to several of the developmental labs and it looks like he's taken advantage of his position as a student." Barrett nodded at Sarah.

Sarah returned the nod and stood up. She tucked a wild strand of black hair behind her earring-studded ear and started to speak. "Normally a student like Steiner wouldn't have access to this type of virus—normally the University of Northern Colorado doesn't work with hazardous diseases. But sometime last fall the Department of Bovine Genetics Research received several genetically engineered embryos. Shortly after these embryos were implanted in a host cow, she developed a mild, mutated form of anthrax—Anthrax 515—affectionately known as the 'Anita virus,' after the researcher." Sarah paused and took a deep breath. "Anthrax, as you know, is extremely virulent and quite deadly. The cow was immediately destroyed. Before the carcass was incinerated, the virus was collected and samples were sent to the Center for Infectious Animal Diseases Control on Plum Island in New York."

"Okay, wait a minute. If this Anita virus was sent to

the island, what's it doin' killin' a bunch of cows? And how did some punk kid like Steiner get it?" Stan asked, folding his hairy arms across his barrel chest.

"Steiner was partnered with Anita Wetherby, an over-zealous grad student. Ms. Wetherby kept enough of the virus to cultivate cultures. Her intent was, of course, to develop a cure and win a Nobel Prize." Sarah winced sardonically. "They were able to develop their research through computer models. Through testing, Steiner and Wetherby determined that Anthrax 515 only affected cattle. And this is how Steiner came to be in possession of the virus. He raided their private stash at the request of his father."

A knock sounded at the door. Travis nodded to Stan, who opened it. The Marine guard acting as their sentry stepped into the room. Jan Steiner entered the room in his wheelchair with Agent Judd pushing. The tall agent flanked them.

"Major Barrett." FBI Agent Judd stepped forward. He pushed the Boer to the center of the room. Jan came to a stop less than a foot from where Travis stood. "Have a nice day, sir." The agent smiled politely. He motioned to his partner and they left the room. The Marine sentry followed them through the door, closing it with a click.

An uncomfortable silence filled the room. Travis stared curiously at the Boer. Stan Powczuk shifted in his seat, and then cleared his throat. Hunter Blake, Eagle Team's ace pilot, leaned forward in his chair, resting his elbows on the table in front of him.

"Welcome, Mr. Steiner. Or may I call you Jan?" Travis's honeyed Southern drawl broke the unnatural stillness in the room. "Won't you have a seat?" He pulled a chair out away from the table. "Oh, look at that"—he shook his head—"you already have one. Hunter, would you remove those from Mr. Steiner? I don't think he's going anywhere."

Wordlessly, the suave pilot stood up and crossed the

room. He took a small key from his belt pouch and un-
locked the cuffs. He pocketed the key again and returned
to his seat.

"There ya go. Would you like a soda? Hunter, get our
boy here a Coke." Travis smiled broadly at Blake.

Hunter returned the smile and fished some change
from his pocket. "Would anyone else like a soda?" The
pilot waited patiently for other orders.

"I'd like one, Blake, if you're buying," Stan said with
a grin.

"Others?" Hunter looked around the room. "Nope.
Okay then," he mumbled and knocked at the door.

When the Marine sentry opened it, Hunter stepped
into the hallway. Travis watched the door close again.
"You've been going to school in Fort Collins, isn't that
right?" He waited for Steiner to answer. Again, silence
fell over the room. He looked at the sullen young man.
He guessed that Steiner must be about six feet tall. His
sandy-red hair and freckles lent him a certain boyish
charm that was visibly at odds with the young man's
size. Although his coloring was fair, his skin was bad
and pockmarked. Angry red boils—too big to be mere
pimples—dotted his face, neck, and shoulders. A sharp
gash across Steiner's forehead had been taped together
with butterfly bandages. Travis took a deep breath. He
knew that for the interrogation to go well, it needed to
be set up just right. "Did you hear me, Mr. Steiner?"
He placed one hand on Jan's shoulder and bent over so
that his face was close to the Boer's. Travis looked him
in the eye unflinchingly. "I said, did you hear me?"

Steiner glared at Travis. "I heard you."

"Good." Travis let go of the man's shoulder and
walked away. "We have some interesting news for you,
Mr. Steiner."

"I've done nothing. You cannot do this to me. I demand to see a lawyer."

Travis could smell the fear of the Boer. "I don't think

you understand, Mr. Steiner. There aren't any lawyers here. You don't have any rights here. No one knows that you're *here.* No one." He pulled a chair close to Steiner and sat down. He let what he'd just said to the Boer sink in. He wanted him to have time to think about his situation.

Several stiff minutes went by and Hunter returned with the soda. He set a can on the table in front of the South African and then looked at Stan. Hunter's eyes sparkled deviously and he tossed Stan his can of soda. He then sat down, propping his feet up on a chair across from him.

"Sarah, please tell Mr. Steiner the events of the past twelve hours." Travis blinked lazily, as if he was bored.

"Yes, sir." Sarah Greene sat up straight and began to speak. She recounted the statistics of the Wyoming slaughter and the death count in England. She paused before describing the events that had taken place in Japan. She inhaled deeply and looked into Jan's eyes and began again. "Operatives were briefed in Japan by an agent there. He gave us the name and point of origination of the terrorist operating there. Our operative apprised us of his train schedule, and his flight plan. The suspect was apprehended before he left Yonezawa and turned over to U.S. agents. Three members of our team were responsible for bringing him back to U.S. authorities. While en route to Edwards Air Force Base, the suspect triggered an incident on the plane and was killed."

Travis watched the face of the young South African as this news was delivered. A much older, more experienced man would have been able to better hide his distress, but surprise and panic registered in Steiner's eyes. "Did you hear that, Jan? Von Heich is dead. The Japanese followed him. They were able to trace him right to those dead cows."

"Travis! Why are we babying this guy?" Suddenly Stan leaped out of his chair. In two long strides, he covered the ground to the seated South African. "Jesus Christ! We *know* that he's the one who stole the virus, we *know* he's connected to Von Heich. Let's get this over with!" Stan grabbed Steiner by the hair and pulled his head back.

"No!" Travis lunged for the angry SEAL's free hand before he could smash it into the startled face of Steiner. "Sit down!" Travis barked. "We're not turning this into a Nazi grilling." He put his hand on Steiner's shoulder.

The younger man had paled. His eyes were round and the blotches on his skin glowed a firey red. He licked his lips nervously.

"Jan here will tell us what we want to know, without any . . . untoward behavior. Won't you?" Travis smiled winningly. He almost laughed when Steiner swallowed hard, his Adam's apple bobbing spastically in his skinny neck.

"I have nothing to say," Steiner mumbled dryly. "You Americans. What do you think you are doing? I know you do this good cop–bad cop thing."

"Excuse me?" Travis leaned close to Jan's face. "You think this is something like you see on TV?" He stood up and looked at the others in the room. Sarah and Hunter both snickered. Stan wore an expression of malicious boredom. "Do you remember, Mr. Steiner, that no one knows where you are? You're a long way from home. Accidents happen in this country all the time. People disappear mysteriously every day. What makes you think you're special? That you're a foreigner here?" He chuckled but the laughter didn't reach his eyes. "We can kill you, Jan. We can torture you slowly if we like. Hell, we can shoot you so full of truth serum that you'll tell us the last time you whacked off if we want to know." He methodically paced across the floor behind Steiner. "Now, Jan, I want to know about the virus. I want to know what Von Heich was doing in Japan. I want to know why the hell you people are killing cows, for Christ's sake."

A firm knock sounded on the door. Travis looked at Stan. Stan looked hard at Steiner before he went and opened the door. In a flurry of paper and noise, a courier charged past the sentry who calmly closed the door behind him, whispered in Travis's ear and passed him a file.

"What are you people doing?" Travis waved a stack of papers at Jan Steiner. "I don't believe this!" The courier handed Barrett a portable radio. "Listen!" Barrett turned it on and fidgeted with the dials. The smooth voice of a radio announcer came through the speakers.

"Once again, we are announcing that a group of South African terrorists are responsible for the loss of cattle in Wyoming. There have been numerous cattle deaths reported in England and Japan. A spokesman from the White House has just announced that the group is demanding Zimbabwe be turned over to them and a white minority government be established or the rest of the world's cattle population will be decimated."

Travis turned the radio off. "This changes everything. The media is adding to the hype." He pointed to Steiner. "And you! Your father held a press conference—this has been picked up by CNN and every wire service in the world!" Travis rubbed his jaw thoughtfully. "Okay. Stan, take him to a holding cell." He nodded in the direction of Steiner. "Sam, better set up a link."

Chapter 3

Glimmering patterns of frost coated the lowest third of the 737's window. Sam stared out the window at the lights of Washington, D.C. No one had wanted the team to fly into the heart of the nation's capital but time was running out. It was the strangest crisis the nation—perhaps the world—had ever faced, the killing of the world's cattle population in an act of desperate terrorism. The plane shuddered slightly in the crosswinds as it turned for the final approach to Reagan National Airport. Once it was lined up, the turbulence dissipated and Sam could feel the tension leaving him. He thought of what the terrorists were preparing to unleash on the world. They've got to be stopped, Sam thought. We're going to have to hunt them down in their own country and if they won't give up the virus then we're going to have to kill them. Burn them. The image of Waco popped into his head. The United States government had burned its own people to death to kill a religious zealot. TALON Force was going to have to lead the world's charge in eliminating these terrorists. They wanted their own country. That's all anyone really wants, Sam thought, a place of their own.

The landing was smooth and Sam switched his mental imagery to what had to be done and the reasons for it. By the time the plane stopped at the gate, his entire focus was on the mission. He knew the other team members hadn't needed to make the same mental switch. Each one of them was so thoroughly trained and equipped for the mission—whatever the mission—that they would never allow any extraneous thought to cloud their mind. From his seat Sam watched the team members clamber into the narrow aisle and then toward the door. They went fluidly, simply, and blended so perfectly with the other passengers that no one realized the person standing next to them was one of the most lethal people in the world. Sam sighed and joined the passengers leaving the plane. As soon as he entered the passenger waiting area he spotted General Krauss wearing a gold cardigan and a pair of tweed trousers. He wore a forest green leather glove over the prosthetic hand. The general looked as though he'd just stepped off a golfing green. Sam started toward him.

"Morning, Sam," Krauss said.

"Sir."

"There are two vans waiting outside. Your bags will catch up to you later."

Sam nodded and walked away. He felt rather than saw the general behind him for a few steps, then Krauss disappeared into an unmarked door. Sam walked at a normal pace, following the throng to the baggage area. He turned away from the claim area and went outside. The two vans waited at the curbside next to a large sign marked PASSENGER PICKUP. As Sam neared one van, the door slid open and he saw Jen Olsen lean out and motion to him. He didn't slow his stride but stepped into the van and pulled the door shut. He wasn't even seated before the ungainly vehicle pulled away. Sam settled into the seat nearest Jen. She handed him an Ultra Palm Pilot. He switched it on and the screen glowed with an eerie light. Quickly he read through an update of the situation.

"Shit, he can't be serious," Sam said.

"Very," Travis said.

"We're running out of time on this one and we just figured out what's going on." Sam frowned.

"Yeah, but it's getting worse. If we don't put a clamp on this soon, we could have a real mess."

"So, has the media scare started anything serious?" Sam asked.

"Try and go out for a steak dinner." The driver grinned. The toothpick that rested at the side of his mouth migrated to the other side.

Sam watched the toothpick bob and weave in the driver's mouth. "You're up on this?"

"Who isn't?" the driver, a beefy man with graying hair and a spare tire, chortled. "Damn thing is on the news every hour and CNN is going hog wild with twenty-four hour coverage until, as they say, the crisis is resolved. They have a logo and theme music—the works."

No one replied. The driver wasn't a team member but they didn't need anyone to paint a picture for them. If CNN and the other cable networks didn't back off on their coverage, Eagle Team's job would be made even more difficult.

Travis looked outside. "Guess where we're going, guys."

"Where?" Jen asked.

"The White House," the driver said into the rearview mirror. "And we're going by way of the secure tunnel."

No one spoke. The silence was dark and eerie. Sam knew what they would be thinking. All thoughts were on the mission. If they were going to be in a briefing with the president they had better have some answers. Problem was, nobody had any.

Sam watched the buildings flash past the window. The serpentine route ended in a jolting halt. Sunlight glared through windows and the driver rolled his window down then flashed his ID to the guard. Sam could see another guard approaching the sliding door. When it opened there were two guards. One held a clipboard. The other, slightly behind the first and to one side, carried an Uzi. Sam felt his stomach tighten. Travis broke the hardened silence.

"Good morning, Tom," he said. The guard in the back nodded.

"Haven't seen you in a while, Major. This must be big if you're here."

"Big enough for you to be holding that on me."

The guard nodded.

"We have our ID."

"Needs to go to the driver, it'll be checked there."

Bodies shuffled back and forth as ID tags were passed forward. Although the military had adopted chip technology for ID tags, TALON Force tags were different. The information the tag would reveal was coded. Only an ID reader with very specific security clearance would see anything other than confirmation of the ID holder. Everything else about the team was classified.

Travis handed the team's cards forward and they sat in silence. No one felt the need to make small talk and the loaded Uzi was a reminder that they were in the midst of a crisis.

When the cards were passed back, the armed guard relaxed slightly. "Okay, Major," the man said, nodding to Travis. "Go save the world."

"Tom?" Travis paused.

"Yeah?"

"Keep the bad guys out 'til we get back?"

The guard smiled and lowered the Uzi.

Jen pulled the door shut and the van lurched as it started up the drive. There was a brief moment of intense darkness while the van rolled into a blackened tunnel and then it burst into the harsh light of the underground parking lot. The van stopped and the door opened. A man wearing a slate-gray suit motioned for everyone to get out. The team followed, noting that the second van was already empty and the other TALON members gone. Their guide hurried to an elevator, guarded on either side by security officers. The closest guard reached around and pressed a button. When the heavy stainless-steel doors slid open, the guide ushered everyone inside. The doors closed with a sickening thump and Sam's stomach lurched with the drop.

"Guess we're going to the basement, guys," Stan Powczuk said. It was the first time he'd spoken since the airport.

"No speaking, please," the guide said. "Security advises that we maintain absolute silence."

Stan nodded.

The other members of the team shifted uncomfortably. When the elevator slid to an unearthly stop, the door opened and the guide stepped into the hallway. A Marine guard waiting for the team took the guide's place. He didn't speak but motioned for the team to follow. Again, urgency encouraged their steps and together they hurried down the hall, turned a corner, and stopped abruptly in front of a door with a scanner in the wall.

"Place your left hand on the scanner as you step to the door. Look straight at that camera. When you clear, you will be allowed to pass. One at a time, please. If two of you try to pass, or you rush, the door will close and you will be detained."

He stepped aside and motioned for Powczuk to start. One by one, each member of the team entered the room. Stan was first and after he was in the small enclave, the door closed behind him. The next time it opened, Sam stepped into an adjacent room, separated from the first by thick glass. It was a fantasy chamber. Digital maps of the world dominated one distant wall. Television screens lined another. Telephones rested on the long, rectangular table in front of each chair. Every telephone had a speaker in front of it for off-the-hook conversations and several video cameras around the room were stationed so any speaker could be put on camera as part of the video-phone system. The head table, obviously for the president, was equipped with three phones. Two of the telephones were secured with locks. Marine guards, wearing 9mm Barettas, stood in opposite corners of the room. The other team members—Sarah, Jack, and Hunter—were already seated.

General Krauss, now in uniform, drummed his fingers rhythmically on the table. "Take your seat, Sam."

That was when Sam noticed that each chair had been pre-designated. Small place cards had been placed before each chair around the table. He found his and sat down.

Krauss nodded. "Under your place card, you will find a name tag. Put it on."

"Yes, sir." Sam stuck the tag to his shirt. By this time Jen, Travis, and Stan were in the room. They followed Sam's lead and found their seats. Sam looked up when a side door opened and three of the Joint Chiefs walked into the room. The team stood up, following protocol.

After they had placed thick folders on the table in front of their chairs they quickly acknowledged the TALON Force members they were familiar with. The people in the room stood behind their chairs waiting stiffly. Another door opened and the president's aide, Jane Whaite-Worthington, entered. She paused and checked the faces in the room. As the team resumed their seats, Sam wondered what kind of talent it took to move so quietly in government-issue chairs.

Whaite-Worthington cleared her throat. "Gentlemen, Operation Bovine has just become the only thing standing between the world as we know it and potential nuclear devastation."

Although Sam didn't turn his head to see who did it, someone shuffled papers. Other throats were cleared with hoarse, grumbling coughs. General Freeman, the man directly across from Sam, pulled a handkerchief from his pocket and nervously wiped his forehead.

"Mugabe, president of Zimbabwe, has ordered the house arrest of every white farmer in the country. He has also announced that if there is another attack on cattle by the Boer extremists anyplace in the world, then all of the white farmers in the country are to be arrested, with their families, and taken to holding areas. Concentration or internment camps, take your pick."

Whaite-Worthington paused and looked at her papers. "And, gentlemen, that is just the beginning." She studied the other serious faces at the table. "In another press conference, Eric Steiner, the self-proclaimed president of New Rhodesia, is seeking support from the countries of the Middle East, his claim being that the Rhodesian people have also suffered from the duplicity of first-world countries. In turn, the government of Pakistan has just announced that it is aligning itself with 'The New Rhodesia.' The Pakistan government's stand is that any attack on Zimbabwe will be considered an attack on Pakistan. They will retaliate with their own missiles and a full-scale attack."

There was another clearing of throats.

"There is more. The Indian government has sent a formal announcement to the press saying that if there is an attack on the cattle of India, the nation will respond with the total destruction of a city in Zimbabwe."

"And South Africa?" General Gates asked.

"The new president of South Africa, Mbeki, has asked for this to be handled wisely. But you see, gentlemen, the shit is getting deep." She paused, inhaled deeply, and put her hands on the table. "Because now the governments of Germany, France, and Spain are demanding that South Africa round up the Boers and farmers—whether part of the movement or not—and end the threat. They want Steiner stopped. Several southern African governments are supporting this demand. But white militia groups in that region are threatening civil war if that happens. I am quoting here." She ran her finger down the edge of a paper. " 'For every white farmer arrested by this government, we will attack and destroy one of the Black Townships.' "

The presidential aide stopped reading and looked around the table. "Is there anyone here who does not clearly understand the severity of the situation?"

No one spoke.

She continued. "Eagle Team, in two hours you will be boarding the X-37 with several containers of your equipment."

"You think," Tavis said, "an experimental rocket plane that doesn't even officially exist won't be noticed at an international airport?"

"You'll be landing in the dead of night. We've arranged for Johannesburg to have an electrical failure until the X-37 can be shuffled into hiding."

"We're cutting things close here," Sarah said.

"That's why, before you leave this room, I want some sort of plan on how we are going to resolve this crisis."

The silence in the room was stiff, awkward. Jane Whaite-Worthington, aide to the president of the United States, had just given the team a mandate. No one knew how to respond.

Finally, slowly, as if he was pulling each word out of some deep recess of his own being, Travis stood up. "Ms. Whaite-Worthington, sirs. Based on the information we now have there are some conditions for this operation that are . . . somewhat unusual."

"Explain," said General Freeman, leaning back in his chair. Again, he mopped his brow with the white cloth.

"Well, sir," Travis started. "We're going to have to try and hit a number of places across the length of South Africa all at the same time, or nearly so, in such a way that the cells cannot communicate with each other."

"Major Barrett is right. But Ms. Whaite-Wothington, General, sirs," Jen said. "You should all be aware of the fact that we've rarely worked in such small units before—

which is what we will need to do now. We are a team. We usually work together."

"If we have one centrally located communications net, a place where the team is being coordinated, it can work," Sam said.

"We will need in-country support for this one," Travis added.

"That has already been anticipated. Arrangements have been made," General Krauss said. "We have asked Mandela to step in and apply political pressure on President Mbeki. He has committed the South African National Police to a supportive role."

"Does that provide us with better intel as well?" Travis asked.

"Yes it does," Whaite-Worthington said. "Here's what we've got. If you'll look at the African screen I'll give you an overview of the country. You are, by now, versed in the political situation that is the impetus for the present situation. This operation is going to be made difficult by the size of the country. South Africa is nine hundred fifty miles across and six hundred forty miles north to south. On the screen you can see that it is one of the better developed third-world nations."

Everyone's attention turned to the screen. South Africa's borders were marked in blue. Roads, towns, down to the smallest village, were depicted as black dots correlating with population size. Several bright red stars glowed on the screen. Three of them had arrows pointing to them.

"The stars represent known terrorist cells," Whaite-Worthington said. "The three with arrows are known to have vials of the virus stored at that location. It is believed that this accounts for all the vials."

"How many is that?" Sarah asked.

"Twelve vials were taken. We know that three have been used. We don't believe they've moved the others out of the country—yet. We believe the cell at Middleburg is planning to move the vials to the Indian subcontinent for a massive kill of cattle."

"That should be our first target," Travis said.

"Agreed," General Gates said. "But the other cells must be hit, too. They need to be hit hard so they can't move the vials. If they anticipate our attack, they will, most certainly, move them."

"Are you sure that each cell has three vials? Not more or less?" Jennifer asked.

"Yes," Gates nodded.

"How can you be sure?" Jack asked.

"I can answer that," blurted a voice from the president's speakerphone.

"Who are you?" Travis demanded.

"Major Barrett, let me introduce you to the director of South African National Police—General York," General Freeman said, his voice quiet but reproachful.

"Hello, sir," Travis said. "I had no idea you were listening."

"Hello, Major Barrett. We're pleased to be working with you—as pleased as one can be under these circumstances," York said quickly. His voice rang with the British accent that marked what he said with aristocratic dignity.

"Yes, sir," Travis replied.

"We have had agents watching these cells for years," York said.

"So you've penetrated them. But then why didn't you know of this plan?"

"We only knew that something was planned. What and where it would take place—we had no idea. We were sure it would be a strike against us, or perhaps, Zambia. It was engineered by one man."

"Eric Steiner," Sam said.

"Exactly."

"So, if you don't mind my asking, sir, why haven't your own forces taken them out?" Jack asked.

"These farmers are scattered across the country. They are each respected men in the regions where they live. If the police force is ordered to move on these farmers, it will trigger a civil war. There are several thousand white farmers who do not believe this government is going to let them keep their land. They will go to war if they believe they will lose it."

"In other words, even if they are not a member of this movement, they might believe it is a devil's advocate operation?"

"Exactly, Major Barrett."

"Will we have your SANP's help?"

"All you need, including armed men ready to fight. But, Major, your team members must be the leaders of the entire operation."

"And just exactly whose authority are we acting under?"

"If you are successful, it is at the request of the South African government."

"And if something goes wrong?"

"You've heard the American expression, 'You're on your own'?"

"Yes, sir."

"Then, Major, you're on your own. You'll have to have a good cover story about being hired by a coalition of international governments."

"Lie?"

"If you must."

Travis turned back to the map. "Are you going to be listening to us as we make our plans, sir?"

"Yes."

"Good, then when it looks like it is going to be a flop, tell me." He walked over to the map. "I need a close-up shot of the target area at Middleburg."

An adjoining screen went blank for a few seconds then a satellite photo filled the screen. "Print copies of this for everyone," Travis said, studying the picture. "This is

Tango One," Travis said. "Mark each photo with that. We'll need small arms . . ."

In less than two hours each target had been identified, the attack planned, and the equipment needed for it confirmed to be in the cargo hold of the X-37. On the other side of the world another half-dozen South African security officers and military men were moving their own supplies and men. When Travis finished he looked at Jane Whaite-Worthington. "Ma'am, do we have the president's permission to begin this operation?"

"Major," the aide said, "from the moment I walk out of this room you have full operational control of this operation. The South African forces assisting will be under your command. Is that right, sir?" she said to the speaker.

"Yes, Ms. Whaite-Worthington. It is correct. Your men are in control. All we can do is pray they are successful."

The presidential aide looked up at the clock for Washington, D.C., time. "As of this moment, Major, you have less than twenty-four hours to prevent a war."

"Then, Ms. Whaite-Worthington," Travis said slowly, "I'd say it's time to get moving."

She nodded. The Eagle Team members pushed themselves away from the table. Each folded their notebooks and put them on the table.

"Your information will be on the X-37 waiting for you," General Krauss said.

The team members filed out of the room under the close scrutiny of the Joint Chiefs and Jane Whaite-Worthington. Sam was the last one to leave. He looked at General Krauss.

"Be careful, Sam."

"Yes, sir," Sam said, then went to the door and left. Outside the team was waiting. When Travis joined them they turned to follow their guide through the hallway. No one spoke. Sam watched them. This was a panic operation. They weren't training for it. There weren't any practice attacks, drills on what to do—no testing of equipment. This was fly into a country, set up a control center, and go on the offensive. He wanted to tell them that this was the *real* test. Having a mission that had to be completed using the intellect of the team members was going to test everything they had practiced and trained for in the past. All of their equipment, from the Low Observable Camouflage Suites to the Unmanned Aerial Vehicles, would be available for them. All they had to do was secure the X-37 in a hangar at the Johannesburg airport, draw their gear, and join the local national police that were supporting them. A helicopter would take each team to its target. Other troops would be on the ground, posing as civilians, waiting for them. The equipment had to work. Every detail had to work without a single test. Sam shuddered.

Chapter 4

Travis caught a glimpse through the cockpit window as the X-37 seemed to drift from heaven into the thick African night. He saw the lights of Johannesburg, then the lights around the airport. The pilot put the plane into a steep dive, losing altitude as fast as he dared. He smoothly eased the nose up and a minute later Travis felt the X-37 thump onto the runway as it landed. There was no roar of engines or reverse thrusters, only the silence of the wheels against the pavement. The plane rolled to a stop. Less than a minute later he felt the plane being jostled as a tug was hooked to it. After a choppy jerk, the plane began rolling down the tarmac. The tug engine chugged and within a few short minutes, they rolled to a stop inside a hangar. Travis picked up his small bag and motioned for the others to follow him. When he opened the door he saw a uniformed officer.

"Major Travis Barrett," a tall white South African said, extending his hand, "I'm Major Thomas Anderson."

"What happened to security?" Travis glanced around as he spoke. There were a dozen or more people looking at the plane.

"Well, security has its place, but so does urgency. This time urgency overrides everything else."

Travis scratched his arm then thrust his hand in his pocket before commenting. "Okay, let's get someplace for an update."

Anderson nodded and turned away. Travis signaled for the team to follow and in a few minutes they were in a small room off the main hangar area. Two South African National Police officers stood up as the team entered. They were introduced as Captains Robley and Schneider.

Travis sat down and looked at the South Africans. "Okay, we know the situation as it was when we left. Do you have an update?"

Anderson nodded gravely. "First, let's say that the situation has deteriorated rapidly. If we don't handle this properly we can expect civil war to break out within forty-eight hours. There are already rumors of war in Zimbabwe."

"What happened?" Travis frowned.

"Two hours ago the Anita virus was released in an Argentine ranching valley. The entire herd of cattle in the valley was dead within hours. President Mugabe of Zimbabwe has issued the order for the arrest of all white farmers. They have been incarcerated in a makeshift holding compound outside Harare. Our last report was that twenty-four families are being held."

"I take it," Travis said, "that not everyone is going peacefully."

"There have been at least four firefights. One ended in the massacre of a white family. The others were finally forced to surrender."

"Anyplace else?"

"There's been a lot of saber rattling." He handed Travis a folder. Captain Robley picked up a stack of folders and passed them out to the team. "Take a few minutes to look over the information," Anderson said, "if you have any questions, please ask them."

Minutes of uncomfortable silence passed until all of the folders were closed. "Questions?" Anderson asked.

"Where's our gear?" Jack asked.

Anderson smiled. "We have a secure hangar waiting for it." He looked at his watch. "Actually, your container load of equipment should be there. The rest of our team is there as well."

Travis nodded. "When do I assume operational command?"

"When we reach the operations hangar."

"Then it's time to get busy."

Anderson nodded and turned to walk toward a door. Travis and the team followed. Outside, a military bus waited, engine running.

After the small group boarded, the driver hurriedly drove past parked planes, then straight across the tarmac to a fenced portion of the military side of the airport. Without slowing he headed directly for a hangar. The door opened as they neared and then closed behind them. Travis stepped off the bus behind the South Africans. The rest of Eagle Team followed. The baggage container that held their hard-sided gear cases had been moved to the other side of the hangar. The doors, Travis noted, were still sealed.

"Jack"—Travis turned to the big Marine—"open the container and equip the team." Travis then turned to Anderson. "Let's meet your team."

By the time Anderson finished his introductions, Eagle Team's equipment was laid out in neat rows. Each piece of equipment would be thoroughly checked by the individual who would carry it. Travis excused himself and checked his gear. Satisfied, he began pulling on his rigging. When he sealed the last Velcro fastener he stood up and walked back to Anderson and the South African contingent of the combined force.

Anderson's brow wrinkled and a grin pulled at the

corners of his mouth. "You look like some bloody cyborg!"

"Yeah, well. This is the future, here and now," Travis said. He reached up and switched on the Low Observable Camouflage. Travis's jumpsuit began to shimmer, and the high-tech camouflage changed color to match the background of the hangar.

"Bloody marvelous!" Anderson said. "You can just walk right in and no one will know. Put an end to this quick—right?"

"We hope," Travis said. "But we've got to get moving." He motioned his team to join him. Each TALON trooper was carrying his XM-29 Smart Rifle, the XM-73 pistol, and either a 9mm Baretta or the new Special Forces .45 made by Colt and H&K.

TALON Force's Battle Sensor Helmets and the utility belts replete with power packs, extra ammo, and communications gear, gave the African operatives a taste of future shock. The South Africans shuffled, visibly disturbed. They wore conventional BDUs. Their weapons consisted of a South African R-4 Service Rifle and two extra magazines—each.

"Our target," Travis said, "is the Steiner Farm. We'll make an airborne assault as outlined in the operational orders. Each chopper will carry six members of the South African police and two TALON team members. You've got your maps, timetable, and objectives. Do you have any questions?"

No one answered.

"The time is now zero-five-fifty. We're on schedule. If there's no questions, let's go," Travis said.

Sarah Greene walked beside him. Just before they boarded the French-made Aérospatiale Puma helicopter, she leaned over and whispered, "Travis, have you ever felt overdressed for a battle?"

Travis smiled. "Not until today."

"We better not screw this up. These guys are looking at us like we're super soldiers."

"We are," Travis grinned.

When Sarah didn't reply Travis filed her silence away for the future. She had a point. Perhaps they should have left some of the gear behind. As he neared the door of the helicopter he turned his mind to the mission.

May 30, 0620 hours
Steiner farm near Middleburg, South Africa

The pilots had been instructed to fly directly to the Steiner farm. They were not to deviate from the path and each team was to be dropped precisely on their assigned landing zone. If anyone was in the way, they were to be ignored. If they didn't move—land on them. If they fired at the aircraft, shoot back and shoot to kill. Travis felt the pitch of the blades alter slightly and the chopper went into a nose-over attitude for a few seconds, then it flared and settled quickly to the ground. The African dust swirled in the blade-generated wind. In his long past life he might have thought about tasting Africa in the swirling dust from the helicopter's downdraft. This time he didn't. He hit the ground at a run. He'd already moved his mouthpiece into position so all he had to do was speak and every team member, as well as Sam in the hangar at Jan Smuts Airport and General Gates in Washington, could hear everything that was being said.

"*Move! Move!* Get your people into position!" Travis barked.

He heard a series of rapid pops. Jen's team was taking fire.

"What've you got, Olsen?"

"AK, one hostile . . . There he is—" More pops sounded, distinctly different from the AK's metallic ping—return fire from a South African R-4 on semiauto. "That one's down. We're moving. Back wall is secure . . . We have the back of the house in our sights . . . *Shit!*"

"What!" Travis demanded.

"There's a kid there. No, two." Travis could hear Jen's breathing as she moved to get a better position. He monitored her team's efforts at the same time his own team rushed ahead, covering each other from forward positions—the traditional bounding, overwatch movement of a team still the best method to secure ground.

Suddenly Jen shouted, "Don't shoot, you'll be—"

Her voice faded, drowned out by the muffled pops of another AK firing on full auto. Travis counted off six shots fired before the South African R-4, also on full auto, returned fire.

"Shit!" Jen said. "Barrett, one of the kids was armed. Both are down."

"Roger that, Olsen. Don't risk your team."

"Roger."

Travis shut the mental image of children in war out of his mind and concentrated on securing the front of the house. He hadn't turned on the camouflage suit's blending ability and was watching his team move forward in short springs when the first claymore mine exploded. Three men in the lead disappeared in a flash of blinding noise. When the smoke cleared, nothing marked their path but shredded lumps of meat. Travis dove into a pile of rocky rubble. *Sure as shit! Someone fucked this operation up!* He hadn't looked at the bodies. There would be no survivors. He checked over his shoulder. Two others had been wounded but made it to cover behind trees. Travis heard Stan Powczuk's voice over his comm links.

"Stan, Front Team has three Kilo India Alpha, two Whiskey. We're operational but not moving until we can figure out if there are any more of those fuckers out there."

"Roger," Stan said. "We're on the deck here. How's the back team?"

"Back Team here," Jen cut in. "I'm putting a Dragonfly in the air. We'll have a scan of the whole area for claymores or other mines. Activate your screens."

One by one each team member rogered their approval. A minute later Travis clearly heard the noise of the UAV's motor as Jen activated and then launched it. He could see the back of the farmhouse as the image was sent directly to his retina via the Battle Sensor Device that folded down from his helmet like a monocle. The view shifted to directly below the UAV. Jen dropped the UAV to ten yards from the ground and began a slow search of the yard around the house, looking for signs of more mines. She saw a small rise in the ground directly in front of a cycad tree.

"There's one," she said.

"Roger," Travis said. "Switch to thermal imaging. See what you pick up."

The BSD rolled with the image change then settled again. The outline of a claymore was easy to distinguish. "Mark it," Travis said. They'd destroy the mine before the team continued.

Jen resumed the search finding three more of the mines before the UAV's fuel began to run out. She was surprised that the UAV hadn't drawn any fire from the farmhouse. When its engine sputtered, she sent a destruct signal and the UAV exploded in the air.

"Think we marked them all?" Jennifer asked.

"Negative," Travis said. Looking up he saw a flicker of movement on the roof of the building. A second or two passed before he realized that the roof wall had been built with concealed firing ports. "There's hostiles on the roof," he said. He pulled his rifle to his shoulder, preparing to shoot when he realized what he was aiming at. From behind a gauzelike covering that made the roof wall appear solid, he scoped into the barrel of a M66

LAW targeting his pile of rubble. Travis quickly noted that there were several of the ports, and from each one LAWs were pre-aimed at designated targets in the yard. The targeted areas obviously had been anticipated. Where else would an attacking force take cover when the first claymores exploded?

The person on the roof had been arming the LAWs—which would probably be fired electronically. The entire team was trapped.

"Fall back!" Travis shouted into his comm gear. "They've got this whole area targeted! *Fall back now!*"

He glanced behind him, back at the South Africans. They were following orders—but not fast enough. As he turned back to check the rooftop, the first LAW fired. The rocket came to life with a burst of flame. The back-blast kicked gravel off the roof of the house in a cloud of dust. The rocket itself seemed to move in slow motion.

Travis turned to look at his South African team. Only Jack seemed to have the instinct for survival. Already he lay sprawled in a small depression, pressing himself flat to avoid the shrapnel that would fill the air when the rocket exploded. The four South Africans, two white men and two black, ran together—they'd just passed a low, small cement building that appeared to be a well covering when the LAW crashed into the center of the small group. Yellow and orange flames flashed brilliantly in the yard. The dust, dirt, and noise slowed, hung in the air, and fell.

The men fell to the ground in a sickening thud, blasted off their feet. Two were blown apart. None survived.

The two explosions wiped out Travis's South African team. He saw Jack roll over, sit up, then turn away from the dead men. He started to head for more cover then checked himself.

"Boss?" Jack said.

"Yeah?"

"We're screwed."

Travis didn't have time to reply. Three more LAWs fired from the roof. Each hit its target and the death toll doubled. The force was crippled.

"Everyone bite dirt," Travis said, then flipped his frequency dial to a circling C-130. "Pilot, mark my signal."

"Marked and locked."

"Fire!"

"Missile launched."

Travis switched back to the team frequency. "Fifteen seconds to impact on the front door of that farmhouse," he said. "We're going to end this now."

He didn't have to remind his team to take cover. For the first time a TALON Force team was employing a newly developed version of the more common Redeye missile. These were fire-and-forget missiles, capable of flying through the window of a house and taking out a steel door. The object was simple. The team needed a system of precise delivery explosives waiting on standby. In the course of any mission, there was always a possibility of becoming pinned down and losing the ability to move without taking casualties. These small, highly specialized explosives wouldn't take out a stadium but certainly packed more punch than hand delivered devices—even with their limited range. Five miles for the mini-cruise missiles was about all they could expect, but Travis believed they would be TALON Force's godsend on future battlefields.

He heard the whisking hum of the missile coming in but never actually saw it. Travis watched the front door of the farmhouse slam open in a burst of exploded bits of wood and metal. He shrugged. The initial explosion wasn't much more than that of the LAWs. But it was more focused and thus more powerful. A large section of wall collapsed and a cloud of debris and plaster dust filled the air. Travis turned on his camouflage and stood up, praying the LOCS feature was functioning properly.

"Team One is moving in," Travis said.

"Right beside you," Jack said.

The two men moved to the shattered entry. Inside, an unrecognizable mass of human flesh lay sprawled against the remains of a wall. Beyond that Travis saw someone moving toward another door. "Halt!"

Instead of freezing, the tall, thin youth turned to fire an AK in the direction of the commanding voice. He saw only a dusty shimmer where Travis and Jack stood. The attackers appeared to be apparitions in the air, or maybe the young man was just weary of battle. Regardless he dropped the AK, letting it clatter to the floor. He put his hands in the air over his head.

Travis turned the stealth camo off and hurried forward to collect the discarded AK. Jack moved beside him.

"Team One is inside," Travis said. "All other teams remain in position until we deactivate the firing system for those LAWs and mines."

Jack took a handful of nylon straps from one of the pockets in his trousers. "Sit down," he said to the wide-eyed youth. Roughly, Jack bound the Boer's hands together and then his ankles. After making sure the restraints were snug, he ran an extra stay through the cuffs and then the ankles and secured it firmly. "Don't think you'll be going anywhere." Jack patted the young man on the head, then moved on. A long hallway led from the living room to the bedrooms, and Travis guessed, to the control center for the defense of the house. They heard men in one of the bedrooms. Jack removed a flash/bang grenade from his belt. Travis nodded.

After Jack threw the grenade, he and Travis ducked back into the main room for protection. Seconds later, the explosion shook the weakened house. Dust fell from the ceiling and smoke rolled down the corridor. Two men staggered into the hallway, coughing and weaving, AKs held in front of them. They blindly fired down the hall.

Both Jack and Travis rolled into a firing position on the floor. With rapid bursts from their rifles, they killed both Boers. Before anyone else could move into the hallway, Travis and Jack leapt to their feet and sprinted down it. They stopped at the open door, preparing to throw a second flash/bang.

A voice called out, "There are children here!"

Travis remembered the two dead children in the yard. Jennifer had said they were armed.

"Send them out!" Travis shouted.

"They're coming," the voice said. When the first child reached the door, Jack grabbed for the boy and jerked him to one side.

Pop! Pop! The quick shots from an AK responded.

If they didn't need these Boers alive to find out where the rest of the virus was Travis would have killed them. Instead he tossed the second flash/bang through the door. He waited for a five count before rolling into the room. The three stunned survivors held their ears. They had been temporarily blinded and deafened by the flash. Travis didn't hesitate. He grabbed the first and pushed him to the floor. Within seconds, the other two followed.

"Where are the others?" Travis shouted.

The man, middle-aged and thick, raised his head to look at Travis. He blinked, trying to clear his vision. Blood trickled from his nose and a split lip. He pointed to a walk-in safe.

Travis hauled him to his feet and shoved him toward it. "Open it, and if the damn thing blows up, you'll be the first to die!"

Without looking at Travis he shuffled to the safe and pulled the handle. The Boer family, looking defeated and frightened, filed out of the door. Other South Africans from Jen's assault force had followed Travis and Jack into the house and they led the family outside.

The women's eyes grew round and the others could feel their stiff silence as they walked past the bodies. When the last woman was out Travis turned to the three men who had survived the final assault.

"Where are the vials?" Travis asked.

"I don't have to tell you anything," the graying Boer, the one who opened the safe, answered. He glared at Travis in defiance and licked the blood from his lip.

"No," Travis said, "you don't have to tell me a damn thing, but you can either tell *me* or you will tell them." Travis motioned to three black members of the assault force. "I'll let them convince you." Barrett cocked his head and eyed the Boer. It was purely a psychological move on his part. He knew that the Boers would be willing to endure a fairly severe beating, but little else would be as bad as being tortured by the blacks they hated.

"We've only got one vial here," the Boer said. "It's too late for the others."

"Explain," Travis said.

"Eric is gone! He has taken the other vials! They have already been distributed to our patriots." The man sneered and laughed, loudly, insanely. "They'll be setting them loose on the world." He stopped and looked at the blacks. "It's too bloody bad you black bastards couldn't keep your place."

Travis glanced at Jack but the big man hadn't moved. He was in control of himself, functioning as part of TALON Force, not a man listening to the backward racial slurs of a backward people.

"Okay, then we'll just have to track them all down." Travis glanced at his watch. He watched the seconds ticking off. Travis knew his patience was thinning. The sound of blood pounded in his temples. *What's wrong with these people?*

He turned to Jack. "Go get his wife."

Jack started to move.

"What are you thinking you will do?"

Travis turned to the Boer. "She has two legs, two arms, two eyes. I figure by the time she's lost one knee and an elbow, you'll tell me where the rest of your patri-

ots are and she'll still be able to walk." He turned to
Jack, who had stopped in the door. "Get her!"

"No!" the Boer shouted. "It's too late to stop all of
our people!" Spittle flew from the man's mouth.

Travis scoffed. Again, Jack moved for the door.

"Stop! I'll tell you! Don't let the bloody kaffirs touch
her!"

Travis grabbed the Boer by the ear. "Know what, you
big son of a bitch?" he hissed. "It only takes three and
a half pounds of pressure per square inch to remove a
human ear . . ." Travis muscled the big man to a table.
"Have a seat."

Travis checked his straight-up satellite link to Washington. "You ready to get this?"

"Roger, Major Barrett," came the reply.

Travis thought about the silence from Washington
when he threatened to torture the Boer's wife. Everyone
in Washington had heard the threat. He wondered if the
situation had become so grim that the leaders of TALON
Force and the United States would have him torture a
woman to get the information.

"All right," Travis started. He faced the Boer so that
every word would be picked up by the communications
gear in his helmet. Travis was surprised when a grim-
faced Major Anderson sat down across from him. Bright
splotches of blood stained Anderson's uniform. For a
moment Travis thought of the South African unit's casualties then pushed them from his mind. This was a war
and in war people died. He took a notebook and a pen
from a pocket inside his camouflage uniform. He'd never
forgotten his training as a young soldier and his notebook
was still the lifeline to facts. He turned back to the Boer.
"Start talking."

Half an hour later the Boer sat back in his chair. "We
will win, you know. Eric Steiner is a great man. He will
lead us to victory—and then ya bloody kaffirs will
know—" He'd recovered some of his composure and he

folded his arms. "If ya daft buggers think you can stop us with force, you can't. God gave us this land. We didn't take it from the kaffirs. We'll get our country back."

"Not from behind bars, you won't," Anderson said. He then looked over his shoulder to two of his men. "Take him and the rest of them to headquarters."

The Boer stood. "We'll win you know. God is with us."

Anderson looked up. "I'm sure he is. He was with Hitler, too. Look what it got him."

The men escorted the Boer from the room. Travis heard the click of handcuffs and the Boer's grunt as he was shoved out the door. Anderson still sat at the table. He waited for Travis.

"Eleven and four," Anderson said.

"What's that?" Travis asked.

"The dead and wounded. All mine, or do you care?"

"Of course I care, Major. But this is a desperate operation."

"Well, Major Cyborg, it isn't so desperate that we can't engage with a bit more finesse. Or do you Americans think of us as expendable because we don't wear hide-and-seek suits?"

"What's your point?"

"My point is that all your fancy techno-crap was bloody worthless. A group of half-witted farmers just about stopped us, *and* killed half my men in less time than it takes to eat a hamburger. And now we find out that the vials are in three different locations, with three different groups of lunatics. How are you going to solve this problem, Major? You're the best in the world. *You're* the one with all the gimmicks and gizmos and techno-shit. How are you goin' to save the world from a group of farmers who want their country back?"

Travis leaned forward and glared at Anderson. "Major, I'll do my job and I'll do it by not losing my fucking head and not believing that I am up against a group of farmers."

A voice in his helmet comm cautioned him to ease off. "Barrett, remember that Major Anderson has lost a lot of men," the voice said.

Travis didn't answer but clicked his tongue to let the listeners in Washington know that he'd heard them.

"Look, Major. We rushed in here thinking this would put an end to the nightmare. It didn't. This will force us to split our forces and go after the other known cells. We don't have time to debate whether it will be technology or brute force that, ultimately, puts a stop to this bullshit. I suggest that we set our differences aside, revitalize the entire assault force, and put our attack plans together—unless you want to continue arguing semantics."

Anderson didn't respond for a moment. Then he said, "We'll finish this operation, Major Cyborg. But don't squander any more of my men with your bloody heroics."

Travis flinched inwardly and set his jaw. The operation had gone wrong. He wouldn't let any of the other assaults go bad. "Major Anderson, let's get back to Johannesburg. We've got work to do."

Anderson pushed his chair back. "Right, and let's not fuck it up."

Travis followed Anderson outside. A team of police officers was preparing to search the entire farm. A tall, thin officer presented him with the contained vial of virus. Travis looked at him and then signaled the rest of Eagle Team back to the helicopters. He glanced at the row of body bags then moved on. In Vietnam, old-timers had told him, the body bags would be laid out in neat rows and the only noise would be the wind rippling the plastic shrouds. War, he knew, had changed. The first assault had lasted exactly forty-five minutes.

Chapter 5

The only sound in the hangar was the voice of General Krauss. The entire assault force, including replacements for the fifteen casualties, listened with an air of desperation.

"India has announced that its entire military, including nuclear-strike capability, has been placed on full alert. They are warning that an attack on their soil will be considered an act of war."

Travis scratched his head. "Why is the Indian government refusing to recognize the action of the Boer extremists as an act of terrorism?"

"It seems most of the world is blaming two governments for this," Krauss said. "The first is South Africa—for allowing this Boer terrorist group to get as well organized as it is; and second—Zimbabwe for not working with the white farmers."

"I don't think, sir, that either government can really be held responsible," Travis said.

"True, Major. But this is an indicator of just how panicked the world governments are becoming over this situation. We've got to finish this operation."

"Roger that, sir," Travis said. "We're ready to roll

on this end. If there are no further orders we're ready to go."

"Good luck, Major, and good luck to your team," Krauss replied. The general paused for a moment before he added in a hesitant voice, "Major, we are going to place additional TALON forces on standby for immediate deployment should the situation deteriorate with additional threats or the discovery of other cells."

"Yes, sir. Do you have any intel to indicate there may be cells we cannot neutralize?" Travis asked, frowning.

"No, Major. At this time you are the entire operation."

"Roger." Travis stood up and walked to the front of the assault group. Anderson stepped to one side. "Each team has its target. Each team understands the mission and you've all been briefed on what happened at the Steiner farm." Travis looked at the assault force—men and women, two nations, different races. They were working together. He wondered why the Boers couldn't find a solution to their problems. When he looked at Anderson, Travis felt the distrust from the South African. Maybe the answer was hidden inside their own treatment of each other.

"You have anything to add, Major?" Travis asked Anderson.

"We've covered the operation."

"Right," Travis said. He studied his watch. "Synchronize your watches with mine."

Every man and woman lifted their arms to set their watch.

"On my mark the time will be exactly zero-nine-ten." He began a second-by-second countdown ending it with, "Mark!" The last detail of the three-way operation settled, Travis picked up his rifle and put the sling over his shoulder. "Ladies and gentlemen, let's rock and roll."

Silently, with the only noise being the shuffling of footsteps and age-old clatter of military equipment, each member of the assault force stood up and started for his or her assigned helicopter. Even as the team moved, the waiting South African Aérospatiale Puma helicopters' twin turbines were winding up. Travis watched his team split and head for their respective ride in one of the six choppers. All of TALON's integrity had depended on the team's ability to function as a unit. Breaking up the team would reduce their effectiveness. Looking over his shoulder he could see Sam with one hand resting on the bank of communication and radio equipment he would be monitoring. His role was essential, and Travis wanted to keep him out of the field where the bullets would probably be flying.

Before stepping up to the deck of the waiting helicopter, Travis checked his communications net. One by one, each team member responded with an affirmative. Sam was the last to confirm the link was operating. Travis asked if the Washington command was receiving.

"Confirmed," Krauss said.

"We're going to launch."

"Roger."

Travis knew that unless something began to deteriorate seriously during the operation, the observers in Washington would not interfere in the operation. He turned back to the team.

"Team Two, ready for launch?"

"Team Two, ready," Captain Sarah Greene said.

"Team Three, ready for launch?"

"Team Three, ready," Lt. Commander Stanislaus Powczuk said.

"Team leaders," Travis said, "you have operational command for your assigned target."

The "rogers" came back to him and Travis settled into his seat in the bowels of the helicopter. He nodded to the crew chief and felt the change in vibration as the rotors gained speed. This is it, Travis thought, we either win or lose in the next two hours.

Sarah pulled her seat belt tight. The helicopter shuddered and lifted from the ground. She looked around. The faces of the assault team were masked with the mission. She fidgeted under her Low Observation Camouflage Suite. "Zoot suit," she mumbled and toyed with her left ear where the four tiny silver rings usually were—a nervous habit. To the South Africans seated around her, the petite black-haired pixieish doctor was an aberration—something strange that snowboarded down from the mountains of Vermont to take over an operation that didn't really make a lot of sense to any of them. As the helicopter turned away from the Johannesburg international airport she put everything out of her mind except the mission. They would follow her orders.

May 30, 0937 hours
South African high veldt farm

Sarah followed the routine checklist for the start of any operation. She checked her equipment, then her communications gear, her biological chip processors, and after reassuring herself that everything was in correct working order, she reported in the affirmative. Her "All systems go" was picked up by the internal mic of her battle helmet and relayed to Captain Hunter Blake. When she heard his "Roger," she relaxed just a bit and turned to the South African team leader.

"Check their gear," she ordered.

He nodded and turned to the team member on his left, checked his equipment and pointed for him to check the next man. In this manner each team member was reassured and his equipment readied. As the helicopter dropped to just above treetop level the perceptible level of tension among the team went up. The pilot turned around and gave Sarah the thumbs-up, followed by his index finger to signal one minute to the LZ. She repeated the signals and watched while each team member made final adjustments. Seconds seemed to drag as the helicopter made its approach, then flared. Dust swirled up and around, briefly disorienting Sarah until the jolting lurch when the helicopter landed.

Training took over for each member of the team and they hit the ground running. They spilled out of both sides of the chopper, running ten or fifteen yards to cover and then dropping to the ground. Sarah dropped behind a large ironwood tree and checked her unit. No one had been hurt and they hadn't taken any fire.

"Hunter," she said into her comm net, "put a Dragonfly in the air and let's have a look around the house."

"Roger," Hunter said, "Dragonfly loose. Watch your BSD."

Sarah was determined not to repeat the first fiasco. She studied the image being sent by the UAV. Hunter maneuvered the tiny surveillance pusher aircraft around the house, using a joystick, then made it hover to check something that appeared out of place. He flew the UAV closer when he needed a better view. There was nothing in the yard to give the appearance that it was anything more than a farmhouse and he said as much on the radio.

"Except for one thing," Sarah said.

"What's that?"

"There isn't a damn thing out here that's moving. Where are the dogs? Chickens? Something, anything?"

"Vietnam syndrome?"

"Roger," Sarah said. Then she heard a voice in her helmet. Someone in Washington wanted to know what the Vietnam syndrome was.

General Krauss responded, again over the satellite, so there wouldn't be any misunderstanding. "It was a tip-off to American troops that something wasn't right when they moved into a village. There wouldn't be any animals or kids around. The troops learned pretty quick that when that happened, there was something else going on."

"Usually a trap," Sarah said.

"You call it," Hunter said.

"I'm going to move the entire team, pull back a hundred meters. I want you to drop me an RPTV. When it's on the ground, we'll send it into the house. See what we're up against. We can't see anything on the ground."

"Roger," Hunter said.

Sarah quickly signaled the team to pull back. There were incredulous looks of disbelief but the men were disciplined and they followed orders. To find cover they had to move nearly two hundred yards away from the house to the top of a small rise. From there the unit could survey the entire area. After a few minutes Sarah heard the distinctive buzz of the Remote Piloted Tracked Vehicle's motor as it swept toward them. Although the RPTV hummed onward in the direction of the house, she hadn't seen the plane drop it into the sky, its glider-chute left somewhere on the high veldt, probably a few hundred yards behind them.

"Hunter, you want to drive that thing?" Sarah asked.

"I got it," he said. For Hunter, the pilot's pilot, driving the RPTV was like being a kid playing with a favorite toy. From his position, with handheld radio controls, he could easily maneuver the tracking robot.

He drove it like the Mars Lander, using the on-board cameras to avoid dangers on the ground. When the RPTV was in the yard and he could see the door on his screen, he snickered to Sarah. "Want me to knock? Or just bust in?"

"Be polite," Sarah said.

Hunter moved the robotic arm. It raised to the height of the doorknob. He then moved it forward to knock on the door. The fireball that consumed the house was bright orange. Blue flames curled from the foundation, licking the air. Debris, appearing like black spots in the fire, flew up and out. The roof went up like a massive solid projectile. It disintegrated in midair, showering the farmyard with splinters. No one had any time to think about the inferno. They only had time to cover their faces. That didn't protect their backs from falling rubble, or from the wall of searing heat that rolled over them from the plastique explosion.

When everything cleared Sarah heard the frantic calls of General Krauss, panicky and demanding to know what had happened. She ignored him and concentrated on the team. A splinter well over a foot long had plummeted from the sky, spearing one man. The piece of wood pierced his leg and, although he was bleeding, the wound was treatable. That was the only injury. The robotic vehicle was gone—vaporized in the explosion—as was the house. What was left, burned. Great billowing clouds of smoke rolled skyward.

"Umm, Captain Greene," the South African team leader said.

"Yes, Captain?"

"How'd you know?"

She smiled at him. "A lesson we learned in another time."

He nodded then pointed behind her. "We've got company."

The trap should have worked—might have worked—and the Boer guerillas who set the trap must have expected it to work because they were emerging from their equivalent of a spider hole. Fully armed, they clearly expected the entire assault force to have been killed in the explosion.

Not one of the guerillas checked the area and Sarah quickly and silently dispersed her unit on the little hill so they wouldn't be seen. She gave the voice command for her camo suit and then ordered Hunter to follow. The two moved down the hill, little more than shimmers against the prairie. When they were in position, she stood ten yards in front of the man who was obviously the leader. He laughed—pleased at their apparent success.

Sarah silently switched off her suit. She appeared in a ripple of atmosphere and background, suddenly becoming visible to the emerging Boers.

"Greetings," she said. "You're all under arrest."

Pandemonium erupted. The Boer howled with rage.

Sarah jumped out of the way when the leader fired a quick burst from his AK-47.

Hunter didn't hesitate—he hardly aimed and dropped the man with a single shot. His comrades saw the bright splotch of red spread beneath his fallen body. Several bellowed, warrior's rage filling them with bloodlust. The battle was now joined.

Sarah gave the voice command of "Stealth on," and scrambled for cover. With the aid of the LOCS, she blended into the rocks.

Six more Boers had poured out of the once-concealed door to the underground bunker and were firing wildly into the bush and onto the hill at the South African troops.

Sarah had lost control of the situation and was trying to regain it when one of the Boers threw an American-made hand grenade at the hill. The grenade fell short, but the warning was clear. These people were not going to surrender. She moved the selector switch on her XM-29 to full auto, brought the rifle to her shoulder, and began pouring three-round bursts of 5.56mm ammo into the Boers. She saw one fall in a bloody crumpled heap and the others spread themselves out, apparently willing to fight to the death.

The fire from the South African R-4 rifles was controlled and deadly. Every time one of the Boers raised above their protective berm to fire, one of the South Africans fired a quick burst and the Boer would fall back, his head shattered by the deadly and accurate shot. When a white flag was gingerly pushed over the berm Sarah smiled. "Maybe," she said, "there's hope for these fanatics."

Sarah kept her camouflage activated while she moved forward. Hunter covered her and she waited for two of the South Africans, also covered by their remaining team members on the hill, to move down and collect the weapons. When the situation appeared to be under control, she said, "Stealth off," and walked forward. The South Africans had disarmed the surviving three Boers and waited, ready to search the bunker. Based on past experience she pulled one of the three survivors toward the door. "You first," she said and pushed him toward the stairs. With the barrel of her rifle in his back she steered him inside.

"My God," she gasped, entering the bunker. "General Krauss, are you picking the audio feed up?"

"Roger, Captain."

"I am going to add video. Make sure you get this. We're not dealing with a bunch of backward farmers."

A few seconds later General Krauss verified that they were indeed receiving the video. Sarah panned the room, stopping to linger her gaze, which was duplicated by the mini TV camera in her helmet. The stocks of ammunition, explosives, and food were startling. Great piles lined the wall. The room rivaled—or bettered—that of any American right-wing fundamentalist groups. Sarah heard the excited buzzing in the Washington command center. She continued her personal tour of the main room in the bunker. Meanwhile, the rest of the team had stationed themselves inside, following her lead. She nodded once to Hunter and turned her attention back to the mission at hand.

"I want the vials," she said.

The Boers were all silent.

"I said," she repeated slowly, "I want the vials,"

"Bugger off, bitch."

Sarah stepped back and switched off the video camera. "I don't have time for this crap," she said and looked around the bunker. "It's got to be here, someplace." She

saw a metal cabinet. "Is it in there?" She stepped close
to the oldest Boer, a man with reddish hair. When he
didn't answer, she reached for him with serpentlike agil-
ity. With one hand in his hair, she jabbed her first and
second fingers into the man's nostrils, pulling his head
down. Leading him by the nose, hair in a vicelike grip,
she bent him over and ran his head into the metal door.
No one moved.

The man drooped in her grip, then spit out what must
have been teeth and a mouthful of blood in a pulpy mass.

"I guess it's not in there, is it." She looked around the
room and caught sight of several cabinet doors under a
counter. "Maybe it's there," she said. Again, she pulled
his head down, lower this time, and ran, full tilt, at the
cabinet. The cabinet door buckled under the onslaught
of the Boer's head.

This time he sagged to his knees then fell over.

"Looks like he didn't know where the vials were."
Sarah stepped over to a younger man, the first growth
of whiskers coloring his chin. "Maybe you do," she said
angrily and grabbed for the youth, who, instinctively,
tried to duck her grasp, only to be held for her by one
of the South Africans.

"I don't have that shit!" he shouted, trying to defend
himself.

Sarah knew she appeared as some kind of warrior god-
dess, decked out in the bizarre camouflage.

"The bloody stuff's in the next room with the rest
of them."

"Rest of who?" Hunter demanded.

"The others from our group. There's four women, six
men, and the kids in there."

"Where?" Sarah demanded.

"There! For bloody Christ's sake!" he said, and
pointed toward a floor-to-ceiling white cabinet. "Behind
that thing is the door."

Sarah turned to two of the South African soldiers,

commanding them to cuff and shackle the prisoners and then take them outside. "Tie 'em to some burning timbers from the house for all I care," she said. "Just get these crazy bastards out of my sight!"

With the Boers safely outside, she turned her attention to the problem of getting into the inner bunker. "Okay, Hunter," she said, pulling her partner over to the door. "What's the best way to take it out without killing everyone inside?"

Hunter studied the door, then grinned. "It's no problem, babe. No problem at all," he said, reaching for his Gerber-Applegate knife. He slid the blade into the doorjamb and began to twist it. He looked back. "Everyone find some cover."

He waited until every member of the team had taken a defensive position, as safe as they could make it under the circumstances. They didn't have the luxury of time for perfect planning or to take great pains in preparation, but they readied themselves as best they could. Hunter pushed the steel tip into the jamb another fraction of an inch and felt the lock. He worked the blade to the end of the lock then pushed it into the lock's mechanism. "Ready?" he said, smiling at the amazed South Africans. When he was sure they were, he let go of the knife. The tip wedged in tightly next to the lock. He drew back his heavy booted foot and kicked the door, jumping back to the safety of the wall in one smooth and swift movement.

The door flew open. Two seconds passed, then three. Then came the long burst of AK-47 fire.

"Y'all are finished shootin' up the countryside. You can put down your guns and come out," Hunter said, in his best Travis imitation.

"Are you Yanks?" a voice asked.

"Yup," Hunter said.

"What's going to happen to us?"

"You started this, we're going to finish it—either with you dead or in prison. Your choice."

"The kids?"

"Not my country," Hunter quit mimicking Barrett. His voice took on the tones of seriousness.

"You always tell the truth?"

"When it's best," Hunter said.

"Okay, we're coming out," the voice said. The sound of scuffling feet preceded the first man as he emerged, hands in the air.

A South African took hold of his prisoner and led him to a wall. He forced the Boer to spread his feet and placed his hands over his head on the bunker wall. Methodically, he frisked the terrorist for more weapons. One by one each of the Boers left their inner sanctum. After they'd all come out, including the women and children, the entire group was methodically detained with nylon straps, courtesy of SANP, and led outside. They were then seated in a large circle so they could be guarded with relative ease.

Sarah approached the group. "Who's in charge here?" she asked.

A tall, bearded man stood up. "That would be me," he said.

"Fine. Where are the vials?"

"Not much on manners, are you?" he said.

"Look, if you terrorists weren't about to start a world war, I'd have time to say please and thank you. Right now, I don't."

"Simpler to give us what we want."

"That's not possible and you know it."

"The world gave our country to the kaffirs. We want it back."

"Dude," Hunter said, "have you ever heard the expression, 'We won, you lost'?"

"No," the Boer said.

"Well, you really need to think about it, because those guys you call kaffirs—well, they won, you lost. And you just lost again so cough it up."

"I don't have a cold," the Boer said, not understanding American slang.

"Nope." Hunter smirked. "I guess you don't. But you keep this shit up, and Captain Greene here is gonna lose her temper and start working your people over again. See, her people won themselves a little country, too. You ever heard of a place called Israel? I have a feeling that she may identify with those kaffirs." Blake said the word with emphasis and continued. "So maybe you better watch yourselves, or all of you—men *and* women—are gonna look like that poor chump," he said, pointing at the Boer Sarah had used as a battering ram.

The passed-out Boer lay on the ground, cuffed and shackled. A gash across his forehead had scabbed over, dry blood matting in his hair.

The Boer swallowed hard. "It's locked in the safe in the bunker."

"Fine, let's go," Sarah said. "You'll open the safe. If it's wired, you're going to eat the blast."

The Boer grunted submissively.

He was, Sarah knew, beaten.

"Captain Greene?" General Krauss's voice sounded in her helmet.

"Yes, sir," Sarah answered. She gestured to one of the South Africans to lead the Boer back into the bunker.

"We've just received word that another vial has been released."

"Where?"

"France, the dairy region."

"Damage?"

There was a momentary silence, then the voice of Jane Whaite-Worthington, the president's aide, said, "The French government is demanding that the southern African nations take responsibility for the actions of the terrorists and make restitution for the loss of their dairy industry."

"All of it?"

"About a third."

"Shit," she said.

"Be careful, but get those vials," Krauss's voice echoed back.

"Yes, sir." She turned to follow the Boer and South African into the bunker. Once inside she motioned for the farmer to open the safe.

He knelt, settling himself on one knee, and began to work the combination. The first time he tried to pull the handle open it wouldn't move so he spun the dial and started over. This time, the handle turned. He started to pull the door open, and at the same time moved to reach inside.

Sarah stood behind him, and although she couldn't see into the safe, she saw his hand move, first toward the lower shelf, then quickly into the upper part of the safe. The black shape of an automatic pistol flashed as he pulled it out.

The South African, a tall and very black man with a ready and friendly smile, even for the prisoners, saw the flash of black. He couldn't believe that even in this last stage of their crumbling plot, the white farmer would insist on trying one more time.

The 9mm Baretta didn't jump in the Boer's hand. Instead, the farmer's hand was steady and the three shots into the black soldier's chest were evenly spaced, each one pushing him backward another step.

Sarah didn't stop to think. She only reacted. Her own gun came up as fast as the farmer's. But the desire to kill, she knew, was on his side and hate fueled his speed and determination. Her first shot came on the end of his third. The bullet from her rifle tore into his right shoulder and down through his lungs. Blood spurted from the twin wounds from the single bullet and he fell forward, rolling over.

He looked up at Sarah and grinned maliciously. "There's your bloody vials," he said.

"Why?"

The farmer didn't answer but looked at the dead black man. "Bloody kaffirs," he gurgled, "never have enough."

Sarah watched him die. She reached past the bloodied body and picked up the three vials. "Vials are safe," she said into the mic of the comm gear. "And this cell's leader is dead."

"Understood," Krauss's voice sounded.

Sarah walked outside. The assault team parted and let her walk through. She handed the vials to Hunter, who quickly locked them in a strong box. She then walked past Blake to the leader's wife.

"Your husband's dead," Sarah said.

"I know," the woman said. "He always said he'd go that way if he didn't get his country."

"Why," Sarah groaned, "can't you people live together?"

The woman looked pointedly at the guards. They were black and white men, one-time enemies now serving on the same team, in the same army. Sarah followed the woman's gaze. The woman looked back at Sarah. Resolution shone in her eyes. "No," she said. "Not with them. It's not natural. It goes against God's laws."

Sarah didn't respond. She only looked hard at the woman and then shook her head. She walked away, slowly. Into her communications link, she said, "General, did you hear that?"

"Roger."

"What happened to 'love thy neighbor'?"

There was a long silence before the general said, "I don't know."

"Roger," Sarah said, then added, "Eagle Team One, mission accomplished."

Chapter 6

Communication between the three teams was kept open, but no one had used it. There wasn't any reason to interfere with the other operations. Each team had received their plans in the hangar, each team had its mission, and each mission needed to be completed. Normally, in an operation of this sort, Eagle Team wouldn't be concerned with the status of the world's powers and the political arena. TALON Force would simply complete the mission and return to the States for debriefing and some much needed R&R. This mission was different. The team was being kept abreast of the world's politics because they were deteriorating rapidly.

"Major Barrett," the voice of General Krauss sounded in Travis's helmet.

"Barrett here, sir."

"Eagle Team One's mission was successful."

"Roger, sir, I monitored."

"You know about France?"

"Yes, sir."

"We sent word to the French government about our successful recovery of the first four vials but the news hasn't changed the situation."

"Changing the situation, sir?" Travis touched his helmet in a gesture of confusion.

"France is blaming England for the Zimbabwe issue, and demanding that England take military action against Zimbabwe."

"Where's that leave us?"

"It leaves us in a position that is even more unstable. If France doesn't get some satisfaction from either the southern African nations or England, they are threatening to blockade the Channel, or even close it down to prevent English exports from reaching mainland Europe."

Travis was silent for several seconds. The mechanical drone of the helicopter became a background for his contemplation of the politics being played out. "We can't hurry the mission, General," Travis finally said. "I don't think anyone counted on this much firepower."

"We understand, Major. All I am telling you is that we're running out of time. Do the best that you can, but do it quickly. As of this moment the presidents of the United States and South Africa have lifted all restraints on the employment of military force. They have authorized me to finish this mission. You now have the authority to take whatever steps you deem necessary to resolve this crisis. Travis, get those vials."

"Understood, sir. But I do have a question."

"What is that?"

"Who's gonna pay the bill?"

"One way or another, Major, all of us will pay for this one."

"Roger."

Travis turned his attention to the assault team and initiated the same equipment check procedure Sarah Greene had followed. When it was finished he sat back and reviewed the target. Like the previous two targets, it was a farm. This one sat in the open high veldt country north of Middleburg—and this mission came with its own set of problems. There was no cover in the area. The helicopter would need to drop to only a few feet off the ground, beginning a distance of about five miles from the target. From there the pilot would follow the ground's contour, using every little knoll and kopje to provide any cover possible. Four hundred meters from the house the helicopter would rise to an altitude of fifty feet and make a run straight at the house. The chopper would flare and drop the first half of the team a hundred meters from the back door, then circle the house and drop the remainder of the team the same distance from the front of the house.

As the helicopter flew the last few klicks, Travis mentally reviewed the chalkboard map and aerial photos of the farmhouse the assault force had used to plan the mission. In his mind he pictured what his team would have to deal with once on the ground.

A four-foot high wall made from a double thickness of brick covered with whitewashed plaster surrounded the farmhouse. Shards of broken glass and a double string of barbed wire covered the top of the wall. It would provide cover for the assault, but then they would need to breach the wall for the assault on the house. How they breached it, what force they used, would ultimately depend on the Boers inside. If they choose to fight, and if this house was as well defended as the first one, it could take a bit of time. Travis didn't have time. There had to be a faster way. Something that wouldn't take as long, or risk so many lives—from both sides. So far each farm had been assaulted in a police-style attack rather than a military assault, although military tactics had been employed, finally, to win the objective.

"Well, hell," he said to no one in particular, "might as well get this mission started with a bang."

Travis turned to Anderson. They needed to discuss their options.

"Major?" Anderson asked.

"You know General Krauss gave us authorization to use whatever force we deemed the situation merited?"

"Yes." Anderson leaned closer to Travis and folded his arms across his chest. "What are you planning?"

"Let's use a little firepower for the opening move."

Anderson nodded.

"Pilot?" Travis said.

"Pilot here," the pilot responded from the left seat.

"I want you to assume a holding pattern, two klicks from the target."

"Roger."

"I'll let you know when to make the assault."

"I understand," the pilot said.

"Sam?"

"Sam here, boss."

"Good. Sam, I want you to have the South Africans scramble aircraft. Here's the target and ordnance requirement."

Anderson and the rest of the assault force waited while Travis manipulated his BSD to study a GPS image of the target. The image was enhanced with map and photos of the target area. The electronic enhancements gave Travis the opportunity to plan his first phase with accuracy and expediency.

First he gave Sam the target coordinates. Then he became specific. "There is a wall, white, surrounding the target house. Instruct pilots that they are to destroy that wall with rockets and machine-gun fire. They are not to hit the house. I say again, limit the strike to the wall."

"Roger," Sam said, then repeated the instructions.

"That is correct," Travis confirmed. Then his voice softened. "Tell them that I think the wall is the trap at his house. I want it reduced to nothing."

"Roger," Sam said.

Travis leaned back in his seat to wait. The minutes ticked off before the pilot spoke to him again. "Major?"

"Yes?"

"Your aircraft are on station and commencing their attack . . . Now."

Travis leaned around so he could look out the window, past the pilots. A column of smoke curled tightly into the blue of the sky. While he watched, two South African fighters dove at the farmhouse and then peeled off, leaving columns of smoke in their path. Each plane made four passes at the target before they turned for home.

"Sam?" Travis said.

"Sam here."

"Tell those pilots I said thank you and that tearing up that wall saved us a lot of time and lives."

"Roger."

"Pilot?"

"Yes, Major?"

"Let's do it."

"Roger." The pilot pulled the helicopter into a steep climb and poured on the power to reach the farmhouse before the stunned occupants could organize an effective defense. Travis watched the ground flash past. When the nose came up for the landing flair, the grip on his rifle tightened. The seconds seemed to slow to a crawl, then the aircraft bounced once.

May 30, 1012 hours
South African high veldt farm

"Go! Go! Go!" Travis shouted.

Major Anderson jumped out the door a full step ahead of Travis. Dust swirled around the men when the pilot pulled pitch and lifted the chopper back into the air, then flew directly over the top of the smoke-engulfed farmhouse. Travis could see the noxious cloud pulled into the curl of the rotor's wash, leaving a swirling haze that rolled onto itself into a tunnel that trailed behind the helicopter. He checked his team, paying close attention to their positions. The assault team stationed themselves around the shattered wall in positions that were not obvious, and although they might have offered less cover than before, the chances of the positions being readily targeted by the Boer terrorists inside the house were slim. Then, almost as an afterthought, Travis looked around.

The fighters had done their work with systematic precision. The outer wall lay in crumbling piles of rubble. Long plumes of thick, black smoke rolled into the sky as the tires on the vehicles in the yard burned, along with the interiors. A gas tank ruptured in the further regions of the compound, sending a ball of flame skyward. Trees were torn from the ground and then turned to splinters that now littered the yard. Not an inch of the farmyard that could have been planted with mines or explosives had escaped the rocket attack. The destruction was total.

"Your boys did a good job of wrecking things," Travis said.

Several seconds of silence met Travis's comment. Major Anderson cleared his throat before he responded. "This is the home of a South African citizen."

"I understand, Major."

"Do you?"

Travis didn't answer. These questions shouldn't happen in the middle of the operation. When it was over, there would be the time to talk about what was right and wrong. He called the C-130 pilot flying support for the mission.

"Support One, go ahead, Team Two Leader."

"Stand by to deliver missile on my target."

"Roger."

Travis motioned for the team to take cover. He then asked Jen to confirm her team's position.

"Team is deployed and back door, secure," she replied.

"Roger. We're going to open up this sardine can,"

Travis said. Then he radioed the pilot. "Lock on my mark."

"Marked and locked."

"Fire."

"Missile is launched, time to impact—twelve seconds from my mark . . . mark!"

"Roger," Travis said. "Everyone down."

The seconds clicked in Travis's mind. He heard the incoming missile first and felt the bizarre sense of history repeating itself. The loud sucking sound of the missile passing overhead gave him chills. Time barely moved until its impact. The missile hit the door of the farmhouse, the resonating explosion immediately followed. A burst of AK fire blasted through the door as the dust began to settle.

This time the Boers had been waiting for the missile assault. They were ready and fighting back.

"I don't think they will surrender without a hell of a fight," Anderson said.

"Yeah," Travis said. "This could turn into a problem."

The sound of more small-arms fire, this time from the back of the house, turned Travis's attention to the unfolding fight.

"Jen, what sort of fire are you taking?" The sound of more small-arms fire and another explosion answered Travis's question.

"At least two automatic weapons," she said. "They also have RPGs."

"Can you take out the RPG?"

"Negative," she said. "The individual is moving along the roof, hidden behind the false front."

"Roger," Travis said. He looked at the door. Another burst of automatic fire came through it, discouraging anyone from a rushing attack. So far no one had appeared on the roof. He wanted it to stay that way. But, the assault team would have to move on the house to put an end to the siege. "Anderson," Travis said.

"Anderson, here."

"You heard about the RPG. We need to get closer to the house."

"Roger."

"I don't want to move in team rushes this time. We move one man at a time. Movement needs to be random so it can't be predicted by the occupants."

"Roger," Anderson came back. "I'll give the name of the man to move. The others can put down suppressing fire until the next man moves."

"That's the ticket. Make sure everyone is on the look-out for signs of the RPG man on the roof. We'll have to worry about taking him out later. First I want to clear that room and get inside the house."

"Understood."

"One last thing, Anderson."

"What?"

"Be sure each man takes cover behind or under something that hopefully isn't targeted."

"I think they understand that problem."

"Right. When you're ready, start the rush."

Anderson nodded. Using hand and arm signals familiar to the team, but not the terrorists inside, he began the movement. After several seconds five of the six men in the front assault force began firing at the house. They aimed at the windows, the door, anyplace where a person could be hiding. The sound of the rifle fire drowned out what Travis knew was happening inside. The upcoming battle, the shots they fired now, each act of violence played its role in destroying the history of a family—the family that lived on this farm. Photographs, keepsakes, the little things that made a family special, were all being shot, shattered, and mangled. By the time the battle ended and the TALON team and the South African police had finished, little would be left to remind anyone of who had been here. The house would be a damaged shell, the family struggling to hold onto their memories

of life, death, and violence—violence generated by ha-
tred and greed.

The running South African—the first to move for position—flopped into a protected post from behind a pile
of rubble. The fallen wall served its purpose well and the
shooting stopped. The quiet in the yard felt unnatural. It
lasted for several long, thick seconds. The South African
behind the wall peeked out from behind his ruins. His
movement was answered by another burst of automatic
fire from the house—a gesture of defiance that clearly
told the assault force that the occupants would not give
up easily. Seconds later the next South African jumped
to his feet. The suppression fire immediately picked up
again. He ran nearly twenty feet before a volley of automatic fire from one of the shattered windows cut him
down—the back of his head exploded in a ghastly wash
of blood and brain matter.

"Stop the assault!" Anderson shouted. "Major, I want
you to listen to the impact of this round."

Travis nodded. Anderson fired a single rough through
the window. The sound of cracking, crashing plaster
echoed from the house, but also the unmistakable sound
of a bullet hitting solid steel.

"The interior walls are armor plated," Travis said.

"That's a surprise to you?" Anderson said. "These
people build their homes to withstand raids by maraud-
ing parties of black guerrillas. They believe that there is
a civil war coming. These aren't homes!" the Major
scoffed. "They're bloody fortresses. They are built for
sieges."

"We've got to take them now, Major Anderson,"
Travis said, frustration lending his voice a crispness that
he didn't like to hear. "If you've got any suggestions,
let's hear 'em."

Anderson paused, weighing his options. "We could call
for armored support. We could burn them out."

Travis vetoed the idea. Armor would take too long—

it was too far away. He also thought ahead to when the smoke of this operation cleared. The world wouldn't be hanging on the edge of war forever. Eventually, someone would find the time to question the force that had been used. "What's the chances those people are prepared for gas?" Travis asked. "Think we could smoke 'em out with CS-Two?"

"No," Anderson said. "Most of the farmers in this part of the world know terrorists have access to gas so they are equipped to deal with it."

"Well," Travis said, "we need some ideas."

"You have any more of those baby missiles?"

"Affirmative."

"Could you put one through the window and into the wall?"

Jen broke into the communication. "Before we put one of those inside the house, let's see if they shut the back door as effectively as they have the front door."

"What's your plan?" Travis asked.

"Look, except for the RPG on the roof, we've taken very little fire. Let this team assault the house, get under the windows, and then see if we can storm it from this side."

"You understand this is an envelope house," Anderson said. "There will be a series of interlocking rooms completely around the heart of the house, which is where the bunker appears to be."

"I understand, Major."

"I'm game," Travis said. "Move on your own when you're ready. We'll put fire into this side and try to keep them occupied."

"Roger," Jen said.

Travis and the rest of his force waited for the assault to begin. When they heard the command "Go!" over the radios, Travis and Anderson signaled the teams. Suppression fire poured into the house.

The din of battle rose in waves around the farmyard.

Hundreds of rounds of ammunition blazed from the barrels of a dozen guns, all at the same time. Travis could hear Jen's calm commands to her force. Her voice, though metallic, was strong and clear. She took care to advise everyone of the net on the team's success on the assault, saying, "First man up—Go! Under the window. Second man up." For the first time Travis felt the relief of success. And then it stopped. With a heavy, coughing "Ugh . . ." from Jennifer, he heard the sound of her body crashing to the ground.

"Jen!" Travis shouted. "Lieutenant!" He wanted to run around the farmhouse and rescue his team member but he held himself steady, relieved when he heard her voice.

"I'm hit," she said, the pain in her voice obvious. Several other grunts and groans followed and then the sound of scuffling as she was dragged to safety. Finally, safe behind some cover, she spoke into the radio again. "The Automatic Trauma Med Pack has kicked in—the bullet didn't penetrate, but fuck me, it hurts! I'm going to have one hell of a bruise!" she chuckled weakly, pain still registering in her voice.

General Krauss broke into the conversation. "Lieutenant, our monitors show your bio-chips indicate that you've sustained some bruising to the front of your ribs near the left shoulder. No broken bones, only tissue damage. Does that agree with your assessment of your situation?"

"Yes, sir," she said. "Sure hurts like hell."

"I understand."

"What's your situation on the back door?" Travis asked.

"My team reports more armor plating inside. The Boers seem to have firing ports built into the walls. That's what got me. Trying to break through that is going to be costly."

"No, it's not," Travis said, then called Washington.

"General, didn't we sell the South African army a bunch of TOWs?"

"Confirmed."

"I want two. How soon can we have them on site?"

A brief silence followed before Krauss returned to the radio. "They are being dispatched now. Should be in your Alpha Oscar within one-zero minutes."

"Roger," Travis said. "Let's back everyone off a bit, hold our positions—if they're safe—and maintain the present situation. Watch for RPG-man on the roof. If you see him, take him out. Otherwise, sit tight." He bit his lip before calling Jen.

"Yes?" she answered.

"How ya doin'?"

"I'm hanging in there," she said. "Won't be wearing anything too low-cut for a while, but what the hell. I didn't have a date tonight anyway."

"Roger."

Travis leaned back and relaxed. He looked over at Anderson. The South African watched him intently. The TALON-led team was resorting to 1970s era hardware to take down the house. Although not truly humiliated, Travis was learning a lot of lessons that he hadn't anticipated when this operation began. In the after-action report, he would most definitely have to address the issue of dealing with this sort of conflict. The technology of tomorrow can always be adjusted to situations. That was what was happening now. His adjustment was to fall back on weaponry designed specifically for the war with the Soviets. A war, he thanked God, that never came. Funny that the weapons built for the war that never happened might save the world from a war that shouldn't have ever started. He looked at his watch. Only two minutes had passed since the TOWs had been dispatched. An occasional burst of fire from one of the windows or the shattered door would harmlessly ping and ricochet off the debris of the wall. Travis watched the South Africans' reactions to the random fire, then realized there wasn't any reaction. They held their position, watching the house for dangers that could be fought or killed. Those minutes of waiting were a part of battle, of being trained to fight and kill. Fight, then rest, then fight and kill. Rest some more so they would have the energy to kill some more.

His helmet radio brought him back to the present battlefield. "Major Barrett?"

"Barrett here."

"We have your TOWs, our ETA is three minutes. Will you mark target with smoke?"

"Roger, will mark with yellow smoke."

Travis checked the house to assure himself that he wouldn't draw fire when he stood up. Satisfied that he was safe, he examined the target window and made sure they had an open path from the window to where the attack helicopter would fire the missile.

"Major Anderson?" Travis waited for the reply.

"Anderson here."

"I will mark the window with smoke," Travis said. "Let's keep the bad guys occupied and their heads down when the choppers get here."

"Roger," Anderson said.

Travis watched Anderson again signal his team of the plan. When Travis heard the helicopter approaching he switched on his chameleonlike camouflage and stood up. "I am going to mark one of the windows with yellow smoke. Pilot, are you in the net?"

"Impala One, here."

"Impala Two, here."

"Roger, Impala. Smoke will be below a window. I need you to put that missile through the window and into the inside wall. Do you copy?"

"Roger. Through the window marked with yellow smoke, into the inside wall."

Travis stepped over the shattered outer wall and hurried toward the window. His camouflage advantage was short-lived. A series of wild, automatic fire erupted from the windows and door, raking the yard around the house. The Boers were onto the plan. They couldn't see Travis but they could deliver enough fire into the yard to discourage anyone from getting too close to the house. Travis pulled the pin on the yellow smoke grenade and holding the spoon against the flat side of the canlike explosive, he raised it in the air and threw it toward the window. The grenade bounced once and rolled toward the house then stopped, fizzled, and popped. A stream of thick yellow smoke spewed from the canister and Travis ran back to his cover, hearing bullets from the house snapping around him. He dropped onto the ground and called Impala One.

"Target is marked. Engage."

"Roger, I have the target," the pilot said. Travis watched the attack helicopter slide into position two hundred yards away. The pilot held the chopper on a steady hover only twenty feet above the ground. He settled the crosshairs of the Tube-launched Optically-tracked Wire-guided antitank missile system on the window and fired. Unlike other missiles, the TOW is slow moving and flies more like a model plane on cables than a missile. Its accuracy comes from the operator maintaining the crosshairs on the target during the missile's flight. Very thin wires, which stream out from behind the missile, carry the electronic commands that keep the missile on the target. If the operator loses the target, or moves the aiming system then the missile follows the aiming system's commands.

Travis was sure the Boers were waiting for this sort of attack and he was stunned to hear Anderson suddenly shouting for his troops to fire at the roof.

The RPG-wielding Boer knelt confidently on the roof, the rocket launcher on his shoulder. He fired at the same time as the pilot.

Travis felt his breath catch as the RPG rocket headed for the helicopter. Luck was on their side. The pilot had seen the RPG fired in his viewfinder and pulled the big Puma out of danger. The RPG whistled past the helicopter and fell into the field beyond, sending up a small geyser of freshly plowed dirt when it exploded.

As the pilot pulled out of danger, a fraction of a second after firing, the TOW missile responded with the movement of the aiming system and turned skyward. If the pilot had been twenty yards further back, maybe the missile would have missed the house to climb into the sky and crash back to earth somewhere in the high veldt. But that isn't what happened.

The RPG operator hit the rooftop running, heading for shelter. Even before he saw the missile streaking toward him, it hit the false wall around the roof and exploded.

Idly, Travis wondered if the Boer was really aware of the force of the explosion that took out a fourth of the front wall of the house—leaving the armored wall inside fully exposed.

"Impala One, you no longer have an RPG to worry about," Travis said. "Can you take out that inside wall?"

"Roger," the pilot said and once again positioned his helicopter to fire a second TOW missile. There was nothing dramatic about the shot. It was textbook perfect. The missile slammed into the armored interior, opening it up like a soup can hit with a .22 hollow-point bullet.

The rifle fire from the Boers suddenly ceased. Anderson ordered the team to rush the house. There wasn't any resistance and the first man inside the house scrambled over the rubble left by the two missiles and looked into the bunker. When he saw that the occupants were still alive he shouted at them in Afrikaans, *"Afkiam! Werker pap, kind eerste!"*

Anderson was the second man to the top. "Open the

door!" he shouted. "Come out the door with your hands in the air."

The Boers, demoralized and defeated, stumbled out of the bunker. Travis watched them, looking for the leader. When a tall, older man with features distinguishing him as a man of influence and power came out, Travis asked if he was the cell leader.

"Yes."

"Good, we're going back inside. I want the vials."

"I've only got two here."

"Where's the third?"

"It was sent out."

"Where?"

"India."

"When is it going off?"

"What time is it?"

Travis looked at his watch. "It's ten-thirty hours."

"Not here," the Boer said, "in New Delhi."

Travis used his radio to ask Washington.

"It's fourteen-thirty," a voice said.

Travis repeated it to the Boer.

"I would say you have half an hour to find it."

"Where is it?" Travis demanded, slamming the Boer against the shattered wall.

"I honestly don't know. Our soldier was simply told that if the world governments haven't responded to our demands by three p.m., his time there, to set it off where it will do the most damage."

"Don't you fucking people know that if that thing goes off it'll start a war?"

"Then give us our country," the Boer said.

"God damn you! You won't have a country left because India is going to nuke you to kingdom-fucking-come!" He paused to regain his composure, then he got a description of the Boer operative in India from his prisoner. "General," Travis said, "have you got that?"

"Affirmative, we have operators who are now looking for him."

"Let us know."

"We will."

Travis pushed the Boer toward the door. "Get the other vials."

The Boer picked his way across the debris-strewn bunker to a safe. Travis was stunned at the level of preparedness of the farmers. Cases of food, an operating well, a generator to provide power, filters to insure fresh air regardless of what happened outside and protect them from gas attack. Against a guerrilla force, attacking the farmhouse with small arms, possibly even a mortar or two, the family would have been able to hold out for several months at the least. They were prepared for war.

After opening the door the Boer stepped away from the squat, metal box. "There they are," he said, gesturing toward the safe.

"Get them out, then hand them to me."

The Boer did as he was told.

When the two vials were in his hand, Travis turned to Anderson, who was standing nearby. "Major, would you please put these in the carrying case?"

"Certainly," Anderson said, and he took the vials then turned for the door.

Travis looked around the room. "You were pretty well equipped for your mission," he said. "But you know you can't win."

"But we are winning," the Boer said.

"How do you figure that?" Travis asked.

"You're here, aren't you? No matter what the outcome of this exercise is, the stage is set and just as Mr. Mugabe started his war by bringing attention to his need for a kaffir country, we are bringing the world's attention to our need for our own country. Eventually, we will win."

Travis didn't answer but pointed toward the door. This

man, he knew, didn't need to be handcuffed. He was a fanatic, but a calculating fanatic. "General Krauss," Travis said.

"Krauss here."

"Team Two has secured two vials. With your permission I am going to go back on the medevac with Lieutenant Olsen."

"Approved," Krauss said. "We'll keep you advised."

"Roger," Travis said. He walked out of the bunker, turned the Boer over to the South Africans, and hurried around the house to check on the team's Minnesota bombshell. He could hear the distinctive "whop-whop" of the HUEY medevac closing in on the farm. Casualties, this time, had been light. One friendly dead, one enemy dead, and one friendly wounded. The medevac landed and two medics jumped clear of the helicopter and hurried toward Jennifer. They carried field medical bags and a litter. For the first time that day Travis began to relax. "Two down, one to go," he said to no one. In return, no one said a word. He looked at his watch, it was now 1036 hours. The operation had taken thirty-one minutes. Stan, he knew, should be closing in for the final assault. We're winning, he thought to himself, we're going to win this thing after all.

Chapter 7

Whatever else Captain Jacques Henri Dubois, better known as "Jack," was, he was not a cruel man. Nor was he a man without a conscience. He would do what he had to do to finish the mission.

The assault force leader, Lt. Commander Stan Powczuk, wasn't cruel either. Both men, Stan knew, had been shaken by the videos of dead cows. He remembered the contorted bodies, the thousands of bovine corpses littering Shirley Basin, the gruesome stacks of dead cattle and the river of milk that had to be disposed of. They'd been forced to question the reason for such a brutal attack. Neither doubted the damage to the world's economy, but something else stayed with both men. It made them nervous about the operation, and although Stan didn't know for sure about how it affected Jack, he knew that his skin prickled every time he thought about it.

These people weren't really amateurs. They were supposed to be, but in the end, he and Jack agreed that they weren't. The extremists had trained themselves, planned for the attacks and the subsequent fallout. Stan believed that the sword rattling going on around the world had been expected by the terrorists. It had probably been factored into the plan. They had to have known that the world wouldn't just turn over Zimbabwe, not without a fight. But if they could trick the world's powers into fighting the battles for them, then maybe they would succeed.

Stan felt the helicopter turn abruptly. He looked forward to see if the pilot was doing anything, then realized the pilot was turning away from their route. Stan checked the volume on his radio. It was fine, but somehow a message had been delivered to the pilot without his being aware of it. He'd have to talk to that little wise-ass Chinese techno-geek about this glitch. He was thinking about what he would say when his radio burst with static and came to life.

"Commander Powczuk," the voice said.

"Powczuk here."

"This is General Freeman."

Stan mentally snapped to attention. The Commander-in-Chief of Special Operations had to be taking things seriously to call the team directly.

"Yes, sir," Stan said.

"Commander, the South Africans have ordered your chopper to the ground until we resolve an issue."

"Yes, sir," he said. The helicopter settled onto the ground even as Stan answered.

"Eagle Team, stay posted for an update. We're getting reports that the Anita virus has been released, this time in India—just as they threatened."

"Yes, sir. What is the situation?"

"We're not sure. India's government is threatening to expel Zimbabwe's and South Africa's ambassadors, but the field reports are keeping everyone confused. No one is sure exactly how many head of cattle are dying in India. Some have, but the virus appears to be attacking some cattle differently than in the past."

Stan heard General Freeman talking to someone in the background and strained to hear what was going on thousands of miles away.

May 30, 0412 hours
Washington, D.C.

General Freeman slammed his hand on the table and glared at the Air Force major who had just delivered a set of photographs printed directly from satellite images. Cattle sprawled in the littered, crowded streets as panicked Hindus ran past them. Other cattle stood nearby, bawling nervously. Obviously, they had survived the virus.

"Eagle Team, switch your BSDs for Internet connection. Broadcast your audio for teams," General Krauss said over the satellite link.

The images of the distraught beasts were transmitted for Eagle Team. Cows milled in wild-eyed terror, occasionally trampling the self-same Indians that thought of them as sacred. The camera panned close to a huge Brahma cow, drooling, front feet splayed as she swayed back and forth.

"Is it dying?" Freeman demanded.

"Sir, we won't know what is going on until we can get some of our people into the area and get tissue samples of the cows. At this point, the Indian government won't allow our people near the cattle—dead or alive."

Freeman sank into his chair, exhausted. "Sometimes I think these people want a war!" he said, then turned to a captain standing nearby. "Any word from Atlanta on the virus? What in the blue *hell* is going on?" Freeman hollered, his eyes bulging with frustration.

"Nothing yet, sir," the captain said. He started to add some sort of comment then stopped when an obviously distraught major hurried into the room, handed General Gates, the head of the Joint Chiefs, a single sheet of paper, and then began adjusting several of the TV monitors. All attention focused on the face that interrupted the coverage of the New Delhi streets.

"Some of you know who I am. Most, however, do not. I am Eric Steiner, the appointed president of the New Rhodesia by the people of the New Rhodesia. Unfortunately, the governments of South Africa, Zambia, Zimbabwe, and other African nations and NATO countries refuse to recognize our right and divine claim to our country. For a century, the English people have suppressed the rights of the Boer nation. Now, we strike back. Let the strike against India serve as an example to the world. The New Rhodesia will not tolerate the worship of the golden calf. New Rhodesia will stand as a power and monument to the memory of Cecil Rhodes. We will be taken seriously. We look to our allies in Pakistan for their continued support. Tomorrow it will be the anniversary of the subjugation of our forefathers. Should New Rhodesia not be recognized at that moment, the pagan world's fate will be sealed with the total and complete annihilation of the world's cattle population. This will be the beginning—the beginning of the end. 'The grace of the Lord Jesus be with God's people. Amen.' " With that, Steiner's face faded from the screen.

"Gentlemen, Eagle Team," Gates said. "We have a serious problem." He waved at the monitors. The image had settled into real-time satellite images. "What you are looking at are several columns of Pakistani troops, artillery moving toward the Indian border. On the next monitor you will see Indian troops moving. On that far monitor you can see the results of a Pakistani attack on an Indian radar installation. The installation, as you can see, has been destroyed. So far India has not responded with military action other than to beef up the border."

Another officer came into the room and handed Gates a second sheet of paper. He visibly paled when he read it and Freeman stood up. The muscles tightened in his stomach. Gates read the paper, "The government of Pakistan has announced that unless the Indian government withdraws from the disputed border region within two

hours, a state of war will exist between the two nations."
Gates looked around the room. "How the hell do we
stop this?"

"There's more," the first major said, adjusting the volume on a monitor that was tuned to CNN. The near-
panicked voice was repeating the announcement. "We
repeat. The government of India has announced that the
cattle terrorists, who are demanding that Zimbabwe be
returned to them as their own country, have just un-
leashed the deadly virus in New Delhi, killing thousands
of cows throughout the city. The Indian prime minister
has announced that this is being considered an act of war
by a group of terrorists who have been sheltered and
trained by the government of South Africa. An emer-
gency session of the government has been called. The
prime minister is asking for a declaration of war on
South Africa."

A stunned silence gripped the entire command room.
Someone asked if they were serious.

"Of course they're serious," Freeman answered.
"Some of you people have been calling this operation an
exercise in muscle flexing. Well, the muscles have
flexed . . . hell, they've fucking morphed. Those muscles
have just become missiles with nuclear warheads!"

Gates turned around and stared at the screens. Every
few seconds the satellite imaging system zoomed in for
a closer look at the columns of troops on both sides of
the border. "What's the South African response?"

"No response so far, sir," the major said.

"As soon as you have one let me know what it is."

"Yes, sir," the major said, then scuttled out of the
room to the communications room.

Freeman stood up and walked to the coffeepot. After
he'd filled his cup he started pouring milk into it. He
stopped, looked into the small pitcher, and thought of
the devastation taking place in the cattle industry.
"Okay"—he set the milk down—"we've got this problem

between India and the rest of the world. Let's get on with the mission."

"We can't, sir," the major said.

"Why not?"

"The South African government has ordered the mission suspended. Right now Team Three is sitting on the ground at the edge of the Drakensburg Mountains waiting for instructions."

Freeman poured sugar in his coffee. His hand trembled and blood pounded in his temples. He had one member of Eagle Team being examined for internal injuries in an African military hospital, another team trapped in some damn helicopter, returning to the CP. And the third team, the one that could put an end to this madness, was sitting on the fucking ground because President Mbeki didn't trust someone . . . he wasn't sure who had this honor . . . and poor Mbeki didn't know who he should trust. "Get Mandela on the line for me," Freeman barked.

Several minutes later, the major handed Freeman a secure phone. He turned away from the others.

"Mr. President," Freeman said, careful to include the honorary title. "I am sure you've been apprised of the situation."

"Yes," Nelson Mandela said.

The softness of his voice, the inflection betraying the weariness of the speaker, pulled at Freeman's heartstrings. He, too, wanted this operation ended. "Sir, our third assault force is sitting on the ground. Apparently the pilots have been told not to move until they receive further instructions."

"That is correct."

"Sir, can you get this operation moving again? We can still get the other vials, prevent any more attacks, and if the situation with India can be brought under control, this whole thing can end in a few hours."

"It is not that easy."

"Sir?"

"Our president has put the South African military on full alert. We know that India has ICBMs capable of hitting all of our major cities. We do not have an effective defense so our military must deploy to protect itself."

"Mr. President, this situation is becoming most grave. Surely you understand that India now has a valid claim in launching an assault against Pakistan. Mr. President, you must understand, India's people will demand that their most sacred beliefs be preserved. An attack against South Africa is justifiable given the religious fervor of the moment."

"What I understand, and what you understand, has suddenly become irrelevant, General. These terrorists have accomplished what others could not. They have brought the world to the brink of nuclear war."

Freeman sat in stunned silence. Then, in carefully measured words he said, "Mr. President, has the government of South Africa sortied any long-range aircraft?"

There was a silence, punctuated by a soft mechanical whirring sound as the voice scrambler waited for sound.

"Mr. President?" Freeman said.

"I am here, General."

"Did you hear my question?"

"There is a saying among many of the bush peoples of Africa," Mandela said. "To hear everything, you must hear the silence."

"I understand, Mr. President," Freeman said. "Would you please advise President Mbeki that Assault Force Three could complete the mission and that we have every reason to believe that we can persuade the Indian government that any sort of military action against South Africa, or its allies, would produce a very strong reaction."

"You can guarantee that, General?"

"No, sir, I cannot guarantee that our president will do

that, but I can promise that I will take every step, use my entire career, and make whatever sacrifices needed, to obtain that promise."

There was another silence, then Mandela said, "General, are you familiar with a lady named 'Jane'? She lives in England?"

Freeman didn't hesitate to answer. He was being given information. "Yes, sir."

"You should really get to know her, she can help you understand so much of the world."

"I'll do that, sir."

General Freeman scribbled on a note pad, "GET JANE'S, GET SAAF Data, LONG RANGE & WEAPONS." He flashed it at the agitated major.

The connection broke and Freeman pushed himself away from the desk and hurried to Gates.

"General Gates," Freeman said, "we need to speak in private."

Gates nodded and led Freeman toward a closed door.

A step before they entered the small, private room, the information Freeman had asked for and a current copy of *JANE'S Military Aircraft* was thrust into his hands. Inside Freeman pulled the door shut, took a deep breath, and said, "Sir, I believe that South Africa has scrambled its long-range aircraft against targets in India."

"They'll be crushed," Gates said.

"Not if they're carrying nukes and the targets are India's ICBM bases that could launch against South Africa."

Gates knew his jaw was hanging open. It was the worst nightmare of the world's leaders—a preventable problem getting out of hand. Something that could be prevented was suddenly unraveling and plunging the world into nuclear war. "I'll advise the president. You keep Eagle Team on the alert ready to resume the operation."

"Yes, sir. I'll advise. Shall we move our status up?"

For both men, this was a tough decision. From the

time the crisis started, the Joint Chiefs had been determined to avoid total official U.S. military intervention. Eagle Team was enough, but ever since the raving lunatic in Waco and the misuse of the military against civilians— in violation of the Constitution—the Joint Chiefs had been gun shy. Even if it were terrorists operating on American soil, the Chiefs maintained that it would never happen again. If the press perceived the military heading for full alert they would pick it up, turn it into more than it was. Still, if the world were about to go to war, every minute the American military had in advance, the more likely it would be to survive the next few hours of what could be nuclear war. Gates nodded. "Go to Condition Yellow, but do not scramble any aircraft. We also need to open the hot line."

Freeman agreed. They left the small, secure side office together. Gates stood in the room for a few seconds before he took a breath. "Ladies and gentlemen," he said gravely. "Order all American military units to go to Condition Yellow, with the following restraints. No aircraft are to be launched, no klaxons to sound. I want a quiet alert of all units. Instruct all military units to be prepared to move from this conditional level to DefCon Two and bypassing Three."

No one questioned Gates, who then turned to Admiral Clay. "Order the fleet to stand by. I suggest you issue a quiet order for any ships of the line not at sea to prepare to get underway."

The admiral nodded and started for his office.

Freemen felt the fear in the tips of his fingers. The president hadn't ordered it yet, and nothing more would happen in this quiet alert until the president did give the order. But, when he did, America would start down the path to war. It could, everyone knew, be the last war humankind would ever fight.

Freeman went to his desk where TALON Force's commanding officer waited for instructions. General Krauss was tugging his coat sleeve down over his prosthetic hand and rubbing his wrist in worry.

"Jack," Freeman said, sitting down heavily. "I want you to send a message, in the clear, to Assault Force Three."

"What's the message, General?"

"The message is this, 'State of War between South Africa and India expected in . . .'" Freeman looked at the page of *JANE'S* that lay open on his desk. It gave the details for the South African aircraft that had probably been sortied. He turned back to Krauss. "'. . . in two hours or less. If war breaks out, expect full nuclear strike between warring nations. U.S. involvement will be an unknown to minimal factor. Suggest if mission not completed, take protective action when you receive our warning.'"

General Krauss finished writing the message. "Anything else, sir?"

"Yes, Jack. Tell the team good luck."

Krauss nodded and walked to the communications desk, picked up the handset, and began reciting the message. Freeman watched the TALON Force commander make a tick mark on a piece of paper. Before Krauss could confirm the message to Freeman, the excitable major hurried back to Freeman's desk.

"Sir," he said, "the Navy has confirmed twelve SAAF fighter/bombers over the Indian Ocean en route to India."

Freeman took the paper. "Does Gates have this?"

"Yes, sir."

"Admiral Clay?" Freeman said.

"Yes, General."

"This is from the carrier task force, is that correct?"

"Yes it is, General."

"Stand by, keep a channel open to the task force. They may have a mission." He turned to the major. "Advise

General Gates that we may have a solution and get Mandela back on the horn."

"Yes, sir!" the major said loudly and hurried away.

"Jack, tell TALON Force to stand by to complete the mission. Have Assault Force One stand by to divert to the third target to support Force Three!"

Freeman didn't take the time to explain but hurried to intercept Gates. "General," he said. "The problem we're dealing with here is that we've tried to pussyfoot around with this issue and it's going to bite us in the ass."

Gates didn't answer.

Freeman knew it was a signal to continue. "General, we've got a whole damn carrier task force sitting between India and South Africa. I suggest we put it to work."

Gates smiled. "Do a 'Tricky Dickey'?"

"Yes, sir, tell both sides that if either one crosses the line, they both die."

"This isn't Russia and China," Gates said.

"No, sir, and that's all the more reason to think it'll work."

"Why?"

"These guys aren't enemies. Hell, they're closer to allies than anything else. Both countries are running scared because their own people are demanding action for religious or racial reasons, not political. Refocus those emotions on a third party . . ."

"The United States."

"Hell, most of the nuts in those countries hate us anyway, what difference will it make, except to prevent a war?"

Gates nodded and turned to a phone that connected him with the president and he quickly outlined the plan. After Gates returned the phone to the cradle he looked at Freeman. "You realize, General, that if they don't back down we will be at war?"

"General, if we don't do something we're going to be at war with the world."

Gates stood up and walked to the edge of the long table in the middle of the operations room.

"Ladies and gentlemen, by order of the president of the United States, all American military forces are now at DefCon Two."

A full colonel dropped his coffee cup. No one spoke. There was only one more step to war. Then Gates said, "Major, open up a link with President Mandela. Connect with President Mbeki, and another link to Prime Minister Shri Vajpayee of India. Tell them the president of the United States will address them."

There was a silence in the room, and then the status board of American Forces that had gone on alert began to light up. Gates looked at Freeman. "Put the TALON team on the horn so they can hear this in the clear. I want it going to every individual BSD. If they get vaporized they might as well know why."

Freeman nodded and in turn looked at Krauss, who signaled that it had been done. The quiet seconds ticked by until a comm board lit up showing the phone links had all been established. The room felt a perceptible change in power when the voice of the president of the United States echoed over the speakerphone.

"President Mandela, President Mbeki, Prime Minister Vajpayee and General Musharraf," the president said.

There were similar formal acknowledgements from the four leaders. The president went on.

"I wish this conference could be under better circumstances," he said, "but we are in a crisis that is heading into a war from which no one will emerge. In the interest of the future of humanity and to prevent the loss of life that would result from a war between your nations I have ordered the armed forces of the United States of America to full alert."

The officials listening coughed and sighed. Nothing was said. They were, Freeman hoped, waiting for a way out of their confrontation. "American naval forces, operating in international waters in the Indian Ocean have confirmed that a flight of long-range South African fighter/bombers are en route to India as we speak."

Suddenly India's Prime Minister Vajpayee broke in to declare that his nation would take immediate action to protect itself.

"That is not necessary Mr. Prime Minister," the president said. "I am issuing an order for our naval aircraft in the area to be immediately scrambled with orders to destroy all incoming aircraft that do not turn back."

President Mbeki broke in, saying that such an act would be a declaration of war against South Africa. The president ignored him and continued with his prepared speech.

"I have also ordered our fleet to take every action necessary to insure that should any ICBMs or aircraft be launched against the Republic of South Africa, that those missiles or aircraft be destroyed."

Before he could be interrupted again the president said, "And I have also issued the following orders to our strategic forces. Should either side succeed in attacking the other with conventional or nuclear weapons then our forces will consider that to be an act of war against the United States of America and we will initiate a full strike against the belligerent parties."

An audible gasp went up in the operations room. Not since Richard Nixon had been in the White House had any American president threatened to use nuclear weapons. Freeman folded his arms over his chest. Either the bluff would work or they were going to war. The silence was palpable.

"Mr. President," the South African president said, "what do you expect us to do?"

"I expect these belligerent nations to order their aircraft back to base and their military to stand down. The United States will maintain its presence and status of alert until the crisis is resolved."

"And how will you resolve the crisis?" the prime minister asked.

"Our assault force will resume its mission in cooperation with South African forces. Our scientists in New Delhi will be allowed full access to all cattle—dead or exposed—by the most recent attack so we can determine the status of the virus."

"And what of our losses, Mr. President?" the PM asked.

"Mr. Prime Minister, I do believe that is something we can talk about after this thing is stopped. Our mission now must be to insure that no more of the Anita virus vials are allowed to escape South Africa."

"I understand," the PM said, "but I believe, when the world judges this entire fiasco, your country is going to be held accountable as the virus was developed by your scientists."

The president paused thoughtfully. Then he said, "That could well be sir, but I do believe the time has come for us to reevaluate the presence of ICBMs in violation of various treaties, and to examine whether some nations—who have claimed they are not members of the nuclear club—in fact, are members."

Freeman let himself smile. They'd won.

President Mbeki said, "I have ordered our aircraft to return to base, however, they will be refueled and remain on alert." He paused for a few seconds. "I have also ordered your TALON Force to resume its mission."

"Thank you," the president said. The Indian prime minister acquiesced as well, ordering the Indian military to stand down, as did General Musharraf of Pakistan. The president thanked him as well and the connection was broken.

There was a flurry of applause in the command center and Gates turned to Krauss. "Get your team back to work, General."

"Yes, sir!" Krauss said, then picked up a phone handset and started talking into it.

Freeman looked up at the TV monitors. He saw the lines of trucks in both India and Pakistan had stopped moving. Some were even turning back. On the digital screen depicting the Indian Ocean, the aircraft that had been headed for India were turning back. He smiled to himself. It was a ballsy move and it worked.

"Assault Force Three," Krauss said. "You have clearance to resume the mission."

Krauss listened then said, "Roger. Good luck."

He put the phone down and looked back to Freeman. "So the game is afoot again, isn't it?"

Freeman nodded. "Let's hope we haven't delayed too long."

The two men returned to the command center and sat down in their customary chairs at the large table. Now all they could do was listen and wait. The operation was back in the hands of TALON Force.

Chapter 8

"Hurry up and wait," Stan said. "That seems to be the way of the damned army, even in this outfit."

"Aw, stop bitching, man," Jack said.

"I like to bitch," Stan said. "That's the thing about us Polacks. We bitch and bitch and never do a damn thing about it until we get tired of bitching. Then we tear the whole system down and . . ."

Before he finished, the command center issued an alert. Both Stan and Jack listened in stunned silence. The mission was not only on standby, the world was headed toward war. When the radio stilled again Stan glanced at the pilot. His knuckles had turned white gripping the stick.

"It's okay, partner," Stan said. "The politicians will figure some way out of this mess. In the meantime we better sit tight and be ready to move."

The pilot nodded. Stan wondered if he was too scared or too worried to reply. In a few hours, unless they figured some way out of this mess, his country was going to be pounded by nuclear weapons from what had always been a friendly nation. Stan sat back and leaned against the cabin bulkhead. He thought about his hot-blooded wife, Angela, in Pennsylvania and how many times he'd come close to dying in other operations. But never, never like this. He would be part of something else, vaporized with most of the world. No one believed it would be confined to Africa and India. From India it would spread to Pakistan. The Moslem countries would come to Pakistan's defense—which would, in turn, drag Israel into the fracas. From there it would become the religious war that everyone feared. One side after another would step in to defend one or another country. All because some nuts want a country of their own, he thought to himself and then about that statement. A country of their own. What group of people in the last two thousand years hadn't wanted their own country? Hell, the Palestinians wanted their own country. So they terrorized the world. What's the difference?

The difference, Stan knew, was that at their worst, Arafat and his followers didn't use trickery to deceive the world. The terrorists' demands were just that. A gimmick to force a nuclear war. Arafat didn't want the remains of a nuclear holocaust. Why would the Boers? These guys are shrewd, he thought. Either way, everyone loses. Some of those lunatic fuckers will survive—they're going to get what they want—the pieces. He pushed his palms together then rubbed them on his camouflage suit. He added up the casualties to date. More than two dozen dead, that many more wounded. Most of them had been the Boers, but they were still people.

"Why the hell do I care?" Stan said to himself, knowing that whatever he said would be heard in Washington and by every member of the team.

"What's that, Stan?" Jack said.

"Nothing, just thinking about how fucked up this operation has become. Who'd have thought a bunch of fanatic farmers could hold up the world."

"Look at our revolution," Jack said. "Look how screwed up it was."

"You callin' this a revolution?"

"I don't know. Maybe it is."

"Jack," Stan said, "I hate to say this, but think about what you're saying ol' buddy. These guys are trying to take a country away from a black government who won it in their own sort of revolution."

"That's the point," Jack said. "Who's right in this thing? Hell man, the government they're trying to get out of—is it all that different than any other?"

"I think so, buddy," Stan said.

Jack was quiet for a minute then he said, "Do you know who Alfred Krupp was?"

"The German arms maker, yeah."

"Back in the 1800s Alfred Krupp wrote, 'How easily a fire can break out, you know, and a fire would destroy everything.' War's like that. One minute you've got peace and the next, war."

"We're not at war."

"No, we're not," Jack said. "But we're dealing with an enemy who understands war. They are inferior in number, in cavalry, and artillery . . ."

"That's Napoleon's Tenth Maxim," Stan said.

"We should pay attention to it."

"There's also his fifty-seventh," Stan said. "When a nation is without establishments and a military system, it is difficult to raise an army."

Jack turned and looked at his friend and partner. "You're missing the point my friend. They have an army, they are an army without a country."

Stan thought about his partner's musings about the mission. If Jack's faith and confidence in the mission slipped away, it would be a problem for the team. He would need to be replaced. "Jack?" Stan asked.

"Yeah?"

"You still up for this mission?"

"For the mission, yes."

"Then what?"

"When this is over, I think I'm going to take some time off. Do some fishing down in Mexico."

"Hell, Jack. You know that after a mission you can do whatever you want."

"Don't want it to be part of no mission," Jack said. "Got some things to think about. Don't worry, Stan, they don't have nothin' to do with the team or the mission."

Stan grunted. The air in the helicopter grew thick and flies buzzed around them. Ever since Jack had returned from Japan he'd been morose about something. Everyone in the team knew that the Boer had said something to him before he'd plunged into the Pacific. Whatever the man had said, his words had been eating at Jack.

He thought about saying something else to Jack—starting a conversation, offering his support as a team player—but the starters on the twin turbine motors began to spin. The rotors began to turn.

In crisp words, the pilot said, "We've been given clearance to resume the mission."

"Fire it up, baby!" Stan said. His focus returned to the mission and what had to be done. He'd worry about Jack afterward. He would watch him. If he started to hesitate then Stan would drop him from the assault force.

The rotors gathered speed and the helicopter began rocking gently as the whirling blades shifted the weight of the Puma around. Until momentum equalized in speed, the chopper would shift and rock. Another minute passed and the pilot pulled pitch and the ground dropped away.

Stan nodded—a gesture that each man should check his equipment—then he checked his own and the man's next to him. When everyone was ready Stan shifted his feet and looked out the door. The country of the African high veldt dropped away as they sailed over the Drakensburg Mountains. The helicopter pitched over to follow the escarpment toward the lower sand and thorn veldt country of the Transvaal. For the first time since he'd arrived, Stan felt he was truly in Africa. Below him, in the openings of the bush country, he could see the wildlife. Small herds of wildebeest, zebras, giraffe, and the occasional rhino dotted the clearings.

The pilot dropped the helicopter to less than a hundred feet over the bush country. He was on a line to the military installation of Hoedspruit Air Force Base. Stan wondered if the bombers sent to India had originally been stationed there. The helicopter swept over a power line, then turned abruptly. This was the final turn. In a few seconds they were over the outer boundary of the game ranch that was the third target. This is going to be bizarre, Stan thought. The target was a lodge—a lodge where Americans were currently vacationing. The assault team had also been informed that although the visitors were Americans, no one had any way of knowing if they could be part of the terrorist operation. No one was to be treated as friendly.

The pilot flew a route that actually took him slightly past the ranch, to an open savanna three hundred yards beyond it. Stan saw several white women in swimsuits sitting around the pool. People milled around the central building as well as the outbuildings.

The women waved. The men stared. Stan saw two men run for the lodge. He guessed they would miss their opportunity to get the vials if they landed at the designated LZ.

"Pilot! Pilot!" Stan shouted into his radio.

"Pilot here."

"Put us down in that yard near the pool."

"Roger," the pilot said. He cranked the helicopter in a gut wrenching 180-degree turn and pointed the nose to the earth, diving toward the yard. He pulled the nose up, flared, and dropped heavily to the ground.

As the wheels settled Stan shouted directions. "Jack, take your team around to the back, drop a man every few yards and seal it up. I'll take my team around the front. Don't trust *anyone.*"

"Roger," Jack said.

Stan could see the women jumping up from their chaise lounges, towels flying, the lounges flung into the pool, and from the nearby thatch-covered bar and dining area, tables of food were being blown over by the helicopter's rotor wash.

Stan leapt from the helicopter, running toward the lodge. His men, all black members of the SANP, were spreading out to secure the area. One man tried to push the scantily clad women to safety in the thatch-covered building. Stan watched him do his work. He was quick and effective, saying as he herded, "Ladies, please take cover. This is a South African police mission."

When his head exploded in a geyser of red pulp, Stan was stunned by the ferocity of the killing. Then he heard a second rifle boom. He looked toward the lodge and a white man in traditional tourist-hunter's garb—bush jacket and shorts—calmly knelt beside the pool. His hand was steady as he pumped more bullets into a huge-bored double rifle.

The man was practiced and calm. A sudden rage fueled the fire in Stan's blood. He knew instantly what drove the man. Like Stan, he'd faced danger before and every time, his calm and accuracy let him win. This time, he would lose.

Stan raised his rifle. He knew the shot would hit the tourist in the center of the chest. The full metal-jacketed bullet would tear through the man's heart and he'd die. For a few seconds, maybe for even a minute, he'd know he'd been shot and that he was about to die. He would know there wouldn't be anything he could do about it—just die. He'd have the opportunity to die heroically like the game he killed, the same way he'd killed the black soldier.

Although he would never know what possessed him, Stan raised his point of aim to the shooter's shoulder.

On impact, the man spun backward. The double rifle flew from his hands.

Stan ran to it and threw the rifle into the pool. "Lay still, asshole," he hissed.

"I'm an American!"

"That's no fuckin' excuse," Stan snarled. "You just shot and killed a South African National Police officer! Not a fuckin' elephant."

The man's face contorted in fear. "I thought you were SWAPO. You know, a terrorist."

Stan stared at the man, disbelief and anger annoying him further. "SWAPO? SWAPO? What the fuck is a SWAPO?"

"Yeah, man—the guerillas who whipped everyone's ass—something like the 'South West African Peoples Organization' . . ."

A woman's scream startled him.

"Larry, Larry. You've been shot!"

The man, Larry, smiled weakly at the woman.

"That your wife?" Stan asked.

"Are you crazy?" Larry covered his wound with his good hand. "My wife hates Africa."

Stan signaled for the woman to come over.

She dropped to her knees beside him. "Sugar, you are so brave," she said. She pushed a tendril of elegantly styled red hair out of her face and touched his brow.

"Jesus fuckin' Christ," Stan muttered. "These people are all fuckin' crazy." He looked around the yard. "Jack, you secure?"

"Roger that. No one is leaving this building."

"You got any civilians there?"

"Negative. I can hear some shouting inside. Might be some inside."

"Well, I've got four Whiskey females here, one KIA by an American tourist."

"Say again?"

"I got John fucking Wayne here. He killed one of my men with a head shot using . . ." Stan turned to the man on the ground. "What kind of rifle you using, asshole?"

"That isn't just any rifle. That *was* a twelve-thousand dollar .470 Capstick."

Stan grunted. "He used a fuckin' elephant gun on him." He looked around the lodge. "We gotta dig these fuckers out of here."

The lodge was roofed with thatch. The previous assault teams had been forced to leave the farms in shambles. Stan didn't want to destroy the lodge. It was a classy place.

"Okay, we're gonna do this the old-fashioned way. We're gonna clear this place room by room, if they want to shoot up, they're gonna be the ones to start it."

"Roger," Jack said. "You want us to hold down the anvil on this operation?"

"That's the plan, my man," Stan said. He turned to the now clustered-together group of guests. "I don't have time to give you the details, but this is a joint operation between the governments of the United States and South Africa."

"What operation?" the wounded Larry said.

"You know, Larry, that's none of your motherfucking business." Stan looked around. "By the way, has anyone placed you under arrest yet?"

"Me?" Larry said.

"Yeah, asshole, you."

"No. Why?"

"Well, consider yourself under arrest now."

"For what?"

"They have charges for murder here, too. You're under arrest for the murder of a South African police officer."

"You're shittin' me!"

"I am not only not shittin' you, I'm wishin' I had blown your fat ass away."

Larry's face fell, puzzled.

Stan looked around the group. "Now, are there any other guests inside the lodge?"

"Larry's partner," the woman said. "He's inside."

"I'll bet he's got an elephant gun, too," Stan said.

Larry answered, "He's got a four-sixteen Rigby, bolt action."

"He as good with it as you were with that cannon of yours?"

Larry smiled. "No, he's full of shit."

"Good. We're gonna try and talk them out of there. Best thing you can do is stay here, out of the line of fire."

Hushed murmurs and a ripple of excitement went through the small group. Eleanor, Larry's friend, announced that the group would stay out of the way. They huddled together, and again, she bent over the fallen man.

Stan noticed that the bleeding from Larry's wound had slowed. He didn't care. To remind himself what sort of person Larry thought he was, all Stan had to do was shift his gaze to the nearly decapitated soldier lying near the pool. Stan turned back to the lodge. He signaled for two of the soldiers to join him on the assault of the house. The others took up positions around the lodge. Stan led the attack, in one-man rushes, toward the nearest door. Once at the side of the building he signaled for the next South African to rush them. Two high-powered shots rang across the yard and bursts of automatic rifle fire through the window answered them. The bullets ripped the window frame to splinters and the fire didn't stop until both South Africans were beside Stan at the wall of the lodge.

Stan signaled that he would take the door down, then enter the building. The first South African would then cover Stan's entrance from one side while the second South African rushed through the door and covered the half of the room Stan couldn't. Once that room was clear, they'd take the next, clearing one room at a time until they cornered their quarry or the Boer terrorists tried to make a break for the outside, in which case the members of the team who surrounded the lodge would net them. When Stan was sure everyone was ready, he checked his XM-29. Quickly, in fluid, deadly motion, he pumped three rounds through the door's lock. Satisfied, he ran at the door, slamming his shoulder into it. A resonating *thunk* filled the air and Stan fell to the floor. He lay on the ground, looking at the still-closed door.

"What the fuck?" he shouted. The door hadn't budged. .

"Sir," the first soldier said. "Perhaps I should have told you that in this country, doors are very strong. Perhaps there is, what you would call, a crossbar across the door and, perhaps, the door is made of very thick wood."

Stan looked up at the grinning soldier. "Yeah, that might have helped." He heard the women at the pool snickering. "Fuck you bitches," Stan mumbled and staggered to his feet. He reached into his leg pack and pulled out a small block of plastique. "We'll just blow the door."

The soldier shook his head. "I believe, sir, if you have disabled the lock, that we can raise the bar inside by lifting this lever." He pointed at the small lever sticking out of the door. "Perhaps it will open then."

"Oh," Stan said. "You lift, I'll rush."

"Fine, sir."

Stan backed up and nodded.

The soldier raised the lever and nudged the door.

Stan rushed the door and burst inside the room, his rifle ready to spit death at anyone who fired at him. In the center of the room a single, khaki and bush coat clad figure was on his knees, hands over his head. He was chanting, "Comrade, comrade, comrade."

"What the fuck?" Stan blinked.

"Comrade, don't kill me. I'm an American."

"Yeah, I guess you are," Stan said, "and a pretty fucked up one at that."

The man looked up at Stan. "Who are you?"

"Yo, bud, hasn't anyone told you that the Cold War is over?"

The man stared at Stan, his face frozen with fear. "You're not SWAPO?"

"Wrong again. I guess comrade is good enough for now. Where are the rest of the assholes who ran in here with you?"

"They have an escape route. I couldn't leave my Melissa with those heathens so I stayed."

Stan couldn't help himself. "Melissa your wife?"

"Oh, no, sir."

"Let me guess, your wife doesn't like Africa."

"No, sir. She's on vacation with her boyfriend in London."

"Ohhh-kayyyy. Where's this escape route?"

"I don't know," the man said.

Stan jerked him to his feet. The man had wet his pants.

"Jack, the guys we want have an escape route. We'll check the lodge, you keep the outside secure."

"Roger," Jack said.

Stan looked back at the newest prisoner. "You got a good lawyer?"

"I don't understand," he said.

"You will," Stan said. He pushed the man toward one of the soldiers. "Take this man outside and let him see his Melissa."

The soldier nodded and took the quivering man outside. Stan watched the two men leave. He shook his head and glanced around the room. He figured the purpose of the room was to be some sort of recreation room, probably for dances or something. There was another closed door directly across from the one he'd crashed through. Stan looked at the soldier with him. Although he'd grinned when Stan bounced off the door, there was an air of business about the man that gave him confidence. "You ready?" Stan asked.

"Yes, sir," the solder said, "but I am not sure about where these doors may lead."

"Yeah, well, what say we find out."

Again, the solder nodded and followed Stan to the first door. They hesitated for only a moment and then once again Stan acted on an instinct rather than what he had been trained to do. He turned the doorknob and stepped to one side. This way he would be out of the line of fire if anyone was waiting, or if the door was booby-trapped. With the firing end of his rifle he pushed the door open and nodded to the SANP—a signal to cover him. Stan rolled into the room. It was empty. He pushed away chairs and tables only to find nothing in the room but another door. The two men repeated the entry into another room.

"Dammit!" Stan shouted to himself. "We're wasting time with this shit!" He walked to the next door and turned the handle. Nothing happened. He rushed into the room.

"Jack!" Stan said into his radio.

"Here."

"I don't think those people are in the lodge. Somehow they got out. Do you see any sort of exit on the grounds?"

"Negative," came Jack's reply.

"Okay, we're running short of time here. There's a group of guest rooms connected to one end of the lodge. Release half the blocking force to start checking those guest rooms. Make sure they are thorough. Check every fucking corner."

Stan and the South African ran through the remainder of the lodge, checking each room thoroughly but quickly. When they reached the end of the lodge Stan stopped and looked back down the long hallway. He couldn't figure out how they'd managed to escape. "We saw the bastards come in. They didn't have time to get out. Where in the hell are they?"

He started pacing thoughtfully, walking around the lodge, looking at the floor and the walls. Then he checked the thatch roof. They couldn't have gone out the roof. Could they? Though it was thatch the woven grass was nearly two feet thick, and the outside was covered with chicken wire to keep monkeys and other animals from tearing it apart. The cathedral ceiling didn't offer much of a place to hide either. Suddenly, Stan smacked himself in the forehead. "Jesus Christ, how could we be so fucking dumb?

"Jack!" Stan shouted into his radio. "Get those women! The Boers didn't need to hide," Stan said. "All they had to do was get on the beams and wait for us to hit the next room. We were looking for someone on the ground—behind an overturned table or some such shit! And then we found Braveheart babbling about comrades!"

"What are you saying, Commander?" General Krauss said.

"They hid on the beams and waited for us to clear the room. Count the women, General, two scatterbrained American bimbos and one that hid behind them. I'll bet anything . . ."

Stan didn't get to finish. The explosion of an RPG, followed by a secondary explosion stopped him. He heard a car engine fire and ran for the door. By the time he remembered the plastique, he couldn't stop himself. With built-up momentum, he cleared the door rolling under a stream of AK rifle fire. Two Boers fired from the back of a speeding Toyota Land Cruiser. Several members of the team fired at the bouncing truck with no effect. Stan scanned the area, searching for the source of the explosions. The helicopter still sat on the ground, the pilot and co-pilot dashing madly about trying to extinguish the flames. An RPG had hit the port turbine. That accounted for the secondary explosion. Flying pieces and parts of the engine had ripped through the second turbine.

"Damn, damn, and damn," Stan said. The Toyota was already out of range, hurtling headlong toward the bush across the savanna. The terrorists had left them two other Land Cruisers parked near the lodge. They'd also blown out at least two tires on each vehicle. The Boers hadn't been shooting at the assault force. They were insuring they couldn't be followed.

Stan heard the roar of an engine erupting from behind him. He prepared to duck for cover but stopped himself and laughed as Jack slid a Land Rover to a stop in the dirt. The Rover didn't have doors, hood, or top. Just two seats and an open back.

"This son of a bitch is built to shit-and-git," Jack said. "Shall we tour the ranch?"

Stan jumped in the passenger seat, on the left side and shouted, "Go." He listened to Jack whoop in excitement with something, Stan thought, that sounded like a wild Cajun rebel yell. The two men were off cross-country after the Toyota, leaving the rest of the assault force and the four Americans to wonder what would happen next in the now-bizarre operation.

Their first victim was the lodge's flower garden. Brilliant blossoms shot from beneath the Rover's spinning wheels with chunks of rock and soil as Stan and Jack disappeared into the savanna.

Stan held his rifle with one hand while he gripped an "oh-shit" handle with the other. Jack aimed the Land Rover across the savanna on what he hoped would be the most direct route to catch the first vehicle. The African grass grew wheel high and thick. Anything that would bring them to a screeching halt would be hidden until they were right on top of it.

Several times the Rover's wheels cleared the blowing, seeded tops of the grass and Stan felt his stomach rise and catch in his throat. He forced any worries from his mind, refraining from those thoughts about what would happen if Jack suddenly hit a rock or sailed off the edge of a hidden precipice. He refused to think about it. When a large warthog jumped up in front of the Rover, Stan gasped, certain that several hundred pounds of angry hog would join him in his seat.

Jack swerved and missed the panicked hog and seconds later they burst out of the grass onto the dirt road. He cranked the steering wheel hard to his left and jammed on the brakes. The Rover slid across the road, bounced off the grassy bank of the other side, corrected itself, and was now pointed in the right direction. Jack jerked it to a lower gear, popped the clutch, and pushed the accelerator to the floor. The Rover's wheels spun in the grass, sending up a dirty rooster tail before they caught traction and shot off down the road and into the bush.

The ranch road twisted and turned. The track didn't follow any sort of reasonable plan. It just meandered toward the river. They topped a small hill and started down toward the river when Stan realized there wasn't a bridge, just a ford.

"Hold on!" Jack shouted.

"No shit!" Stan said. "You with us, General Krauss?" He shouted unnecessarily loudly into his helmet mic.

"Krauss, here."

"Stay with us . . . ugh. Shit, stay with us, we're chasing those guys . . . ugh." Stan groaned then gave up trying to explain and just held on. As they crossed the ford, the spray of water drenched both men. The four-wheel drive propelled them through the mud then pushed them up the far bank. A dissipating cloud of dust hung over the road.

"We're closing in," Jack said.

Stan nodded and released his death grip on the oh-shit handle. He brought his rifle up. He'd start shooting as soon as the Toyota was in sight. At the top of the embankment the road made another sharp turn to the left and suddenly they were in the open bush country of the sand veldt. The acacia thinned, providing them a clear view of the road as it ran straight up a hill toward the dominating kopi of the ranch.

"They're trying to make the highway up there," Stan shouted and pointed at the top of the hill.

Jack grunted. The straight road was rough, but it gave him an opportunity to pull out all the stops on the Rover's speed. They could see the white Toyota nearing the gate at the highway entrance.

Although they were at least eight hundred yards behind the Land Cruiser, Stan pulled the XM-29 to his shoulder and laser-aimed above the Toyota, hoping to compensate for the bullet's drop over the distance. He began firing three-round burst of automatic fire, changing his aim as the distance closed. From two hundred yards he could pick out targets, one man fired back at them, the other struggled to open the gate. Stan tried to aim in the bouncing Rover and fired a long burst, dumping the last round of the magazine toward his target. He was just as surprised as the Boer when one of the bullets found its target and the man flopped onto the ground.

Jack covered the remaining distance in seconds and slammed on the brakes. He turned the steering wheel so the Rover covered Stan while he changed magazines. By the time the Rover slid to a dusty, dirt-scattering stop, Jack was on the ground, rolling to safety while Stan ordered the female driver to put her hands in the air.

The second man, hidden by the Toyota, started around the vehicle. "Freeze!" Stan shouted. "Put your hands in the air!"

Instead the Boer fired his AK in a long burst at Stan, the bullets pinging into the metal of the Land Rover.

Stan dodged behind the Rover. The Boer, seizing his opportunity, ran into the bush.

Jack leapt from cover and chased the terrorist.

After watching his team member sprint off behind the

Boer, Stan ordered the woman out of the Toyota as he walked toward the downed man.

The woman, a lanky blonde, asked if she could help her friend. "He needs attention."

Stan kept the muzzle of his rifle in her stomach while he roughly searched her for weapons. Before he let her kneel beside the wounded Boer, Stan searched him too, removing a compact 9mm from the small of his back and a knife from his boot.

"Don't you people ever give up?" Stan said. He motioned for her to help him. The Boer, a bald smallish man, had been hit in the thigh. Fortunately the wound was not serious and bleeding was minimal. Stan didn't feel bad about handcuffing the two of them to the bumper. When they were secure he moved into what he felt was an adequate defensive position. Since Jack had disappeared into the bush he hadn't heard a sound. He felt the African quiet settle around them and time seemed to stand still. The silence shattered brutally with the sound of several shots from an AK and an answering shot from Jack's rifle. A second shot sounded from Jack's rifle, slightly further away. Stan tried to follow the chase. He expected Jack to say something into the helmet radio but the big man was silent in the bush.

When Jack's voice came over the helmet's radio it was calm. There wasn't any evidence that he'd been running down a fleeing terrorist. "Stan?"

"Yeah, Jack."

"You secure those other two?"

"Secured."

"Follow my radio to me."

"What's the situation?"

"He's dead."

Stan didn't answer. He assumed Jack's last shot had been the one that dropped the fleeing Boer. He followed Jack's radio signal through the bush, weaving around the thorn bushes and staying alert. He saw Jack standing, staring at the ground. Stan walked to him. The Boer was on the ground. Blood pooled under his neck, soaking into the dry ground and matting the dead man's hair.

"Hell of a shot," Stan said.

"Didn't shoot him," Jack said.

"Who did?"

"No one," Jack said. "He ran into a poacher's snare." Jack used the muzzle of his rifle to point to the wire.

"Umm," Stan said, "I'll bet it was quick."

"Quick enough." Jack stuffed his free hand into one of his pockets. "That ain't it though. There are no vials on him. Nothing," Jack said. "Have you checked the Toyota for the vials?"

Stan shook his head. Then he heard Krauss on the radio.

"DuBois, are you sure there are no vials on that man?"

"Absolutely, sir."

"Check the vehicle, the woman, and the other Boer. We need those last three vials."

"Roger, sir."

"What about him?" Jack said.

Stan looked down at the body. "You find anything on him?"

"No." Jack studied the dead man's face. "Hey, man, look at him . . ." Jack stooped next to the body and cupped the dead man's chin in his hand. "Isn't this—"

"Holy Jesus, Mary, and Joseph!" Stan blurted and knelt next to Jack. "That's Steiner!"

Krauss's voice came over the radio again. "Gentlemen, you're sure that you have the body of Eric Steiner there?"

"Yes, sir. It's him. I'd recognize him anywhere," Jack said, his face pulled into a tight sneer.

"Leave him for now. We'll send someone out for the body," Krauss said.

The two men returned to the vehicles. The woman was softly sobbing. "Ma'am," Stan said, "was he your husband?"

She nodded.

"He was caught in a poacher's snare," Stan said.

"It doesn't matter what killed him," she said.

"What do you mean?"

"We will all die."

Stan knelt and rested one knee on the ground. "You better explain that."

"What you're looking for. They aren't here, haven't been for hours."

"Where are they?"

She looked at Stan's face. "You're an American, aren't you? You've got your own country. His country was taken away by those monkeys." She spat the word angrily, staring at Jack. "He never forgave them."

"Ma'am," Stan said, composing himself. "I really don't care about the politics. What I do care about is recovering those last three vials before they are turned loose somewhere else and it starts a war."

"That's what's going to happen," she said. She checked her watch. "In a few hours it'll be over."

Stan studied the ground. He wasn't getting anywhere. He looked at the wounded Boer lying beside her.

"You know where the vials are?" Stan asked.

The man nodded.

"Where are they?"

This time the man looked up at the sky. "Like she said, the bloody things are gone."

"General?" Stan said.

"Krauss here."

"Sir, the vials are not with them. Is there any chance of stopping all outbound aircraft?"

"We'll do it," Krauss said. "They might be bluffing. Search everything. Talk to the staff, and those Americans. I want you to tear that ranch apart if that's what it takes. If any of those vials are there, find 'em. If we miss a single one, they'll still have a weapon. We'll go to the airport . . ." Suddenly Krauss paused. "Powczuk, stand by."

For a full minute the radio was silent. "DuBois?"

"Sir."

"We know who is missing. A photo has been relayed via satellite to Sam. South African radar has reported that no private aircraft have been in the air since the operation began. We think he may be en route to Johannesburg airport. Captains Greene and Blake are being diverted to the airport. The SANP is putting their full resource into trying to stop him outside Johannesburg. We're also flooding the airport."

"Roger that, sir," Stan said. "We're going to pick up the body and return to the lodge. Start the search."

"Do that, Stan. Also, regarding the four Americans?"

"Yes, sir."

"There will be a South African police car coming to pick them up."

"What's going to happen to them, sir?"

Krauss didn't respond for several seconds then said. "They are being detained by the South African police There's talk of a murder charge. The two women will be returned to the United States. The men . . . we'll see what we can do."

"Yes, sir."

Jack and Stan returned to the dead man and removed the poacher's wire around his neck. Jack picked the body of Eric Steiner up, arranged him on his shoulders, and started walking. Stan followed the big man and thought about what Krauss had said in reference to the four Americans. Would they be returned to United States?

"General Krauss," Stan said.

"Stan?" said Krauss.

"Regarding the four Americans?"

"Yes."

"They were just caught up in the thing. Didn't know what was going on. Shouldn't we at least provide them with some defense in a trial?"

"You think so?"

"Yes, sir."

"I'll take care of it."

"Thank you, sir," Stan said, then added, "You know, sir, they really believed they were being attacked."

"I know," Krauss said.

Stan walked in silence. He watched Jack place the Boer's body in the back of the Toyota. Jack assisted the wounded man into the back of the truck and cuffed him to the rollbar. Stan handed the woman up to ride next to her wounded friend. She glared at Jack and refused to take his hand. Stan climbed in the back and watched the two prisoners. Before Jack had finished turning the Toyota around he heard Hunter saying that the elusive Boer had been spotted inside the airport's international flight lounge. Stan and Jack listened to the chase as the three TALON members tried to ferret the Boer out of the bowels of the airport. The chase was not going well. They could hear Sam's heavy breathing as he chased the Boer. While events in the airport were playing themselves out, Stan and Jack listened in silence.

Jack wanted to ask Sam what he was doing, where he thought the Boer terrorist was hiding. When they heard Sam shout for the Boer to freeze, then threaten to shoot him, he stopped the truck.

"Go get 'im, Sammy!" Jack said, rooting on his little friend.

"I got him, Jack," Sam said. "I . . . shit!"

Jack didn't look back or say anything, but Stan could see his grip tighten on the Toyota's steering wheel. Stan was looking forward to searching the ranch. It might take Jack's mind off what was happening in Johannesburg.

Don't get yourself killed, you crazy Chink, Stan thought. As a lapsed Catholic, he knew this was the time to pray for Sam.

No one had heard Sam's voice over the comm gear, now, for over a minute.

Chapter 9

Sam didn't know if he should be scared or excited. He'd listened to every phase of the operation and knew the last Boer was running with the vials. When Jack started after what everyone believed would be the last of the terrorists, Sam was elated. Once again, he laughingly thought, TALON Force has saved the world. He doubted that he had been the only one who received a shock to his system when they discovered that not only did Eric Steiner not have the vials on him, but that the damn things may have already been taken out of the country. He knew, however, that Eagle Team would deal with the problem and find a way to retrieve the missing vials.

"Sam," General Krauss said.

"Yes, sir," Sam said.

"You're going to have to hustle across the airport and help the team search for the Boer," Krauss said.

"Yes, sir."

"Sam, we're sending you his photo. His name is Lars Gruenwald. He may be wearing a disguise. Hell, he might even be armed. We don't know what we're dealing with here but this has come down to you, Blake, and Greene. They are on their way now. The two of them will be working with airport security. Are you wearing civilian clothes?" Krauss waited for an answer.

"No, sir."

"Well, change. We want you in civvies—less attention that way. Wire yourself for communications support. Take your Baretta. Wear a shoulder rig. There'll be transport waiting for you outside the hangar."

"Yes, sir."

Sam pushed himself away from his communications console. The photo of the last terrorist appeared in his BSD. He committed the image to memory. He picked up his 9mm Baretta and its shoulder holster. Although the other male TALON troopers carried the heavier OHSW .45, Sam carried the lighter Baretta along with Jen and Sarah. He began wiggling into the rig. Sam stuffed the pistol into the holster and pulled on his jacket. "Well, shit," he said to himself, "let's go to war."

Outside, a security Jeep waited for him. The driver took Sam directly across the runways, speeding over the tarmac to the terminal. Sam jumped out of the Jeep when the driver stopped.

"That door," the driver said, pointing to an obscure entrance in the side of the building, "is the end of a service entrance. Go through it, up the stairs, and there'll be a security guard at the door. He'll let you into the main terminal. Then, it's up to you."

"Thanks," Sam said. He opened the door, hurried along the corridor and up the stairs.

The guard was indeed waiting for him and he opened the door. "Don't let anyone out through this door," Sam said, feeling less convinced than he sounded.

The service door opened into the main terminal's departure area. Lines of travelers idly milled about, waiting to check bags, pick up tickets, clear customs, and solve the dozens of other perplexing problems of international travel. Sam closed his eyes and forced himself to recall the terrorist's image. Satisfied that he would recognize the man, he started walking. He walked slowly.

Every few steps he'd stop and study the people around

him, looking for the face. He didn't look for the whole face. He looked for the eyes, or the chin, or the nose, or the mouth. He didn't look for a nervous person. Every person seemed nervous—nervous about leaving the country with illegal bits of ivory, or stones, or money, or just getting on the airplane. And they had every reason to be. Sam didn't waste time looking for a man carrying three vials of the deadly virus that could start a world war. He tried to focus his search on the details he could see in a person's face.

As he checked the details of each face, Sam slowly became aware of a commotion at one of the airport's many side doors. For a few seconds Sam thought his terrorist was trying to escape and had been cornered by either his fellow Eagle Team members or the South African police.

His guess was close but not quite right. The doors were being sealed by South African security and no one was being allowed to leave the airport without producing a passport or some other form of identification. Okay, that takes care of that escape, Sam thought. He turned back to the line. All right, Sammy, slow down, he thought, take your time. This badass isn't going to get out of here all that easily. He reminded himself to look carefully at each face in each line. He needed to be sure it didn't belong to the man Eagle Team had been told to find. He knew that by this time every gate to departing aircraft had been secured. No one could leave the country without proving who he or she was and why they were leaving the country.

The clamor of disgruntled passengers continued to grow. Sam checked the lines of people. Each step became another face; each face passed by was another one that was innocent. He saw a group of men more nervous than the others and one man among the group looked right. Sam removed his glasses and squinted in the group's direction. He knew they were too far away to see clearly.

He polished his glasses with the bottom of his shirt and settled them back on his nose. He focused his attention on the men. They saw him coming and turned away, pretending to be preoccupied.

Sam walked with purpose. The one man—the one he thought looked overly jittery—the one who appeared to have the matching build, the matching hair color, even the beady eyes that matched the image—tried to edge away from the other men.

"I may have him." Sam touched his cheek to cover his mouth. "You guys wanna give me some support?"

"We're here, Sam," Hunter said. "I see you. I am on your nine o'clock. Do you copy?"

Sam turned and looked to his left. Hunter stood there, fifteen yards away and closing the gap. "Which one is it?" Hunter asked.

"The one in the middle of the group," Sam said. "He's turning away from us now."

"Got him," Hunter said.

"Sarah, you got him pegged yet?"

"See him," she said.

The three TALON troopers closed in on the suspected terrorist. Sam glanced around and could see South African security forces, in and out of uniform, closing the gap. His confidence began to climb—something that definitely hadn't been there when he started. If the guy didn't run they would be able to finish this operation in the next few minutes. He'd be on his way home to visit his parents in Queens by nightfall.

The circle around the group tightened, every possible escape route sealed off. The man would have to see that his situation was hopeless and surrender. Sam sensed the anxiety that swept across the group. They were like cornered deer, or since they were in Africa, antelope. The men milled around, cross glares cautioned others to retreat and move away. Together, as a herd, they seemed to wait for a danger signal—a warning to flee. A time to run. Direction didn't matter. Whatever was in the path didn't matter. They simply had to run, to find an escape from what would be certain death. Sam watched the flickering glances of the men's eyes. They were searching for the escape. Their options were narrowing. The closer the net came and closed in on them, the more frightened the men became.

An alarm bell started to ring in Sam's head. A terrorist, even an amateur terrorist, wouldn't be giving himself away so easily. Something wasn't setting right.

And then the man in the center suddenly broke. He pushed another man out of the way and ran directly at Sam. The force of the fleeing man knocked Sam backward. Both reeled and the suspect stumbled into a startled line of waiting passengers.

Sam collapsed in a startled heap on the smooth marble floor. All of Sam's doubts disappeared in the rush of adrenaline. Sam saw Hunter pushing people out of his way, trying to chase the rapidly disappearing man.

But the crowd of people, scared and startled as a flock of pigeons suddenly in the shadow of a goshawk, didn't give way. In screams of terror, the crowd ran aimlessly, trying to escape an unknown horror. Conditioned by the world's violence televised on every nightly news program, they expected to hear the sound of gunfire, see the spray of blood streak across the marble floor. Some froze or dropped to the floor. Some cried, or shouted. The commotion became increasingly out of control.

Pandemonium spread through the passengers and Sam, in imminent danger of being trampled, fought mightily to regain his balance. He could still see the man, running, pushing, shoving violently to get through the crowd. He ran, trying to reach the door but already airport security was closing the door and moving toward him. He had no opportunity to escape. Sam struggled to his feet and bolted after the suspect through the milling throng. He watched the Boer's confusion. The man must not understand that he had no chance for escape. All he must see is the door and what he thought would be freedom.

From behind, Sam heard Sarah commanding someone to freeze. He resisted the urge to turn and look back, but knew that Sarah had taken command of the security forces that had surrounded the other men. He heard her bark orders for them to lie down, to put their hands over their heads.

Sam kept pushing and running. He darted past fleeing travelers, wove in and out of the crowd. The man he was chasing had turned at the last minute—apparently giving up when he saw the door was blocked.

Instead of escape, the Boer ran into a huge black man, a passenger who wasn't afraid. The big man stood his ground. In a flash of motion, the black man's fist connected with the Boer's nose.

Sam saw the man's face contort in pain.

A bright red stream gushed down the suspect's face and he crumpled to his knees. He wobbled, stunned as much by the blow as by the change in fortunes. He let his arms hang heavily at his side, blinking to clear his vision. Finally, he put his hands in the air.

"You people are crazy," the man said as Sam neared him.

"We're crazy?" Sam repeated. "We're crazy!" he shouted.

Hunter was already there. He pulled the man's hands behind him while pushing him toward the floor.

Sam hollered again, "We're crazy! You're the crazy ones!" Then he stopped. "Where are they?" Sam shouted. For the first time, he fought the urge to do bodily damage to another human being.

"In my pocket."

Roughly grabbing the lapels of the suspect's bush coat, Sam reached into his pocket. His hands trembled as he removed a small bag and opened it.

"What the fuck!" Sam held the bag up for Hunter to

see. "He's carrying rocks! These are nothing but God damn rocks!"

"Yeah, well, if you fuckin' DeBeer spooks weren't so selfish and kept trying to keep the little guys out of the business we wouldn't have to . . ."

Before the common smuggler could finish, Sam threw the fortune in diamonds on the floor.

Hunter stood up, his foot resting comfortably on the man's neck.

A police officer, his pistol drawn approached. "Wrong bloke?" he said in a thick English accent.

"Yeah," Hunter said, "he's all yours." Hunter removed his foot and with Sam, started surveying the passengers, who were also regaining their composure. He asked Sarah how she was doing.

"Well, we just busted up a ring of diamond smugglers for the South African government and saved DeBeers a bunch of money."

"Screw the Dutch," Hunter said. "Do you see anything?"

"Negative," Sarah said.

Sam felt like an idiot. He felt his cheeks begin to burn and heat prickled at the back of his neck, making him flush under his collar. He wanted to apologize to Hunter, but TALON Force members were trained to take setbacks in stride.

Already Hunter was giving instructions. "There's a chance he cleared departure and is sitting in the international lounge," Hunter said. "We've got the gates closed off but he might be willing to wait us out—see if we don't give up and figure he made it out of the country."

Sarah and Sam both agreed.

"Okay, we'll split up and cover the international departure lounge," Hunter said, leading Sarah and Sam through the departure control, flashing his identification at each of the security officers they passed.

Fewer passengers wandered through the international

lounge area. Hunter radioed his South African counterpart to shut down the entrance to the area. Once completed, he turned to Sam and told him to go to the far end of the departure area and begin working his way back toward the center.

"The exits are secured," Hunter said. "I'm betting that if he's in here he'll break and run when we start to close in on him." He told Sarah to take up a position where she could watch the terminal while he started at the other end and worked toward Sam. "I've got that feeling, Sammy boy," Hunter said. "I think he's in here."

"I hope so," Sam said. As he neared the far end of the closed terminal Sam made a broad turn and began a slow walk back, weaving from side to side in the hallwaylike terminal, going into each of the little shops lining the terminal walk. Sam checked each person he encountered. Some of them stared back at him with open hostility. A few smiled. Most of them ignored him, turning away quickly so they didn't have to endure the discomfort of their features being scrutinized by a stranger. Sam became systematic in his approach. He glanced at the women, reassuring himself that his target wasn't trying to pass himself off as female. Then he studied the men. The obvious faces he dismissed quickly—black faces, mulatto faces, colored faces. Gruenwald could have shaved his beard or colored his hair. He looked for the eyes or the nose, features he could be sure of.

Each shop became a chore and they seemed to stretch endlessly through the lounge. Sam fought the urge to hurry. He lingered for a second at the entrance to the men's toilet. "Hunter," Sam said into his radio. "Want me to check the head?"

"Roger," Hunter said. "Let Sarah get in position to see if Gruenwald tries to get into the area you've already cleared while you're in the head."

"Okay," Sam said. Then he added, "How do I check the stalls?"

"You get on your hands and knees and look under the door, Sam," Blake said.

"Uh-huh," Sam said, his lack of enthusiasm obvious in the tone of his voice.

Sarah snickered and Sam ignored her. When she said she was in position, he pushed the door open and went inside. He carefully walked through the men's bathroom, checking each man at each urinal, then the men washing their hands. Finally, reluctantly, Sam began checking the toilet stalls. Fortunately there were only three in use and after Sam had put his head under the divider of the last occupied stall, a tall, well-dressed man near the door paused to question him.

The man reached for Sam, firmly grasping the small Chinese-American by the shoulder. "Excuse me, just what do you think you're doing?"

"Police business," Sam said.

"You don't look like a cop to me. You look like a weirdo."

Sam turned away.

"Bloody queer, aren't you?"

This time Sam lost it. His frustrations piled up and boiled over. Angrily, he jerked out of the man's grasp and pushed past him. "Bug off, you stuffed shirt," he snarled. Satisfied, Sam turned to the door then looked back at the man. "If I were you, I'd have a seat. Stay awhile. You don't want to mess your pretty suit." The man sputtered and his face turned red but Sam didn't hang around to trade insults.

Once outside the men's room, Sam told Hunter the toilet was clear.

"You get on your knees and check those stalls?"

"Sure did. But Hunter, didn't anyone ever tell you, if you're going to put your name and phone number on the bathroom wall, it's supposed to be in the *ladies* room?" Sam chided.

"Why, Sammy?" Hunter said. "Was it spelled wrong?"

Sam chuckled and turned to the next set of shops. They were on his right as he walked and the first one was a candy shop. Two men lingered in the shop. Sam carefully checked their faces and continued on. The next shop sold women's clothing and several women milled around, in and out of dressing rooms, shuffling through racks of intimate nightgowns, talking to one another, but no men. The absent men loitered outside the shop, smoking and pacing back and forth across the entrance. Again, Sam examined the face of each one as he passed by. He followed the same routine in the next store—a leather shop. Before starting into the shop, he studied the faces of passengers sitting in the rows of chairs that filled the center of the long terminal. He looked beyond the end of the first row where he could see into the bar area of the international lounge and restaurant. A small group of several men sat at the horseshoe-shaped bar. Three of them had beards—like their suspect. All three sat together.

For a full five seconds Sam studied the men. Their faces were blank. They didn't seem to be interested in anything but their beers, but as Sam turned away he caught a glimpse of movement by the man on the left. Sam turned back around. The man turned on his bar stool so he was now sitting at an angle. It's not him, Sam thought. The man was too obvious. He wasn't hiding. He was in the public, facing the open entrance to the bar. Every police officer and security person who walked past could easily see him. Sam tried to convince himself that the man who had pivoted on his bar stool was not the man they wanted. And then a lesson from his college days hit him and he remembered a line from literature about "hiding the thing most precious in plain sight."

"Who the hell said that?" Sam whispered, turning around.

"Said what?" Blake said.

"Hide it in plain sight."

"Poe," Blake said.

"No, it was Sherlock Holmes," Sarah said.

"It doesn't matter," Sam said. "I've got him."

"Sam . . . are you sure?" Hunter asked.

"Yes," Sam said, "and he knows I've got him."

"Don't spook him," Hunter said.

"He's spooked. He's coming out of the bar and lounge area," Sam said. "He's wearing a khaki bush coat, long pants with cargo pockets."

"Look around, Sam," Sarah said.

Sam heard her brushing past people. He didn't take his eyes off of Gruenwald.

"Why?"

"There must be fifty or sixty men wearing bush coats, it's gotta be a national requirement."

"Yeah," Sam said, "I guess you've got a point." He moved at an oblique angle that would allow him to intercept his target in another two dozen steps. "But hey, how many of them are carrying metal briefcases?"

"Only one," Sarah said, "and I see him. You're right, Sam. That's him. No disguise, nothing. Wonder how many times we missed him?"

Sam didn't take a guess. Instead, he alerted Blake and Sarah that the man had changed direction and was now moving across the terminal hall. "He's headed for the gates."

"Let him," Sarah said. "They're secured."

Gruenwald moved quickly, briefcase in hand. He picked up his pace and began to roughly push people out of his path.

A South African Airlines employee at the ticket counter became aware of the steadily advancing man. Sam watched as she stepped out from behind the counter to stop him. The door behind her, Sam knew, was locked. He couldn't escape. Once again Sam felt the rush of relief and of having accomplished the mission. In seconds it would be over. Sam hurried down the corridor, closing the distance.

What happened next caught everyone unexpectedly. The target slowed, opened his briefcase and removed another metal container—a boxlike thing Sam was sure contained the vials. The bearded Boer jammed the smallish box into one of his many pockets then held the suitcase in front of his face—his every movement controlled precision, fluid, and athletic. Using it as a battering ram, he ran full speed toward the glass windows that gave passengers a view of departing aircraft. He had to be gambling it was glass, and at first he gambled wrong.

The glass window didn't shatter and break, but vibrated with the impact. A spiderweb of cracks appeared. The man backed up and, still holding the metal briefcase in front of his face, hit the glass a second time. This time the glass bulged. He threw his weight behind the suitcase and pushed, backed up, ran at it, and pushed again. The window frame cracked and groaned in protest. In the matter of three short bursts of pushing and straining, the entire window buckled and popped out of its frame, crashing to the ground. The Boer, intent on his escape, looked down, stepped up to the bottom of the gap and jumped.

Only seconds behind him, Sam reached the window. He saw Gruenwald climbing out of a large trash container.

"How'd he know?" Sam sighed. Then he climbed onto the window frame and jumped into the same Dumpster— still seconds behind the Boer, who was by this time running headlong into the baggage handling area. Sam thrashed awkwardly among the trash bags and climbed out. He told Hunter and Sarah where he was going and sped toward a door that was closing.

Sam hadn't expected to find the confusing array of conveyor belts, baggage carts, and milling people. The subterranean world of the airport was ablaze with bright lights and punctuated with dark shadows. Every ten feet or so gave birth to another blackened hiding place—

place where the Boer could disappear into the inky darkness. Sam radioed Hunter to tell him where he was, adding that he sure could use the BSD's infrared capablity. Sarah and Hunter each responded, saying that they were on their way and would try to block the target's escape. Sam slowed down and began to search for the man. He crawled under the conveyor belts that were moving bags of luggage from one mysterious point in the sprawling airport to another. There were belts he couldn't go under, and he had to go over them, or around them. The further he worked his way into the bowels of the luggage area, the harder the workers stared. This was their world, not his. He was an interloper, invading. No one asked what he was doing just as no one offered to help. None of them pointed to a direction Gruenwald may have gone. Their black faces appeared blacker and more sinister to Sam as he followed what he was sure was the path of the Boer.

"We're inside, now," Hunter said.

"Roger," Sam replied.

Suddenly all the moving belts stopped. The stillness of an underground death descended on the baggage area. No one moved. Sam froze in his tracks. He was lost and confused. Then he heard the muffled scrape of shuffling feet. He didn't hear the sound of cheap tennis shoes on the feet of black workers—those who were still struggling to be equal. What he heard was the sound of leather soles—a farmer's boot—on a floor where they didn't belong. It was as intrusive as the scrape of soil and shit being ground into the terra-cotta tiles of an expensive restaurant.

Sam turned toward the sound. "You hear that?" he whispered into the radio.

"Yeah," Sarah said. "I'm moving toward it."

Sam moved slowly, trying not to make a sound. The contrast of glaring light and pitch darkness confused his eyes and he couldn't see into the murky concrete depths.

He passed a patch of blackened wall then heard what didn't belong in the darkness—the hushed sound of breathing. Sam crept forward, stopped, and looked around hoping to appear lost and confused. Without warning, he whirled and jumped into the darkness. He felt the body of another man falter and stagger. Sam grunted and grabbed at the anonymous man, forcing him into the light.

"Son of a bitch!" Sam shouted, "you're not him!"

The startled and slender black man blinked at Sam. The brown face was weathered and didn't belong in the cavernous darkness. Silently, intently, he stared at Sam. He darted out of his captor's grip, scuttled back into the darkness, and hurried away. Sam heard another burst of rushed activity and hurried toward it. This time there was no mistaking the man they were after.

The Boer had climbed onto a conveyor belt and was pushing baggage out of his way. Sam saw the blurred movement of Hunter beyond the terrorist at the same instant the Boer saw Hunter. He jumped from the belt, crouched to run beneath another, and then hurried across an open area to disappear into the blackness of the shadows. Hunter warned him to stop and Gruenwald turned and aimed a pistol at him. The shot echoed through the baggage cavern. Sam ducked.

"That, my friend," Hunter shouted, "was a damn stupid thing to do."

The Boer could be heard pushing bags out of his way, trying to find an escape route. More voices could be heard as the South African police and airport security officers joined the pursuit. The net was again closing down and Sam's adrenaline was still driving him. His heart thumped and he moved steadily toward the noise of the lone Boer's frantic search for an exit. Twice more Gruenwald fired at his pursuers but no one returned the fire. Once Sam thought he had a pretty clear shot bu this had become a game of honor. Somehow the Boer had to be taken alive and uninjured.

Working his way toward the Boer, Sam thought he saw his opportunity to intercept the man. He thought that Gruenwald was working his way along the back of the baggage handling area. A number of South African officers could be heard working their way toward him. The only possible route of escape would be to use the shadows along the wall to conceal his movements until he could find a place to hide or escape.

Pulling his Baretta free, Sam held it with both hands. He didn't really intend to shoot the Boer, unless he had to defend himself, but he wanted it in his hands. He moved slowly along the edge of the conveyor. He could hear the voices of the others. The Boer's noise was so distinctive that Sam could easily follow his progress and plot his interception. Stopping near a concrete pillar Sam crouched down. Gruenwald would have to move across the open, lighted area between Sam and a solid wall. The sound of the Boer's feet on the floor, creeping closer to him, worked like a pump sending adrenaline into his body. Sam could feel his kidneys and his back muscles strain. Sweat dripped from his upper lip. His hair was plastered to his head.

When the Boer appeared at the edge of the open space, Sam was ready. He raised the gun, holding it steady with both hands. Gruenwald started to move into the open, to scurry across the clear cement floor, when Sam stood up and shouted for him to freeze.

The man stopped and turned to face Sam. "You going to shoot me?"

"If I have to shoot you, I will."

Gruenwald raised his hands. "Then you've got me." He started toward Sam in cool, methodical steps.

Sam moved into the open where the Boer could see him.

"Not many places to go down here, is there?"

"Just stay where you are and keep your hands up."

In his ear wire, Sam heard Jack say, "Go get 'im, Sammy!"

"I got him, Jack," Sam said. "I . . ."

He managed to shout, "Shit!" as Gruenwald rushed him. The Boer's fist slammed into his face and Sam fell back against the pillar. The Baretta clattered against the wall and slid into the shadows.

Gruenwald leered and reached for Sam, happy to finish his work.

But not before Sam struck back. Instinctively, he pulled his fist back and let it fly. The blow was blind, the landing, perfect. His fist caught the Boer under the solar plexus and he stumbled back, staggering from the blow. Immediately, he doubled over, gasping for air. Sam didn't relax or give the man time to think. Instead of searching for his gun, Sam rushed the Boer, slamming his head into Gruenwald's groin and propelling him backward with the blow. After regaining his balance, he reached for the stunned Boer's hair, grabbed a handful, and pulled Gruenwald's head up, exposing his chin. Sam drew his fist back once again. He threw his full weight into the punch as it connected with the Boer's chin. The man sagged to the ground. Breathing hard, Sam started to sit down next to the terrorist then thought better of it. He scrambled into the darkness and found his Baretta. Knees still wobbling, he tottered closer to the Boer and put the muzzle to the man's head.

"Move, you S.O.B.," Sam said, "and I'll blow your brains out."

Gruenwald grunted in submission and lay still.

Sam heard Hunter and the others hurrying to join him. When they had surrounded the beaten Boer, Sam looked up at Hunter and Sarah.

They grinned at him and nodded to each other.

"Looks like you handled it just fine," Sarah said.

"Yeah," Sam said. "Jack, you there?"

"Here, buddy."

"*Now* I got him."

Jack laughed and every member of Eagle Team heard the laugh.

Hunter reached down and handcuffed the Boer, then hauled him to his feet. "Give me the vials."

"I don't have them."

Thick silence dropped over the group.

"What the hell do you mean you don't have them?"

"I hid them," he said, "back there. Under one of those belts. In the shadows."

"Where?"

Gruenwald shrugged. "I don't know. You find them."

With one hand, Hunter jerked the Boer forward. He brought up his free hand, formed a fist, and started to slam it into the man's face when Sarah stopped him.

"Don't," she said.

Hunter stared hard at her and then lowered his fist, still holding the limp Boer like a rag doll.

Sarah brought her face close to Gruenwald's so she could see his eyes. "All of these people would like nothing better than to tear you into very small pieces and stuff your maimed and dismembered carcass into outbound luggage. Why don't you just tell us where it is."

He looked at Sarah and blinked. "I really don't know where they are. I hid them under one of the belts."

Sarah looked at him, then at Hunter. "Know what I think?"

"Babe, I never know what you're thinking."

"I think he's telling the truth."

Sam looked at the cluster of people. "Then I think we better find it."

Two South African police officers took the Boer from the baggage area and Blake took charge of the search. "Okay, we'll search the place starting from here," he said. "Everyone fan out, form a line."

Under Hunter's supervision the searchers retraced the

Boer's steps. They hadn't been searching for more than ten minutes when one of the security officers shouted that he'd found the vials.

"Don't touch it!" Hunter shouted. "Maybe he booby-trapped it."

Before touching the package Hunter checked it from every angle. The Boer had carried the vials in a padded nylon case. It looked like the carrying case for a pair of binoculars.

"These guys don't seem to think too far ahead." Finally, satisfied that the Boer hadn't the time to do anything other than stash it in the shadows and run, he reached for the nylon case.

"Here goes," he said. After picking it up, Hunter carried it into the open. "Washington, you on-line?"

"Krauss, here."

"Okay, sir," Hunter said. "We've got the last member of the terrorists in custody and the last of the vials right here."

"Check the vials," the general said.

"Yes, sir." Hunter pulled the Velcro flap open. The vials were wrapped in plastic bubble wrap and he took them out of their snug carrying case. "They're wrapped up," Hunter said, "I am unrolling them." After a pause Hunter said, "Sir, we've got a problem."

"What's that, Captain?"

"There are only two vials here."

"Stand by."

"Roger."

The minutes ticked off before Krauss was back to Hunter. "The police have questioned your last terrorist and are convinced he had all three of the vials when he went into the baggage area. The police are sending down more officers for you to search the baggage area. The best we can figure is that he dropped it in the baggage handling area . . . Find it."

"Yes, sir."

May 30, 1700 hours
Jan Smuts International Airport, Johannesburg, South Africa

The search for the missing vial lasted nearly four hours. After the search team had gone over the area, dogs were used for another search, but the vial was still missing. Hunter, Sarah, and Sam sat together on one of the baggage carts surveying the mess.

"Anyone have any ideas?" Hunter asked.

"Nope," Sarah and Sam answered together.

"Are you sure there were three vials in that package?" Hunter asked.

"We've accounted for every vial but one," Krauss said. "We're also convinced it is no longer in the airport."

"What next?" Hunter asked.

"We're not sure. The rest of Eagle Team is in the hangar. Join them and stand by."

"Roger."

Hunter stood up and looked at the others. "I have a gut feeling that we might have lost this one."

"Hunter." Sarah frowned. "You're Mr. Cool, Mr. Optimist. How can *you*, of all people, say that? It's not over yet," Sarah said.

A few minutes later a South African military van stopped in front of the three and they silently climbed inside. They rode to the hangar in weary silence. When they joined the rest of the team, a sense of failure permeated the atmosphere. The other Eagle Team members sat around the communications center. Hunter asked Travis if he had any word on Jen Olsen.

"She'll be fine," he said. "Some deep bruising so the Air Force is bringing a transport over to fly her back to the States. She'll be down for a few days."

"This fuckin' mission has been screwed from the start," Stan said, slamming his battle helmet on a table. "I've never seen a more cockeyed deal."

"Back off, Stan," Travis said.

"*Back off!* Have you kept a count of the number of people who have been killed on this fuckin' thing? It's been a nightmare. We're so good we didn't need to train, we just drop into South Africa, take out a few farmers, pick up the vials of some virus some college kid in our own country stole, and then we're outta here! In the meantime half the fuckin' world is ready to go to war with the other half, sending nukes that supposedly don't fuckin' exist against a country that was their ally!"

Travis took a step toward Stan. "We can't cover every base, every possible thing that can go wrong," he said. "No one knew for sure what we were up against. We're lucky we got this far. There's one vial missing. We'll find it."

Stan's head dropped in frustration. "Sorry," he murmured. He sat down with the others.

May 30, 1930 hours
operations hangar, Jan Smuts International Airport,
Johannesburg, South Africa

Several hours dragged past with only an occasional communication with Washington. Major Anderson returned and walked through the hangar to the waiting TALON members. He went straight to Travis.

"Major Barrett," Anderson said.

Travis stood up. He didn't speak.

"We've got a problem," Anderson said.

"What's the problem?"

Anderson looked at the communication equipment. "I take it you've got your commanding officers in Washington listening in."

"Yes," Travis said.

Anderson turned toward the desk and in a loud voice said, "We know where the third vial is."

"There's no need to shout, Major," General Freeman said. "This equipment is designed to pick up a whisper—if that's what we want."

"Understood," Anderson said.

Travis leaned toward Anderson and whispered, "He's a general, they're all generals."

"Major, my rank isn't the matter at hand presently," Freeman said. "Let's get on with this."

"Yes, sir," Travis said.

"Generals," Anderson said, "we know who took the vial."

"Who?" Freeman demanded.

"A Namibian."

"You need to explain yourself."

Anderson pulled an empty chair over and sat down in it. "It seems that while our people were busy trying to capture our last terrorist, a bushman took it. This bushman isn't your average individual. He was once a member of SWAPO, and is still somewhat revered by the former guerrillas who fought for South-West Africa during the revolutionary period of the seventies and eighties. Apparently he plucked one of the vials from the bag, walked out of the airport, got in his car, and drove off. We suspect he is on his way to Namibia."

"You've closed the borders?" Freeman asked.

"Of course, General."

"What can we do?"

Anderson leaned forward. "General, with all due respect, we'd appreciate it if your Eagle Team would pack up and go home. There is one vial left and we believe it is now a matter for the South African government."

"With all due respect, Major, I think that order will have to come from higher up."

"With all due respect, sir," Anderson said, "I believe you should be getting confirmation of that request."

Washington was silent for several seconds before Freeman's subdued voice was heard in the hangar. "Major Barrett," Freeman said.

"Sir."

"Pack your team. You'll be flying back on a C-141. Captain Olsen will be on it as well."

"Yes, sir," Travis said.

"We're breaking the net down in five minutes," General Krauss said.

"Breaking down," Travis repeated, then unhooked his combat pack and dropped it on the table. He noticed Anderson staring at him. "You have anything else, Major?" Travis asked.

Anderson shook his head. "I am sure that on the right mission your team functions perfectly."

"We've had our successes."

"Are they always as bloody?"

"What's your fuckin' problem, Major? We're supposed to be soldiers here. Hell, these people weren't just common soldiers before they were picked for TALON—they were the best! So, what's your fuckin' problem?"

"There are more than two dozen dead South Africans, farmers, police, and military stretched halfway across our country."

"It's better than a nuclear war," Stan said.

"There were no nukes on those planes," Anderson said. "We were only trying to make a statement."

"Bullshit, Major. You're spouting party politics now."

"Perhaps you should look at your own history, Commander. Your country did a good job of hurting a lot of poor people with its embargo against South Africa."

Stan stared at him. "Is that what you're angry about? The politics of fifteen years ago? The politicians who voted for that aren't even in office anymore!"

"South Africa suffered under that embargo, mostly the poor, black *and* white, while high-minded American im perialism was your justification. Your country didn't suffer. Your politicians grew richer with our misery."

Stan started to step toward Anderson and Jack pulled him back. "Let's stow our gear and get out of here," he said.

Anderson looked at the team and the scattered equipment. "We'll keep some guards outside the hangar until your aircraft arrives."

"Thanks," Travis deadpanned.

Anderson nodded and walked quickly out of the hangar. When the door slammed shut, Sarah drop-kicked a trashcan across the floor.

"What's that for?" Jack asked.

"We don't get a thank you or kiss my ass, just booted out of the country."

"Well," Travis said. "At least we're all leaving in one piece."

"Yeah," Stan said. "At least we can leave."

Sam watched Jack start breaking his equipment down. Usually his big Marine buddy was a bundle of laughs, even in the worst times, but on this mission he'd remained mostly silent. He didn't have time to brood about Jack's problems. Instead, he turned to the task of breaking down the equipment. The equipment was compact and designed for quick deployment but it still took longer to break down than set up. After it was packed in its containers and readied for loading on the airplane, Sam walked over and joined the others at a long table. They were drinking coffee and each one seemed lost in their own worlds.

When the door slammed open and Anderson returned, they expected him to tell them when their aircraft would be arriving. Instead he stopped at the end of the table and looked at the team.

"You've got something on your mind?" Travis asked.

"The vial is in Namibia," Anderson said.

"Well, go get it."

"It's not that easy."

"Why?" Travis said, pushing himself away from the table and standing up.

"It seems Mr. Sam Nujoma, the president of Namibia, doesn't trust the South Africans and has refused to allow our security forces into the country to track down the person who has the vial."

"What's that got to do with us?"

"He will allow an American security team to do it."

"Okay," Stan said, "a job for TALON Force."

"Hold it, Commander," Anderson said, stopping Stan halfway out of his seat. "The Namibians don't trust the Americans any more than they trust the South Africans, even with a black government here."

"Why don't they trust us?"

"Your government wasn't a friend of SWAPO, either."

"That's ancient history," Sarah said.

"Not in Africa. You're from the first world and you keep slamming doors on the rest of us."

"So, what's the deal?" Travis asked.

"Just this. President Nujoma has agreed to allow two members of your team to enter the country with the express mission of tracking down one former SWAPO member by the name of Benjamin Moses."

"We can do an insertion, HALO in, whatever it takes. No one will know we're on the ground."

"No," Anderson said. "The Namibians will be watching for that sort of trick. They don't trust you."

"Okay," Travis said, "we pick two members of the team and they go get this guy. What's so hard about that?"

Anderson laughed. "For one thing, Mr. Nujoma has heard of all the exploits of your team. He is sure that you are serious about your work, and even someone to be sort of trusted. However, he does not wish to offend any of the ethnic groups in his country so he has chosen the two who will go after Moses."

"Who's that?"

"Captains Wong and DuBois."

"Sam?" Travis said. "Really?"

"He caught the last terrorist, and as an Asian-American, is the least offensive. As for Captain DuBois, the feeling is that as a black man in a black country, he might have the best chance of convincing Mr. Moses to hand it over."

"Hand it over?" Travis shouted. "Hand it fucking over? What are they goin' in there to do? Negotiate some sort of peace treaty?"

"That's the deal. They will be allowed to take communications equipment so they will be in contact with their headquarters in Washington. They will each be allowed to take their sidearms. No aircraft standing off with cruise missiles. No robots."

"We wear our bio-gear and camouflage?"

"That's approved," Anderson said. "No smart rifles, hand grenades, or any of that stuff."

"Why all the restrictions?"

Anderson looked at the team. "Mr. Moses is a bushman. The Herero people are very special in Namibia. They have become a national treasure to the Namibian people. They are also the world's greatest trackers and are experts at camouflage and concealing themselves. If Mr. Moses doesn't want you to find him, you won't."

"When do they leave?"

"There will be a civilian jet outside the hangar in half an hour. It'll fly you to Windhoek. From there you'll be provided with a Range Rover equipped with water and supplies. You'll be given the last known location of Mr. Moses. As you will have your GPS maps and other technological gadgets, we expect you will be able to find your way around the country although the police will give you every possible assistance."

"In other words," Jack said, "we're gonna be on our own."

Anderson turned to him. "Essentially, that is true." He turned back to the others. "The rest of you will be confined to this hangar until Mr. Moses returns the vial, or the chase is given up."

Travis looked at Jack and Sam. "We'll set up a communications net here . . ."

"No, you won't, Major," Anderson said.

"What do you mean?"

"A representative of the government of Namibia has been ordered to monitor your communications from inside this hangar, and not allow you to leave. He'll be in communication with his embassy here, and they will be in communication with Namibia. Captains DuBois and Wong will be allowed to communicate with Washington and from Washington, to you. There is to be no direct communication between them and the rest of TALON Force."

"Whose idea was that?" Travis demanded.

"This was a demand of the Namibian government," Anderson said. "Namibia has a somewhat tenuous hold on peace. Namibian officials want as few military interventions as possible." Anderson smiled coldly. "And won't it be interesting to have to put your cyborg goodies away for a while?"

"Listen, you two-bit tinhorn, I've put up with your cyborg shit this whole mission. There isn't a member of this team who wasn't a damn fine soldier before the TALON Force was created. The difference is in their dedication and belief that laying it all on the line is worth the risk if that's what it takes to keep the world from blowing itself up. We don't make the rules or set the politics, and so far I haven't seen anything from you that is very fucking impressive except a lot of bullshit and whining."

Sam could see the anger in Travis's eyes.

Travis turned to Jack and Sam, ordering them to ready their gear.

"I am going to set up my link to Washington, if you don't mind, Major," Travis said.

"I don't mind," Anderson said. He checked his watch. "Your plane will be here soon. I suggest you get yourselves ready. The Namibian desert is quite hostile to those who don't understand it."

"Do you?" Jack asked.

"Do I what?" Anderson replied.

"Do you know the desert?"

Anderson looked at him. "I've been to it," he said. "I don't ever want to go back."

"Then make sure you don't change your mind for this mission either," Jack said.

Anderson stared at him. "I'll be waiting for you to fuck up."

"I'm sure you will, Major."

Anderson turned and walked to the door, banging it behind him.

"What was that all about?" Travis asked.

Jack looked back at him. "He's on our side—but just barely." He shook his head. "Just barely."

Travis nodded, then picked up a box to set up the net. "We'll be with you, guys," Travis said. He opened the box. "We'll be with you even if it is long distance."

"Let's get this shit together," Jack said, looking at Sam. "We've got a mission to finish."

Sam stood up and walked to the packing boxes to retrieve his gear.

Chapter 10

Jack looked across the aisle of the British-built jet. Sam appeared to be sleeping. He'd propped a pillow against the window, made himself comfortable. Jack knew that Sam must be exhausted. Normally his slightly built friend struggled to relax, and in truth, sleeping would be the best thing that either of them did under their present circumstances. He reached across the aisle anyway and nudged Sam's shoulder to see if he was sleeping. Sam turned and looked at Jack.

"What's up?" Sam asked.

"Nothin' much, I just can't sleep."

"Why?"

"I'm wound tighter than a cheap watch."

Sam sat up in his seat and faced his friend. "What's eatin' you, big guy?"

"This mission. This mission is buggin' me. It should be over. The whole fiasco is being kept alive, dragged out by something that no one seems to have any control over."

"We'll get Moses and that'll be the end of it," Sam said. "How hard can it be? I bet the Namibians even know where Moses is right now."

"That's what I mean, Sam. We don't have nuclear wa looming large and bad on the horizon, the countries tha lost all the cattle—they're getting things under contro

Most of the carcasses have either been burned or buried. The only question left is the legal one. Who's going to pay the farmers for their losses? Which country is going to prosecute the terrorists?"

"That's more than one question, Jack."

"I know, Sammy, that's what I'm getting at. This damn cow thing was like manure hittin' the fan. We all got splattered, but everyone is still running for cover!"

Sam waited for Jack to continue.

"Look at what those assholes at CNN were broadcasting just before we pulled pitch! The insurance companies are claiming the attacks were an act of war—won't offer a settlement for the dead cattle. It's the same in England and France—this thing will end up in international court yet. Shit, mon, TALON could end up in court, too."

"Come on, Jack. We're soldiers," Sam said. "This is what we get paid the big bucks for—doing our duty."

"Yeah, well, where have you heard that number before? Don't forget the Nazis and all that happy horseshit. Something about this mission doesn't feel right. It's like we're cleanin' up a mess that was left by the politicians," Jack said, then rubbed his temples. "Sammy, shouldn't someone have cleaned up the first mess and not let that broad back in that university lab? She's the first fuck up—and then that Steiner kid—he's the second. And what about the limp-dick who decided to move the virus to Plum Island instead of just whacking it right then? That was another one."

Sam didn't respond at first. He wondered what was really eating at his friend. Several minutes passed before he said, "Well, Jack-o, maybe we had to clean up the mess, but we also had to stop the Boers. I don't think our government deserves to be held responsible. How can our government be accountable for the rest of the world? Come on, Jack."

"You know what really bugs me?"

"What?"

"TALON Force has just saved the South Africans' butts but our guys are still stuck in that hangar, the two of us are going on some kind of wild-goose chase. You know what I think?"

"What?"

"I think we're going to take the heat for this mission. You and me. And you know what else?" Jack paused and raised one eyebrow in skepticism. "I don't think it's going to make any difference. We did what we had to do—we're still doing what we have to do. The thing is, those people are still going to want their own country. They're still going to fight. Believe me, Sammy, it ain't over . . ."

Sam turned and sat back in his seat.

"It ain't over." Jack leaned back in his own seat. Then he said, "I gotta tell you one other thing, buddy."

"What's that?"

"You did good on Lars, real good. Kept your head and brought him in. That was first class."

"Thanks, big guy."

"Yeah," Jack said, letting his thoughts drift. "You did a good job there."

"Hey, Jack?" Sam said.

"Yeah?"

"What'd you think of that South African claim—that they'll work with the disenfranchised Boers, help 'em find new homes, build new lives, find 'em some place where they could live in peace and practice their religion?"

"Sounds good on TV," Jack said, "but I'll believe it when I see it. The Boers didn't do dick for the blacks when they had the power. What makes anyone think that once power's changed hands that anything will be different?"

"Maybe you're right," Sam said.

"Yup, same shit, different drummer. That's all."

"You know my mom and pop own a laundry in Flushing, right?"

Jack looked at Sam quizzically. "What the fuck you talkin' about?"

"Just that my parents own a laundry. You know what they say in the laundry business?"

Jack threw his hands up in exasperation.

"It all comes out in the wash!" Sam grinned at Jack and punched him in the shoulder. "Get some rest, big guy."

Jack rolled his eyes, nodded, and turned to the window. He and Sam were on another mission—a strange one to be sure. He thought about what he'd learned before leaving the hangar. They were to track down a bushman in the Namibian desert and convince him to turn over the last vial of the Anita virus to them. Nobody knew why he'd taken it, or why he'd hurried back to Namibia with it. The Namibians gained their independence from South Africa on March 21, 1990. The country had actually enjoyed a fair degree of prosperity under Nujoma—at least prosperity of a sort when compared to the other southern tier African nations. Mr. Moses, Jack reasoned, surely wasn't going to attack the white Namibian farmers' cattle. Nor would he be planning an attack against some other tribe. Whatever it was that the bushman was planning, Jack and Sam had to stop it. We will, he thought, we'll track him down, get the vial back, and end this clusterfuck. He turned back to the window and watched the African night outside the plane. After a few minutes he turned back to Sam.

"And you know what else, Sammy? I want to know why no one in the whole fucking world but the two of us will go after this guy."

"Ask 'em when we get to Namibia," Sam said.

"I will, Sam. I will." Jack felt tension knotting the back of his neck.

The pilot began the descent to the Windhoek airport.

The landing was smooth and the plane taxied to a part of the parking apron to one side of the terminal building. Someone from outside opened the door and lowered the stairs for Jack and Sam. As they deplaned, their gear was being unloaded from the cargo belly. Jack watched two police officers remove the equipment, place it in the back of a police car, and drive off.

A short bald man with a thick chest and neck hurried toward them. His voice echoed the same power as his physique. "Don't worry, Captain," the man said. "They are taking your equipment to a car that is waiting in the parking lot for you."

"Who are you?" Jack asked.

"Sheidley." The man beamed at the Americans. "Major Nigel Sheidley. It is my duty to get you started on your mission. Why don't we have a spot of coffee, something to eat? I will brief you then."

Jack and Sam nodded, then followed the major into the airport. He guided them to a public cafeteria inside the airport.

"If you are worried about security, please don't," the major said. "Most of the country knows that you are in pursuit of Mr. Benjamin Moses."

"What?" Jack snapped. "What is this, some sort of showboat operation?"

"I assure you, it is not a showboat. My government is making a real effort to be cooperative with the United States and the government of South Africa."

Major Sheidley led them through the cafeteria line. "You don't have to pay," he said. "You are the guests of my country. Everything is being done to make your visit enjoyable. Actually, at this time of night the airport is closed, but we've opened it for you."

Jack followed the major through the line and then to a table where they sat down.

"Eat well." Sheidley smiled. "I am sure that Benjamin

is going to lead you on quite a merry chase, quite different than your recent wild Boer hunt, ha, ha."

Jack took a big gulp of coffee and closed his eyes. He gently set his cup on the table although his knuckles had noticeably whitened. "Okay, Major. Give me some straight answers about what is going on and give 'em to me quick."

The major, now startled and not quite sure how to proceed, put his fork on the plate. He looked at Jack, carefully trying to gauge the other man. And then he did the same to Sam.

"Okay, I'll tell you what the situation is." He sobered in expression and tone. "Somehow your country was unable to hold onto a number of vials of a virus—Anita, isn't it?—that has proved to be very deadly to cattle all over the world. A South African fanatic managed to obtain it from one of your universities. He then managed to get it to another South African fanatic, who, in turn, managed to get it out of the country and into South Africa. These very enthusiastic individuals then divided up the vials. Some stayed in South Africa and the rest went to various parts of the world where Anita was set free. Many thousands—or is it hundreds of thousands?— of cattle died, triggering what almost became a nuclear war." Sheidley's eyes narrowed and he continued in his heavy, clipped English accent. "But your team managed to blow up a number of farmhouses, killing lots of people on both sides. Then, just before the last terrorist, Mr. Lars Gruenwald, who happens to be a farmer—a rather common man without even the benefit of a secondary education—is able to slip out of South Africa to spread more of the virus, quite remarkably, Captain Wong"—he paused to take a breath as much as acknowledge Sam—"wrestled Gruenwald to the ground. But it was too late. He'd hidden the vials, and while Captain Wong pummeled the terrorist, our own SWAPO hero of the war for independence managed to steal one of the vials. Is that correct?"

Jack nodded. Nothing sounded very good.

"Good, well, now let me continue. Mr. Moses managed to get back into Namibia. He has rejoined some wandering bushmen, who still live pretty much the same way that bushmen of this part of the world have lived since long before your country was even a place that had a name in Europe."

"What's your point?" Sam asked.

"My point is this, Captain," he said. "Your TALON Force is a group of the most bloodthirsty, technology-driven cyborgs who have ever walked across the African soil. None of us really want you here, but none of us really want to go into the desert after Moses ourselves." Sheidley's nostrils flared. "You must understand, Moses is not really so bad. You must also understand that nothing would really happen to us, but as a people we are learning to live together. If a Namibian soldier or police officer were to capture him, or bring any harm to him, there would be hell to pay in this country. Now if you big, strong, powerful Americans happen to capture Moses and get the vial without hurting a man who is a national hero to most of the blacks, then more power to you." Sheidley folded his hands in his lap and leaned back into his chair. "That means that you get to keep the reputation as being the most powerful nation in the world. Bully for you."

The major waited for the stunned Americans to move. Both Sam and Jack sat at the table, dumbfounded. Suddenly he pushed his chair away from the table and stood up. "Come with me. I want to show you what you are up against."

He led them out of the cafeteria and into the main terminal. At a brisk pace, he led them to a large glass display case. "This is what you are up against." He pointed to some human wax figures inside. They were of a man and a woman, smaller in stature than most people. He held a tiny bow and some small arrows. She was digging at a root.

"These are bushmen. Officially these people are the Khoi-San. They still don't like to carry modern firearms, although they will—hence you are being allowed to carry your sidearms. But, they prefer their own little bows and arrows and they have different kinds of poison on them. Some kill in minutes, some in days, some don't kill at all but they will keep you in one place. These people know how every blade of grass in the desert grows. Their most precious possession is the wood they find. They live in small bands, family groups, and roam the desert. In the last few years each of these groups has been given about eight hundred square miles of territory they call their own. They live in the caves and sometimes will set up a little thatch hut for a month or so. In those hundreds of square miles there is nothing growing. They carry their meager but highly prized possessions with them when they are traveling. They know how to survive in the desert, as I am sure you think you do. But, Captains, trust me. If Moses wants you to die in the desert, you will. If he wants you to find him, you will."

"You called these people the Khoi-San," Jack said. "I thought the guy we're up against is Herero."

"Good point, Captain," the major said. "He's not really either. Moses's mother was San, his father was Herero, hence his participation in the war."

"SWAPO?"

"Yes, quite a vicious soldier in his time. Quite capable of killing with any weapon. Led a number of highly successful operations against our people. We're quite taken with his capabilities."

"Ever arrest him?"

The major laughed. "We tried—tried many times, but Moses was never one to be caught."

"What makes you think we can catch him?"

"Oh, you'll catch him. He may lead you on a chase and have a bit of sport with you, but he'll eventually let you close enough for whatever it is that he wants to do."

"What do you suggest, Major?"

"Well, I think you should finish eating and then we'll go out to your vehicle, I'll give you some maps that show where he has been seen and other landmarks."

"Then what?"

"Why, go after him. When you stop for food there will be no bill. Same for petrol, a place to sleep in town. Whatever you need."

"Why?"

"Why what?" the Major answered.

"Why all this crap?"

Sheidley smiled at Jack and Sam. "I would have thought you would have figured it out by now."

"What is that?" Jack asked.

"Humility, Captain. A very small man, with a very long name in his native language, has decided to teach the greatest power on earth a lesson in humility. And there isn't anything I"—the major thumped his chest and then pointed to Sam and Jack—"or you, or any of the other world powers can possibly change . . . Let's finish our dinner. After that we'll let Benjamin Moses start his chase."

Jack and Sam followed. They both peeked at the major while they ate. The idea of learning some humility hadn't been mentioned before but Jack thought it was a hell of a good idea—win, lose, or draw.

"Sammy," Jack said. "We're going to need a miracle to mark this mission up in the win column."

"Yeah," Sam said. "It's going to take a huge miracle."

Thirty minutes later Jack and Sam stood on either side of Major Sheidley looking at a fully equipped Land Rover. It was decked out with spare fuel cans, water cans, a steel-mesh deck cargo-carrier on top, with much of their gear already strapped on.

"Well," Sheidley said as he patted the sides of his stomach. "There you are, Captains. This is your transport into the wilds of Namibia. You've got water, food, petrol, lanterns, a tent, two cots, and blankets. Of course your radio and GPS equipment is in the back seat. We'll let you set that sort of thing up." He reached into a pocket of his bush coat and removed a small envelope. "Here are directions to the last place Mr. Moses was seen. We believe he's headed toward his family group, which is normally found in the area of Herero Land, which would be to the east of the Waterberg Park."

Jack took the envelope. "So we start there?"

"No," the major said. "I think you should follow him, see where he leads you."

"Well, where in the hell do you suggest we start?"

"I think I'd go north out of Windhoek. About forty-five kilometers north is Okahandja. Take the road to Usakos, which will be to the west toward the Skeleton Coast. During his SWAPO days Moses had a contact in Usakos. He now works at the Total petrol station. Perhaps he's left some word there that might be useful."

Jack nodded and started toward the Land Rover then stopped and turned around. "Major, I've got a question for you."

"Yes?"

"This whole thing sounds to me like some kind of setup. I think you know where Moses is, and I think you know what he's up to and why he wants that virus."

"I think you may be right, Captain. But this isn't between you and me. This is between your government and mine. My government doesn't want Moses to turn that virus loose in this country. If he did turn it loose, then the white ranchers would be able to tell the world that the black government isn't taking any steps to provide any safety. And if we send our own people after this half-San, half-Herero, then many of the native peoples will claim the whites of Namibia are still controlling the government. So, you see, Captain, things are not as clear-cut here as they are in other countries. We're trying to build a nation of tolerance and your country has created this virus and allowed it to get away, which isn't helping us a bit. So, you're on your own. We won't help you with troops or airplanes or anything of a military nature. We will also not stop you from capturing Moses and getting your virus back and out of our country."

"That's big of you," Jack said.

"There's one more thing, Captain."

"What's that?"

"If either of you happens to kill Benjamin Moses, or any other bushman, you'll be charged with murder."

Jack nodded. "Come on, Sam. Get the comm gear up and running. I'll drive."

"Right," Sam said. He opened the door to the back seat and wedged himself among the bags and metal boxes.

Jack opened the door. Maps, instructions, a letter of introduction that informed the reader—in German, French, Spanish, and English—that the bearer was on a mission for the welfare of the people of Namibia and should not be charged for any services. The bills for the services provided should be sent to an official office in Windhoek. "Looks like we've got everything we need," Jack said.

"Yeah," Sam said. "Give me a few more minutes and I'll have the radio gear working."

Jack started the Land Rover and backed out of the parking lot. As he drove past Major Sheidley, the man saluted.

"Good luck, Captains."

A few minutes after Jack was on the highway and headed toward Windhoek, Sam had the satellite phone powered up and ready. He punched in the code for TALON Force Operations in Washington. The speakerphone buzzed once before General Krauss gruffly answered.

"We've been waiting to get this link back up," Krauss said.

"The net was ordered down by the South Africans and this is the first opportunity we've had to reestablish it, sir."

"Understood, Sam," Krauss said. "Now, have you been briefed on this operation?"

"This is what I have so far," Jack said, then repeated what they'd been told since landing in Windhoek.

"Essentially you have the facts, Captain. As for the killing of Moses, Major Sheidley is correct. It would not be politically astute to let anything happen to Mr. Moses."

Jack heard Krauss clear his throat and someone's voice muffled in the background.

"One other thing, Captain." Krauss paused.

"Yes, sir?"

"We feel that you should know something about your Major Sheidley. He is a veteran of the SWAPO wars—fought a lot of terrorists, but when the new governments came in, he swore his allegiance to them."

"Sir, what if we have to defend ourselves?"

"You shouldn't have much trouble taking down a bushman armed with a bow and arrow."

"Thanks for the vote of confidence," Jack said.

"Don't mention it," Krauss said, then added, "I assume you're headed for Usakos and the Total gas station?"

"Yes, sir."

"Well, the man you want to find is the day manager, Mr. Jacobs. Jacobs is a white man who supported SWAPO during the war."

"Yes, sir," Jack said.

"One more thing, DuBois."

"Yes, sir."

"Anita is still the target. A lot of governments are nervous and won't relax until all the vials are safely returned to the United States to be destroyed."

"I understand, sir."

"Be careful, Captain. No one, and that means no one, really knows why this Moses took the vial. For several years he's been content working at the airport. He hasn't given anyone any reason to think he was dissatisfied."

"Yes, sir," Jack said. The conversation was apparently finished. He turned his attention to the highway. The drive to Windhoek was less than an hour and Jack followed the highway, B1, into the heart of the small city, then north. On the south side of Okahandja the road forked and Jack turned onto the B2, toward the coast.

"You're not saying much," Jack said to Sam.

"Not much to say."

"Yeah. Guess there isn't."

Time dragged ahead of the two men like the desolate country they were driving through. The further west they drove, the more desolate and rocky the country became. Two hours later Jack pulled the Land Rover into the Usakos Total station. A young black man wearing a Total Service Center shirt hurried out and asked if he could fill the tank. Jack nodded. Briefly, he watched the attendant scurry around. He noticed that the young man wore tennis shoes without laces or socks. Are things really all that different here? he thought as he shook his head and then went looking for Jacobs. He spotted a wiry-looking white man watching him from inside the service station's office.

"Sam, keep an eye on things here," he said and crossed the parking lot to the office and went inside.

"You Jacobs?" Jack asked.

"Yes, are you Captain DuBois?"

Jack nodded.

"You are an awfully big man," Jacobs said.

"I eat a lot."

"I suppose you do," Jacobs said. "Benjamin left this for you." He handed Jack an envelope. Inside was a crude map of the region to the west, to the coast.

"Where is this leading us?"

"Your guess is as good as mine, Captain. Benjamin is going to take you on a tour. He wants you to follow that map. Your first stop will be in the Spitzkoppe Mountains."

"What do you mean, 'a tour'?" Jack's temper flared. "Listen, Mr. Jacobs. I'm not here to take a fuckin' tour because some guy with a bad case of governmentitis wants to play games. I want that vial. I want it very soon, and when I have it, then he can start another fuckin' revolution!"

Jacobs smiled and shook his head. "Sometimes, during the war, he would lead the South Africans on a similar chase. Only he would leave clues so they could follow him. He knows you don't have the time so he's leaving little flags, like this one." Jacobs held up a scrap of black cloth. "When you see one of these, Moses wants you to stop and go to the flag. He will have left instructions for you at those places."

"This is crazy," Jack said, grabbing the envelope and starting for the door.

"Captain," Jacobs said, stopping Jack.

"What?"

"The government is paying for your petrol, but the boy who pumped your gas isn't paid."

"So?"

"He depends on tips."

Jack grunted and walked to the Rover. The boy who'd pumped the gas stood silently watching. Jack dug in his pocket for some bills and handed the boy a five-rand note.

"Boy, aren't you a big spender," Sam said.

"What do you mean?" Jack said, a discernable growl in his voice.

"Five rand is less than a buck, cheapskate."

Jack looked at the dejected service boy. He took out another five-rand note and gave it to him. "There," Jack said, "now I don't feel quite as ugly." He handed the crude map to Sam. "See if you can plug this stuff into your GPS map. That's where we're headed."

Sam took the map and looked outside. The sun was coming up and they were driving through the morning glow of dawn. "You know, Jack . . ." Sam said.

"What?"

"Right now, with the sun just breaking through, this is sure some pretty country."

"Give me the swamps of Louisiana."

"You sure?"

"Yeah," Jack said, "I'm sure. I don't like Africa."

Jack drove on, Sam giving directions to follow various tracks, relying on the GPS to guide them through the desert mountains. When Jack saw the little flag in the middle of the track he slid the Land Rover to a stop and jumped out. He hunted around the flag, then either side of the road for some sort of instructions. He couldn't find anything and went back to the Rover. Sam waited beside the passenger door, his hand on his Baretta.

"There is supposed to be some sort of hint or something around here. Something for us to do," Jack said.

Sam walked to the flag and looked at it. "Jack," he said, "I think the flag is the instruction."

"What?"

"It's in the middle of the road. Like a roadblock. Maybe he wants us to stop here. Make camp, you know, that sort of thing."

Jack looked at Sam and smiled. "Could be right, little buddy. That's the only thing that makes sense."

The two men checked over the area for a place to park and camp for the rest of the day and night. Ten yards off the road, the rocks had been scraped away to form a small clearing, free of the scrub thorn bushes that dotted the countryside. In the middle of the clearing, a pile of sticks had been arranged with kindling for a small fire.

"I guess you're right, Sam. He's even left us wood for a fire."

In the space of about an hour, the two men unpacked their gear, set up the tent and cots, and unrolled their sleeping bags. They spent the entire day around the camp, wondering if they were being watched and what they were being used for. To get the vial, which meant to find Moses, they had to play his game. That evening Sam dug through the canned foods they'd been given by the Namibians and picked out their dinner—a can of beans and a can of an unidentifiable meat product. He also found some warm beer to wash the food and dust down. While the food warmed on a small Sterno stove that had been packed with the food, they lit the small fire and sipped their beers.

"It's quiet here," Sam said, warming his hands on the fire. "It's quiet and when the sun goes down, it turns cold and humid."

Jack didn't answer, but stared at the fire.

"Look at that sky," Sam whispered. "I've never seen a sky like that."

Jack looked up. "I have, in different places." He looked back at the fire. "Sam, this ain't no TALON mission. This is something else and I don't know what it is."

"We'll find out," Sam said. "Krauss wouldn't have agreed to this unless there was some purpose for it."

"Yeah," Jack said. Then he sank into himself. He didn't want to talk to Sam anymore. When the food was hot Jack took his and ate in silence. Later that night he told Sam there wasn't any need to worry about setting up any sort of guard schedule.

"Why not?" Sam asked.

"Moses is leading us around by our noses," Jack said.

Sam stood up and stretched. "Then, in that case, I'm hitting the sack. Wake me when the war starts."

Jack nodded and stared at the fire. He fed the small pile of sticks into the fire. He watched the yellow and orange flames lick the wood and thought of what Sheidley had said. The bushmen carried their little stores of firewood with them as they wandered through the desert. He plucked the rest of the sticks away and let the fire burn down to coals. In the darkness and the cold of night, Jack sat outside the tent. When he finally went to bed, his feet hanging over the edge of the cot, sleeping bag pulled over his shoulders, he still felt the melancholy sense of loss, or maybe something more indefinite than loss. Something gnawed at his brain and wouldn't go away.

May 31, 0600 hours
the Namibian desert

Sam woke first. He sat up and rubbed his eyes. Jack's steady breathing sounded calm, and he felt better knowing that his friend had found some peace in his sleep. Sam picked up his boots and looked inside. He turned them, one at a time, upside down and thumped them against the cot to knock out any small critters that may have taken up temporary residence inside. When he finished, he pulled the boots on and walked out of the tent.

The little black flag that had been in the road was now tied to the Land Rover and a piece of paper had been stuck under the windshield wiper.

"Jack!" Sam called out. "Come on, big dude! Sun's up!" He waited, leaning on the Rover for Jack to stumble into the morning light.

Squinting against the morning sun, Jack emerged from the tent. Together, they went through the campsite. The wood Jack hadn't burned had been taken. The empty cans they'd eaten from were gone. When Jack unfolded the paper from the windshield, it was another map. This time it marked a cross-country trek, starting with the campsite then going up the face of a mountain. Jack folded the paper and put it in his pocket.

"Well?" Sam asked.

"Let's advise Washington we're going to be on foot."

After confirming the plans with General Krauss the two men sat down. In silence, Sam heated two cans of hash while Jack filled their water canteens. Each man would carry a small pack that would enable them to survive several days if needed. Jack decided to add a satellite phone to his pack. Each of them packed energy bars for lunch and extra ammunition for their sidearms. And then they started walking.

Several times Jack stopped to check the map. What had appeared crude at first soon revealed itself to be a highly accurate, though somewhat stylized, map. At midmorning they reached the first flag. Another map was pinned to it. The directions led the two men up the mountain and, if the map was to be believed, to a hidden cave. The climb to the mouth of the cave, according to the map, should take another hour. But, when they reached what they had both figured to be the mouth of the cave, it wasn't there. They looked around, poking at bushes and rocks but didn't find it. Frustrated, they sat down on some rocks.

"Now what?" Sam asked.

"How the hell am I supposed to know?"

"Call home. You can bet they're watching us with satellites."

"Yeah, well, they can watch all they want. It ain't helping us find squat," Jack said. Then he stood up looked round. "Where the hell is it?" He kicked a rock off the mountain and it bounced once before it stopped against large boulder. Jack walked toward the boulder, stopped

near it and turned around to look back at where Sam
was standing.

"It's right there, Sam."

"Where?"

"Get down on your knees and look up."

Sam saw a large rock outcropping. But he didn't see
a cave entrance.

Jack hurried back. Standing beside Sam, he reached
out, grabbed the rock outcropping, and pulled. It fell
apart in his hands in a cloud of dust. They could see a
small, blackened portion of what must be the cave's entrance. The men pulled away the rest of the rocks and
dirt from the mouth of the cave. When the opening was
large enough for them to crawl through, they took small
flashlights from their packs and went inside. At first there
was only a small passage, leading slightly downhill. They
cautiously crawled along the passage.

"Jack?" Sam broke the eerie silence of the cave.
"Aren't you curious as to why two TALON troopers are
doing this?"

"Yeah, Sam. I thought about it, too. But until someone
gives us an order to stop following Moses's scavenger
hunt, I'm going to stay the course."

"Right," Sam said. A second later he heard Jack suck
in a lungful of air.

"I'll be damned," Jack said. "Look at this."

Sam heard the awe in Jack's voice and crawled up
alongside the big Marine.

Jack washed the beam of his flashlight over the wall
in front of them. Sam followed his lead and then he, too,
gasped. The cavern was huge, perhaps as much as fifty
yards across and twice as high. The floor was right below
them and Sam started to crawl onto it. Jack pulled him
back.

"What'd you see?" Sam asked.

"Nothing," Jack said. "But look at the floor of the
place."

Sam looked. The floor was covered in powdery-fine dirt. A trail of smallish footprints had been left on the cave floor. "Looks like someone has been here."

"No," Jack said, "I don't think so. I think those footprints are old. Real old. Look at the walls."

Sam looked at the walls of the cavern. It was covered with drawings of men and animals, sailing ships and more men.

"You know what this is, Jack?"

"It's the history of the San. These people have been coming here for generations and doing their art work, recording the history of their people by carving it into the walls of this cavern."

"You think we'll be part of that?"

Jack began pushing himself back. "We are now."

Outside there was another flag. A piece of paper weighted down with a rock was under the flag. A careful drawing of the Land Rover was on the paper.

"Guess it's time to go back," Sam said. "Shall we wall this up?"

"No," Jack said. "I think they'll do it. Let's go."

They reached the Land Rover in early afternoon. Another flag was tied to the Rover and after lunch they packed their gear, loaded it, and started following the new map. Through the afternoon they were led on a trip around the western desert country. They drove along the Skeleton Coast, stopping at various flags where they saw more rock drawings or a hidden mound of bones. By the time the day was nearing its end, they had driven hundreds of miles but never once had they seen their bushman, or any other bushmen, for that matter. They finally found a black flag on a narrow track a few miles from the Okaukuejo entrance to the Etosha National Park. After setting up another camp they warmed their dinner and built a fire with the wood that had been left for them. In the quiet of the night Sam asked Jack what he thought the purpose of the day had been.

"I just don't know," Jack said. "This crazy little dude is leading us on a chase all over the country, leaving us maps and flags and crap where he wants us to be. And all the while, he's carrying around enough of that cow bug to kill half the cattle here."

"There's a reason," Sam said.

"Yeah," Jack said, "I'm sure there must be some sort of reason for this nonsense." He looked around. They could hear the noise of tens of thousands of flamingos on the Etosha Pan.

"Tomorrow," Jack said, "we're going to put an end to this shit. I'm going to bed."

Alone, Sam sat beside the fire, feeding the small supply of sticks to it until the last one burned. When the fire had burned down to coals, he climbed to his feet and went to bed. Sam had never been so confused.

June 1, 0630 hours
near the Etosha Pan

In the morning there was another note on the Land Rover. "Get your maps," Jack said, looking at the hand-drawn map. "We're going to a place called Okakarafa."

A few minutes later Sam had the GPS system on the Land Rover's hood and had pinpointed their destination. "It'll take three hours to get there," Sam said.

Jack nodded. "Today, we end this thing."

Sam agreed. Within minutes they had checked in with Washington, loaded their gear, and were driving across the sandy bush country of Namibia. Jack drove silently, concentrating on the road. Whatever was driving Jack was something that he refused to share with Sam. Every time Sam tried to engage Jack in conversation, he'd mumble that he was thinking about something and wanted to be left alone.

After leaving the B2 and turning onto the gravel-paved C22, Jack slowed the Land Rover.

Sam thought he was looking for something but Jack refused to tell him what.

"There it is," Jack said, smiling. He slowed and turned onto a narrow road that led to a hunting lodge.

"What's this place?" Sam asked.

"Where Moses is hiding."

"How'd you know?"

Jack didn't answer. He stopped the Land Rover in front of a whitewashed lodge. The thatched roof was baked a silvery brown by the Namibian sun. A tall white man emerged from the office and stood in the shade of the porch, his arms folded. Jack walked toward him, Sam behind Jack.

"You know Benjamin Moses?" Jack asked.

The man nodded. "Many years I've known him, his family."

"He's here, isn't he?"

The man nodded again, then said, "Somewhere out there in Herero Land but I don't know where."

"You have an idea where to start though, don't you?"

"Yes, of course. I'll get you a map. One that we use. It has the tracks that don't appear on other maps." He looked at Sam and Jack. "You might as well have something cold before you go into the bush. It might be a while before you find him."

Sam and Jack followed the man into the lodge and he directed them to a large sitting room. The room was filled with hunting trophies and pictures of hunters with the animals they'd killed. It was the kind of room where men who had money to spend would sit and sip sherry, talk about their investments and their affairs with women who weren't their wives. Sam sat down in an overstuffed leather chair. The rich, brown leather felt cool and smooth after their long days in the African sun.

Jack walked around the room, staring at each photograph. When the owner returned, carrying a tray of drinks, he set them on the table in front of Sam and then went to stand beside Jack, who was staring at an older black-and-white photograph.

"That's him, isn't it?" Jack said.

"Yes, before the war."

Sam started to get up and join them but Jack signaled for him to stay seated.

"He worked for you?"

"Off and on. Mostly to guide us on hunts, such as this one. That was my father. We had a lion on the ranch that was causing quite a problem. Moses helped us track him down. Quite a tracker."

"You were friends with him?"

"Grew up with him."

"Boyhood friends?"

"Of course."

"You wouldn't let anything happen to him, would you?"

"No."

"Then why the chase? Give him time to get away?"

The man smiled. "The least I could do for my friend."

"Why?"

"No war is really over until the hate ends. And the hate hasn't ended. Not here, not any place. Moses thought that if he took a vial he could force some of the ranchers who still want to push the San off the land to listen to them, give them room to live."

"It didn't work."

"No," the man said. "All it has done is create more tension, more distrust, but Moses is a proud man and he must play out his role."

Jack turned to look at another picture. Several white men were standing behind a pile of human bodies—all black.

"And this one?"

"A bushman hunt."

Jack looked at the white man.

"Years ago, it was common practice for the whites, and some of the blacks, to go on hunting parties to flush out the San people and kill them. They were thought to be a higher ape, or monkey, if you will. Take a look at them. So small, they don't look like the rest of the blacks. Everyone hunted them, killed them. They were killed in war. They were killed for sport." He pointed to another picture frame.

It held a document and Jack leaned over to read it. "This shit for real?"

The man nodded. "Not one of mankind's greater moments, is it?"

Jack read it again. "A license granting the bearer the right to kill bushmen on his property."

"A hunting license for humans," the man said. "It belonged to my grandfather. When he died and my father took over the estate, he put a stop to it and allowed the San to live on the land we controlled. Of course it took a long time for them to trust us and when the war started, my family was in great danger. But it was Moses, and the fact that he is half Herero, that saved us. He stood between my parents and the AKs of Sam Nujoma's guerrillas."

The man paused, letting what he told the Americans sink in. He stepped closer to the wall and examined the license. "On that piece of paper is the blood of Moses's grandparents, great-aunts, uncles, second cousins. A whole generation of bush people, destroyed."

Jack stared at the framed document. "Why do you keep it here?"

"A reminder of the way things should never be."

After looking at the license a little longer Jack went to the table and picked up a drink. He sat down. "Who is Major Sheidley?"

"My brother-in-law."

Jack didn't respond at first then said, "Different sides in the war?"

"Yes, but he's loyal to Namibia. It's been a very hard lesson for all of us."

"I've got to get that vial," Jack said.

"Yes, yes you must go after him . . ."

"Mr. . . ." Jack hesitated.

"Humes," the thin man said.

Jack nodded. "Mr. Humes, I don't want to hurt him."

"I'm glad of that," Humes said. "He's a good man. He wanted to put an end to something that needs to be ended."

For half an hour, Humes told Jack and Sam everything he could that would help them find Moses. After he finished he led Sam outside while Jack went to the bathroom.

Soon, Jack joined them outside. He shook hands with Humes.

"I assume you have everything you need," Humes said.

"Yes, sir," Jack said, "we've got what we need."

Humes pointed to the towering Waterberg Plateau. "You'll see the road to the Waterberg cutting off this road. Go past it about a kilometer. On your right you'll see another track. It'll appear to go nowhere but turn off onto it and you'll be headed into the heart of Herero Land. There's not much there but somewhere out there is where Moses is waiting for you."

"Thank you, sir," Jack said; then he opened the door to the Land Rover. He leaned out the window. "One question, sir."

"What's that?"

"All the little diversions. Yours?"

"Oh no, that was the San people at work. Did they show you the cavern?"

"Yes," Jack said.

Humes smiled. "I remember when Moses took me

there. He showed me the history of his people, all on
the walls of the cavern."

"We didn't walk on the floor," Jack said.

"That's good," Humes said, then leaned forward. "Did
you notice, Captain, the cavern still has a lot of room."

"Yes, there is room."

"More history, wouldn't you say?"

Jack nodded.

"Perhaps, Captain, someday a San will paint your visit
on the rocks."

Jack didn't answer but put the Land Rover in gear
and drove toward the road.

Sam waited until Jack was on the highway. He waited
until Jack seemed to be comfortable and then asked him
what the disjointed conversation had been about.

"Sam, my friend," Jack said, "now I know where to
find our Mr. Moses."

"Where?"

"At the end of that road. He'll let us find him. We
may have to walk a few miles in the sun, but Benjamin
Moses is leading us to him."

Sam leaned back in the seat.

"How did you know about the lodge?" Sam asked.

Jack laughed for the first time since arriving in Namibia. "It was an accident. When you drew that line to connect up all the places we were led to, they formed an
arrow that pointed to the Waterberg Plateau. There is a
straight line from where we camped at Etosha, to the
Etosha/Waterberg lodge. If we hadn't figured it out we'd
of been led there sooner or later."

"Just like you said, we've got rings in our noses."

Ten minutes later Jack turned off the road onto the
track. At first the track was easy to follow, and they
made good time. After the third dry wash, the track became twin ruts across the desert. They were still able to
follow the path, but the going became increasingly difficult with each dry wash they crossed. When the track

finally faded to nothing, Jack turned off the engine and sat still, looking at the seemingly endless desert.

"Well, buddy," Jack said. "Let's see if our Moses has left his footprints in the wilderness."

Walking in a circle around the Land Rover, Sam picked up the bushman's tracks.

Jack confirmed them and they returned to the four-wheel-drive vehicle. "This time, we're going to meet Moses, and not do some sightseeing," Jack said. He struggled into the Low Observable Camouflage Suite with bio-sensors, then pulled on his pack. Lastly, he put on the pistol belt with the .45.

"Think we'll need guns?" Sam asked.

"Let's put it this way. We have a mission to finish. The United States government has promised the world's powers that we will get the last of that virus and return it to the States. We're going to do that and if someone gets in our way, we'll have to do what is necessary to finish our mission."

"Sounds good to me," Sam said, then asked if Jack wanted the camouflage suits turned on.

"No, let's save the battery juice until we need it."

Sam found Jack's new determination refreshing. Whatever had been bothering the big man seemed to be gone. After Sam finished strapping on his own gear the two men set out, following the footsteps of Benjamin Moses into the bush of Namibia. With each step they took the lifeline connection to the world they called home became more distant. After two hours of walking, following the bushman's footprints across the sand and around the rocks, they stopped to rest. Sam put his pack in the shade of a large boulder. Jack sat across from him in what shade he could find. They sat like that for ten minutes, comfortable in their reliance on each other and secure in their belief that no harm would come to them. When the little arrow, less than two feet long, sailed silently across the clearing and stuck in Jack's leg, the surprise was complete. The tiny arrow moved slowly, but from the needle point to the near paper-thin edges of the broadhead it slipped between the fibers that were designed to stop something much larger and faster. Jack grabbed at the arrow stuck in his thigh. Teeth clenched together, sweat beading on his brow and rolling down his face, he started to pull the short shaft of the arrow out and then fell back in agony. The pain was excruciating and he rolled onto his side. The bio-sensors seemed to be going haywire.

Sam crouched next to Jack, looking for the source of the attack.

Jack gulped loudly, pulling deep breaths into his lungs. Finally, he stopped struggling and rolled onto his back. "Sam," he said, "I can't move my legs. They've stuck me with some sort of poison . . . I can't move."

"But it won't kill you, Captain," a voice said. "It will only keep you there for about twenty hours. You can't really do anything. Not even crawl around. I suggest you just make yourself comfortable."

Sam tensed, still crouching in the middle of the clearing and next to Jack, his Baretta in both hands. He couldn't see the bushman.

"Captain Wong, you should really put your gun down. I am not going to kill you but if you keep pointing it at me, I will give you an arrow as well."

Sam looked at Jack lying flat on his back. Perhaps Moses would let him call for a medevac. He put his gun down and backed away from it.

"That's better," the voice said.

"Mr. Moses?" Sam asked.

"That would be me," the voice said, then the small bushman appeared on top of a rock ten feet from the Americans. "And I would say that I've bagged two prisoners."

Chapter 11

Sam pushed the gun toward Moses. The heat of the afternoon sun had already baked the sand hard. Scooting the
gun across the ground, his hand stung as if it were on
the tray of a warming oven. Satisfied that the pistol had
been moved far enough out of his grasp, Sam scuttled
backward a few steps toward the now-paralyzed Jack.

"That was very good," Moses said, jumping down from
the rock he'd been perched on.

Sam recognized the smallish man he'd tackled at the
airport. He wasn't sure what he expected Moses to be
wearing now but the bushman looked pretty much like
anyone else. He wore khaki pants and a faded blue
T-shirt. A small quiver of arrows hung across his back
and in his hands he carried a traditional bushman's bow.
He had nocked an arrow and it was ready for use. The
point of the arrowhead, a barbless broadhead, had been
made from thin metal. Something glistened on the honed
tip. Moses looked down at Jack and smiled.

"I hated to stick you with that arrow, Captain," Moses
said. "But you are a very big man and you appear to me
as the sort who can be rather violent. Frankly, I didn't
want to really hurt you."

Jack glared at the bushman.

"You will be able to speak in another few hours, but

it will be twenty hours or more before you will be able to move, let alone walk." He examined the arrowhead and grinned at Jack. "Very good nerve agent, wouldn't you say?"

Jack nodded weakly.

Moses turned to Sam. "The worst part is that if a person panics and tries to fight the effects . . . well"— he shrugged—"then it can kill them. The best thing to do is to just lie there and wait it out. Of course, we'll be here to keep the jackals and hyenas from getting at Captain DuBois."

"What do you want, Mr. Moses?"

"What do I want? Well, that is a fair question. Sometimes it is not so easily answered. You see, I didn't have a plan when I copped the virus. I really didn't know for sure what it was until I put the cattle killings together with the raids on the Boer farms." He wrinkled his forehead in thought. The sun-dried skin looked aged and tired. "That was more damage in one day than my unit did in the entire war. You guys are really very well equipped."

"Answer the question," Sam said.

Moses's eyes crackled when he looked at Sam. "Don't presume to command me," he snapped. "I've had all the commands and demands that I will ever need from anyone. I have been commanded by my government to put aside the things I heard and saw and suffered. I have been commanded to be at peace with my enemy. I have been commanded by the whites to cut their crops, plow their fields, water their gardens, mix their drinks, and carry their baggage. So, don't command me. Do not command me to do shit!"

Sam's eyes were round by the time Moses finished. He nodded. "Okay, but will you please answer the question and tell me what it is you want?"

"I will have to think about it."

"Well, how about this," Sam said. "You give me the

vial, I'll call my government, get a medevac out here, and we'll get Captain DuBois to a hospital where he can be treated. You can go off into the desert and do whatever it is you do."

"I do not like that idea," Moses said. "But I am intrigued by the idea of you being able to call your government. I assume you will use a satellite phone."

Sam nodded.

"Well, I am not ready to give you the vial, and when I decide what it is that I want and of how to state my demands, then we will call your government."

Sam shifted his weight on the balls of his feet and looked around the small area they were in. Boulders surrounded them. Other bushmen could be waiting beyond the rocks, ready to cut him down if he did anything. He'd have to be careful, but he had to get the vial and get Jack out of the desert. Sam noticed the beads of sweat on Jack's forehead and upper lip. He reached over to wipe them off.

"I'm going to give him a drink," Sam said. Moses didn't answer. When Sam raised Jack's head and lifted the canteen to his lips he whispered that he was developing a plan. Jack's eyes widened slightly and Sam read that as approval. He poured a little water into the palm of his hand and dabbed it on Jack's face to cool him off, then took a drink himself. Turning around, he offered Moses a drink. The bushman shook his head and walked back to the shade of the boulder and scrambled up the side. The Baretta was gone.

"Do you know the story of the San people?" Moses asked.

"Some. I read a bit and listened to Mr. Humes talk about it."

"Humes is a good man, a brother with light skin. His grandfather, however, was one of the men who tried to kill us."

"He killed your family, didn't he?"

"Yes, most of them. We have rebuilt our family but the blood isn't pure. My blood is mixed but my heart is all San." Moses slid down the boulder, his back to the rock, the bow still in his hand. "You can understand that, I think."

Sam nodded. "You speak English so well. Refined, almost. Why? How?"

Moses laughed. "I am a bushman, a poor black African tribal man, only a little better than an animal—is that right?"

"I didn't say that."

"No," Moses said, "you did not say that but your culture makes you think it. I speak four white languages: English, German, Spanish, Afrikaans and, of course, my own languages and several dialects. But that is not so unusual. A lot of black African people speak more than one language. It is the way we learned to survive in the white world."

Sam was frustrated. "Look, I've asked you what you want. Tell me what to do and I'll use the satellite phone to contact Washington, see what options we have."

Moses was obviously thinking the offer over.

Sam's hopes rose.

Finally, after what seemed like minutes, but was only seconds, he raised his eyes and looked hard at Sam. "The Boers wanted their own country. They wanted Zimbabwe returned to them, didn't they?"

"Yes."

"Well, I want the same thing."

"You want your own country?!"

Moses laughed with rolling, full guffaws.

Sam couldn't resist joining the bushman's laughter despite his anger.

"Not my country! I want you to give the Boers *their* own country. Go ahead and carve out a little of Zimbabwe, a chunk of South Africa, maybe some of Zambia. Give it to them. Let them have their own country. All the crazy Boers who think that blacks are animals, call us monkeys, the Boers who want us to work in their homes and perform like pet dogs for their parties—let them have their own country. That way we will always know where they are. We will even call it Boerland."

When he finished outlining his request, Moses started laughing again and repeated the name, "Boerland" several times, making plays on the word. "Boering land, Wood Boer land. The land of Boering people!" His laughter finally played out, he nodded at Sam. "Yes, that is my request. If your government wants this vial returned then that is what they must do." Moses looked at Jack. "What do you say, my immobile Captain? Boerland for the Boers?"

"Are you finished, Mr. Moses?"

"Huh?" Moses mumbled looking back at Sam. "Oh yes, make your call."

Sam moved slowly to the packs and carefully began to rummage through both. While ostensibly looking for parts to the satellite phone, he hoped to find a weapon. Sam removed the satellite phone. Although it could be used as a very high-quality speakerphone he made sure the speaker function was turned off. He placed the phone in the sand and adjusted the pop-up antenna so it pointed directly overhead. He knew that Washington had been tracking them through their sensor chip implants and that Jack's biochips had been sending out panic alarms about his paralysis. Hell, Washington had probably watched the entire episode, wondering what was going on.

Sam finished setting up the phone and picked up the handset. Turning on the power he listened to the phone scan for a satellite, pick it up, lock on, and begin sending a signal. The time between the signal starting and General Krauss's controlled, calm voice announcing that Washington was on-line couldn't have been more than a few seconds. Sam's heart pounded with the fear that the plan would fail.

"Sir," Sam said, trying to control his own voice, "this is Captain Wong."

"Situation report!"

"Yes, sir, Captain DuBois has taken a hit from an arrow tipped with some sort of paralyzing agent. According to Mr. Moses, the effect will wear off in approximately twenty hours with no side effects."

"We've monitored his condition and unfortunately there is nothing his health sensors or health pack can do for him. Keep him calm and relaxed. We're monitoring here. Before we update you on the situation from this end, please advise your position."

"Yes, sir," Sam said. "My situation is that Mr. Moses has another one of those arrows pointed at me. He also has the vial with him." Sam stopped for a few seconds and looked at Moses. Now Sam had to be careful and frame his comments so General Krauss would understand him, and Moses would not suspect he was being set up. "Mr. Moses has made some demands that are consistent with the situation. I cannot talk him out of them or into giving me the vial and letting me go at this time."

Sam heard some mumbling on the receiver end and before Krauss could respond, he said, "You want to speak to Mr. Moses personally, sir?"

"I didn't ask . . ." Krauss said.

Sam heard the general take a sharp breath and say, "Sam, you need to know . . ." But Sam couldn't wait for the general to talk him out of taking action. Moses would be vulnerable while holding the handset.

"Yes, sir, he's only a few feet from me. I can give him the phone."

"Sam, don't!"

"I'll give him the handset, sir." Sam started moving toward Moses.

At first Moses started to stand up and step back, still holding the bow and arrow pointed toward Sam.

But Sam had guessed that Benjamin Moses had developed an ego with his success in escaping from South Africa, capturing the two of them, and the adulation he seemed to enjoy as a bushman hero of the SWAPO wars.

Moses took his hand from the bow and reached for the phone handset. Sam raised to his toes as he squatted, coiling the muscles in his calves and thighs for the strike like a cobra. He gauged the distance to the poisoned arrow tip, still pointed at him, and Benjamin Moses's face. When Moses's hand was ready to close on the phone Sam lunged. His first move was to whip the cord connecting the handset to the base around Moses's hand. He didn't need more than one wrap around the bushman's wrist to pull him off balance. At the same time, he sprung into Moses's face, bringing the top of his head into the bushman's chin. While he vaulted up and toward Moses, Sam brought his left arm up to block the arrow pointed at him.

The bow and arrow flew from Moses's hand and he tried to sidestep Sam's assault, but, instead, he toppled off balance, jerked by the phone cord around his left wrist.

Sam's head smashed into the bushman's face. Sam felt the warm spurt of blood gush from the injured man's nose and mouth.

Moses moved to his right, toward the bow.

Sam altered the angle of his attack and pushed Moses backward, to the bushman's left, keeping him off balance so as he fell, his left hand would still be tangled in the phone.

Moses fell, his left hand pinned beneath him.

Sam grabbed his immediate opportunity and smashed his right hand into the bushman's face, adding more confusion to the fracas, not giving Moses the time to respond and counter the moves. After his fist collided with the bushman's face, Sam rolled to his left, over the bushman's free arm, pinning that arm to the ground. Sam grabbed the phone and wrapped the cord twice more around the bushman's wrist then released the phone. He fumbled for the small shoulder bag that Moses had carried around. Ripping it open Sam saw the vial. He reached for it. He didn't see Moses flex his left arm and swing. The phone swung loose at Sam's head. The blow missed but the momentum carried Moses's fist past Sam's head. The wildly swinging phone caught Sam's hand and knocked the vial free.

Sam watched the vial, filled with the milky-white gel that was home to the virus until it was mixed with a bit of water and sprayed into the air to seek its bovine prey. The vial tumbled end over end as it sailed away from him. It should have landed softly in the sand. There, it would become another piece of human flotsam on the desert's sea of grit. Instead, Sam watched it land on a small, partially buried rock. He heard the musical tinkle of shattering glass as the vial broke into three large pieces and rolled onto the sun-hardened gravel. The thick, milky liquid sunk into the ground.

"Shit!" Sam shrieked. "What the fuck is going to happen now?" He looked wildly around, his gaze settling on Moses's bleeding face. Although blood still trickled from his nose, Sam could read no more urgency in Moses's features—not even anger registered in the bushman's calm visage.

Sam had stopped him, taken away his only reason to fight. The resignation of defeat was in the bushman's startled face. The recognition of what he'd done sunk into Sam's mind and then he heard the frantic voice of General Krauss coming from the handset. Reaching for the phone, Sam gently unwound the cord from Moses's wrist, pulled himself into a sitting position, and, looking at the still wet sand around the rock, said, "Sam here."

"Sam! Don't touch that vial!"

He heard the frantic fear in the general's voice.

"Sir," Sam said slowly. "The vial is destroyed."

"How?"

"I tried to get it away from Mr. Moses, there was a scuffle and it was broken."

"Sam, did you spill any of the liquid on yourself, Moses, or Jack?"

"No, sir," Sam said, suddenly feeling a growing sense of panic. "No, sir, it spilled in the sand."

"Okay, Sam," the general said. "I want you to move away from the virus, get Moses away from where it spilled. Don't touch it. Make sure Jack is away from it."

"Sir, I . . ."

"Goddammit soldier, this a fucking order!" Krauss snapped. "And put that fucking handset down and switch on the speaker, I want that fucking Moses to hear this, too!"

"Yes, sir!"

Sam scooted back, away from the still-stunned Moses, who was lying on his back, fingering the injuries to his face. Before Moses could protest, Sam grabbed his arm and dragged him away from the vial, then switched the phone to speaker mode.

"You're on speaker, sir."

"Good, now listen carefully, all of you. I know Jack can't respond but I want you all to hear this, including you, Mr. Moses."

Moses turned and looked at Sam.

Sam saw the bewildered expression on the bushman's face.

"If you recall, with the last use of the virus in India, not all of the cattle died."

"Yes, sir."

"We didn't want to alarm anyone, and we were hoping the virus was dying but we needed to examine the dead and sick cattle. When the crisis was resolved we did just that. Sam, our researches have some very, very bad news."

"Sir?" Sam said.

"The virus wasn't dying, it was mutating." The general paused. "Sam, we've got some people from the Center for Disease Control in Atlanta here with us. I'll let them tell you what needs to be done and what is at stake."

"Yes, sir." Sam glanced at Moses. The bushman sat with his knees pulled beneath him, blood dripping from his nose. He, too, listened.

A new voice came over the speaker. "Captain Wong," the voice said gravely. "It is absolutely essential that you, and anyone with you, remain absolutely calm while we explain what has happened and what you must do."

"Yes, ma'am."

"Anthrax 515 has mutated. It no longer attacks only cattle. Now it attacks humans, too."

Sam didn't answer.

"We're working on a cure. Using computer models and advanced simulation, we're gaining ground. At this point, we don't know if we'll have time to find a cure for the Anita virus or even manufacture it. Are you with me so far?"

"Yes, ma'am," Sam said glumly.

"The Anita virus is incredibly tenacious. It can survive a lot but requires moisture to move. We don't know how long it will live but indications in India are that it was able to survive much longer in its mutated state. According to our satellite monitors the humidity where you are is zero. Two things, the dry air and the heat, contain the virus. However"—the woman's raspy voice began to crack, the strain apparent—even over the speaker—"as soon as the sun goes down, the humidity from the Atlantic will begin to move over the desert, reaching you about an hour after sundown. At that time the temperature will be low enough, and the humidity high enough, for the Anita virus to grow. It will become mobile on molecules of moisture in the night air."

"How dangerous is this virus?" Sam asked.

There was a pause then the voice continued. "We've

worked out a computer model of what will happen if the virus gets out of the desert. Everyone at Okakarafa would be dead within two hours of sundown. The virus, if it gets into a human host, will then be able to multiply and grow. As the first human host dies, they will be vomiting, sneezing, bleeding, and rubbing their eyes. More of the virus will get into the air, or, in the heat of the day, lie dormant until nightfall. Otjiwarongo would be gone about five hours later. There's enough host there to produce and spread the virus."

"Can't you evacuate, contain this area and come in and destroy it if it is dormant right now?"

"It's not that simple. It seems the mutated virus can live in virtually any mammal. That means it could live in a field mouse there in the desert. The mouse could give it to another. Eventually it would get into a town. The virus will now only kill humans. It's our DNA that leaves us without a defense. The difference between a human and an ape, for example, is enough for the virus to attack and kill a human but leave the ape virtually unaffected."

"What are my orders, sir?"

General Krauss came back on the connection. "Sam, there is a chance for you to kill the virus and get out of this mess."

"How's that, sir?"

"You've got to collect all the sand in a three-foot radius of where the vial broke. The CDC scientists say that if you do that, then you'll get all of the virus, anything that might have bounced into the air when the vial was broken. You've got to put all that sand in a shallow metal container and build a fire on, under, and around it. You must maintain that fire, a good fire, for six hours at a temperature of at least 400 degrees Fahrenheit throughout that time. That will kill the virus."

"What if we can't do that, why can't you just evacuate us?" A silence of several seconds followed his question.

"While you're keeping that fire going, we'll monitor

your bio-sensors," Krauss said. "If you've been exposed
and it hasn't infected you yet, there is a chance it will
tonight. If it infects you there is nothing we can do on
this end to save you."

"Sir," Sam said, "can you just give us the bottom
line?"

"Okay, Sam. You've got to get that fire going before
the sun goes down. You've got to keep it going. Even
as we speak, the Namibian and South African militaries
are sealing off an area—a one hundred mile radius from
your position. They're evacuating as many people as they
can. But Sam, if you fail . . ."

"Yes, sir?"

"We're going to monitor your fire. If it drops below
400 degrees for more than ten minutes, we're going to
have to take control of the situation."

"You mean napalm, sir?"

"No, Sam, not napalm. We need to ensure that there
is no chance for that virus to escape into the air, or for
it to be picked up by anything—even a field mouse . . .
No, Sam, nothing conventional. Do you see contrails in
the air?"

"Yes, sir," Sam said slowly.

"Those are our aircraft. The choice is between the few
dozen human lives in the desert and the entire human
race."

"Could it kill that many?"

"Sam," the general said, his voice weak from the emo-
tion. "If that virus breaks out, the estimate is that in ten
days, sixty percent of humanity will be lost. Thirty days
to total extinction."

The silence was the desert and the sun. Sam looked at
Moses, whose face was lost in his own thoughts. "Sir, if
we fail, how big an area will be scorched?"

"We will," Krauss said slowly, "vaporize every living
thing in that hundred mile radius. We must be absolutely
certain that nothing survives."

"Are you sure, sir?"

"Sam, if anything—even that one field mouse—is exposed to that mutated virus and escapes into the desert, then the human race is doomed. Do you understand?"

"Yes, sir," Sam said.

As if he could no longer contain himself, Moses stood up and approached the phone. "General," Moses said, "what were your people planning to do?"

"From what we know of Anthrax 515, it only killed cattle, Mr. Moses, not people."

"No General, it used to kill cattle, but you forgot something."

"What's that, Mr. Moses?"

"Nature has her own plan."

"Mistakes were made, Mr. Moses, by everyone."

"Yes, sir," Moses said, "by everyone."

Only Jack didn't speak. All he could do was lie in the shade of the deepening shadow of the boulder and watch.

Sam glanced at Jack, then said, "We'll do our best, sir." He turned off the phone.

Chapter 12

Sam turned away from Moses. He knelt next to Jack, took out his canteen, and gave the Marine a drink. He studied Jack's face and then looked across the desert. Their only hope of survival would be to get the Land Rover to their small clearing. Sam remembered the two-mile hike that he and Jack had taken. He could drive it here, park it close to Jack. He needed to use whatever he could from the Land Rover to build the fire, starting with its hood as a large baking dish for the contaminated sand.

Moses was irritating him, insisting that Sam couldn't make the run.

"I am supposed to trust you?" Sam said. "Based on past performance I think you want to take the Rover and shag ass out of here—put as much distance between you and this spot—which just happens to be ground zero—as you can."

"Maybe," Moses said, "you better trust me or we're all going to die."

"Why should I?"

Moses faced Sam, spreading his feet to strengthen his position. He folded his arms across his chest. "Remember those few dozen people in the desert who are going to die?"

"Yeah," Sam said. He frowned at the bushman. "What about them?"

"That is my family, the San people, out there."

Sam shrugged. "I'm going to trust you, Benjamin Moses. But if you don't come back—"

"There wouldn't be a damn thing you could do about it."

Sam flushed with anger. He wanted to yell at the bushman, tell him that he should feel the same guilt that he, himself, felt. Instead, he reached into Jack's pocket and took the keys to the Land Rover from it. He tossed the jangling ring to Moses. "Here's fate in your hands," Sam snarled.

The bushman nodded and without answering turned and trotted out of the circle of boulders. Sam watched the little man disappear over the horizon. Turning back to Jack, who was lying motionless in the shadows, Sam said, "We have a fighting chance to see tomorrow, or we're going to be dead in a few hours." He shook the canteen, gave Jack another drink then took a long swallow himself. He stared at the now dried spot in the sand, trying to visualize the virus in the grains. "Look at that sand, big guy. All those little 'bugs' are waiting, lying there, dormant. Hard to believe that virus is harmless right now. Think about it. Even dormant, the Anita virus is waiting. It's not moving, but with every minute it comes closer to life—to lashing out." Sam's eyes glazed over, imagining the potential horror that lay ahead. "Think about it, Jack. It'll move into the night and begin its rampage against the human race. How bizarre . . ." His voice trailed off. "It's going to wipe out the race who created it—gave it life." He shuddered. A tale from his mother's kitchen flashed in his mind. "My mother has a saying. She says, 'When you shiver in the sun a ghost is waiting on your grave.' You know, big guy, sure hope she's full of shit!"

Sam had nothing to do but wait. He leaned against

one of the weather-smoothed stones and closed his eyes. The image of the virus cluttered his mind. Tiny bugs that he couldn't see, that he would never feel crawling over his skin, lurked only a few yards away inside a circle of boulders. He thought of Moses. The bushman, an hour earlier, could have—no—would have killed them for the vial. And now the fate of the human race lay in the small man's hands. Sam refused to look at his watch or to think about the time. He knew that Washington was watching, tracking Moses. If he didn't return with the Land Rover, they knew Sam would have no real chance to kill the virus and the strike would be ordered.

Sam didn't want to know. He resigned himself to the unknown. Minutes stretched, piling on top of each other, and Sam began to lose himself in thoughts of what might have been. He thought of the friends he had, the friends he'd lost, the girlfriends he'd never had time to make. He thought of his immigrant family back in Queens, New York—of all places. He thought of the life he'd lived, the choices he'd made. He drifted in time and started when he heard the sound of a motor in the desert. A few minutes later the Land Rover came to lurching stop, with dust settling around it. Moses jumped out and slammed the door. Sam watched him and for the first time, let himself smile.

"I was about to give up on you," Sam said.

"Hey, there isn't a road to this place."

Sam nodded. "Let's get started."

The two men rummaged through the Land Rover for tools. Underneath all of the remaining gear in the back, Sam found a small toolbox. Moses opened the hood and together, they studied the hinges.

"We need a wrench," Sam said.

Moses grinned and waved a large adjustable wrench at Sam. "This and a little muscle will do it."

He went to the front of the Land Rover. Methodically, he loosened the heavy bolts of the hood's hinges. Side

by side, Moses and Sam worked for ten minutes to free
the hood. When it clattered to the ground, Sam dragged
it into the clearing in the boulders. He dropped it in the
sand then walked back to the Land Rover. He began to
work the straps that secured a shovel to the passenger
side of the truck. "Good thing you Africans are always
prepared when you go into the bush." He grinned weakly
at Moses.

The bushman nodded and went to the clearing. He
stood, waiting at the spot where the vial had shattered.

"The general said all of the sand in the three-foot
radius had to be dug up and put in the hood," Sam said.
He drew a circle around the rock and the shards of glass.

"The other thing we've got to do is make sure that we
don't touch a grain of that shit." With the shovel, he
began to scoop sand into the overturned hood of the
Land Rover. He dug in a circle, stretching so he didn't
step into the circle. Digging closer to the rock and the
broken vial, he turned and told Moses to start ripping
out the seats.

"We'll burn one of the two spare tires first, build up
the fire with the material from the seats then another
spare. After the seats, take the tires off. We'll burn them,
too. Anything on or in the Rover that'll burn, pull it
out."

Moses found a folding knife, a Gerber-Applegate, in
Jack's pack. He went to work on the seats and lining
while Sam finished digging up the sand.

When Sam finished he looked at the pile of combusti-
bles and spare tires that Moses had dragged into the
circle. "Okay, we'll pile this stuff on, but we don't wan
to touch the sand or knock any out of the hood."

"I will start taking off the tires," Moses said and re
turned to the Land Rover.

Sam picked up chunks of padding that had once beer
inside the Rover's seats and placed it carefully on th
contaminated sand. As he added each bit of padding an

pieces of cloth, rubber, carpet, anything that would burn, he had to remind himself that the virus was dormant in the heat and couldn't hurt him. When the pile was ready, he retrieved one of the petrol cans, opened it and poured a generous dose on the pile. He pulled a box of matches from his pocket. Before he lit the match, he thoughtfully fingered the olive-drab plastic box and reminded himself of their need for success. He removed a match, struck it on a rock, and tossed it onto the pile.

In a roaring "whoosh," the fumes of the gasoline burst into bright blue tongues of heat and then settled into a steady burn. Flames burned through the sand and licked at the rags. In seconds, they smoked and then flamed. Sam dipped other pieces of rag in the gas and then dropped them into the greedy fire.

When Moses walked back into the circle he was carrying a tire. He'd used the knife and a hatchet to cut it free of the wheel. Sam helped him put the mangled tire on the fire. The rubber began to burn and the thick smoke rolled across the desert. When Sam was sure the fire was burning firmly, he used the cell phone to contact Washington.

"We've got your fire on the monitors," Krauss said.

"Yes sir, can you tell me the temperature?"

"You're well above the four-hundred-degree minimum."

"Yes, sir," Sam said. "The battery on this phone is limited. I'll put it on standby. If we drop below temperature you'll have to let us know."

"Roger that," Krauss said. "How's Jack doing?"

"He's just lying there enjoying the fire."

"Yeah, well, we'll keep our eyes in the sky on you," Krauss said. "By the way, Sam, you do understand that if the fire falls below four hundred degrees for a period of ten minutes, we'll have no choice . . ."

"General Krauss, we're grown people here. We take on these missions because we want to. We know the risks. You do your job, we'll do ours."

"Roger, Sam."

Sam didn't respond. He broke the connection and put the phone on standby.

Moses walked over to the growing pile of what was burnable. "We've got five more tires to cut up," Moses said.

"I'll help," Sam said.

Sam piled more of the debris on the flames then went to help Moses dismantle the Rover. He stopped, shocked, when he saw it. The little bushman had torn the expensive vehicle apart. He watched as Moses pulled the wheel free to let it fall so it lay flat on the ground. He picked up the hatchet and hacked at the tire until the battered tire began to hiss as the air escaped. Working from the initial tear, he continued hacking, opening the gash until he was able to pry the mutilated steel-belted radial away from the wheel. Within two minutes of the first whack, the tire was free and Moses cut it into burnable chunks. He glanced at Sam.

"You want to carry that to the pile? I'll get the next one. Then I think we should drain the oil and soak some of the stuff we pull out of here."

"Yeah, yeah," Sam said. He went back to the fire with his load of rubber chunks.

Gradually, in less than an hour, Moses had stripped the Land Rover of everything combustible. He walked into the circle of firelight. The smoke, thick and choking, rolled into the night sky.

"This is not enough to last," Moses said. He turned around and looked Jack. "I am afraid, Captain, that I am the one who got you into this mess and now you could not escape if you wanted to."

He turned to Sam. "I'm going to leave you for a bit. There is nothing else to strip from the Rover. I am going to look for something to burn."

Sam nodded. He didn't believe the bushman, but he couldn't blame him for trying to save his own skin, and maybe the skins of his family. Maybe, Sam figured, there were some caves in the area. Maybe Moses was going to tell his family to take cover there, hoping they'd be safe from the nuclear holocaust that Sam now believed was inevitable. He watched the bushman walk out of the fire's light and into the darkness beyond the boulders.

When Moses disappeared, Sam sat down beside Jack. "We're going to lose this, you know. I guess I made some mistakes. Shouldn't have gone for the vial, just disarmed him. Who knows?" Sam stopped talking and leaned back to watch the fire. "You know, Jack, this has been a good run. But, the way everything is burning I figure we've got about five hours before we run out of fuel. The fire will burn down. If we had some sort of pump we could pump gasoline on the fire, spray it on, maybe, by thickening it with some oil."

Jack could move his eyes. His jaw was starting to loosen up enough for him to mouth words.

Sam leaned over and tried to hear his friend's whisper.

"Trust," was the only word Jack managed to form.

Sam could see the effort the huge Marine was making to say something more. He leaned closer.

"Bushman."

"Yeah," Sam said sitting up. He climbed to his feet to add more debris to the fire. "Don't trust the bushman. Well, no need to worry about that. He's gone."

Sam piled more of the Land Rover's upholstery and pieces of tire onto the fire, arranging them so they covered the widest area of the sand, keeping the heat on the virus. He stood beside the fire. When he moved a few feet away, he felt the desert's night air. It was cool. And moist. "That's the death we're fighting," he murmured to the fire. "The moisture that cools the desert at night and gives life to what little lives here." He laughed. "How ironic. The humidity brings life to the desert but it is going to kill us."

The flames had started to die down and he went to

the fuel pile and picked up two more pieces of rubber, some scraps of cloth, and torn chunks of the ceiling liner. Most of it was gone. There would be only one more trip to the pile. He piled it on and went to the satellite phone, switched from standby to on, and waited for the connection to Washington.

"Krauss here."

"General, this is Sam."

"Yes, Sam?"

"What's your eye in the sky picking up?"

"Your bushman left. We lost him two hundred yards from your position. We're focused on you and the fire."

"Yes, sir," Sam said. "You picking up the health from the biochips?"

"Jack's improving. Three more hours and he'll be able to move around a bit and talk."

"General, we don't have three hours."

"What do you mean, son?"

"Sir, I've got enough debris left for one more trip to the pile then we've shot our wad."

There was a silence on the line. "We've thought about bringing you fuel to burn. Wood, dropping it a few hundred yards from your position. You could get it that way."

"Won't work, will it, sir?"

"Too much risk. If there's any virus in the air and someone picks it up . . . we've lost. Total containment is the only way and it's got to be the full six hours or we take it out."

"I understand, sir," Sam said. Then, slowly, he said what he'd opened the connection for. "Sir, I'm going to put the last of the burnables on the fire. You'll know when it goes on. Your eyes will pick it up. We'll let it burn, but that's all we've got. Everything else is gone. Moses hit the road, I'm sure to save himself—maybe his family. Jack and I know the score. When I break the connection, I'll put the rest of the fuel on. I'm going to sit with Jack. After that, sir, this is in your hands. Washington will know when the time's come to make the strike. No reason to drag this out any longer. You wait too long, something else could go wrong—hell—this mission has been cursed from day one. Maybe from before that. We don't need any more mistakes."

"You're right, son," Krauss said.

"Yes, sir. We've all got letters in case of loss in the operations safe. You'll take care of that for us?"

"I will."

"Fine." Sam paused. "Enough said."

"I understand," Krauss said.

"It's been a pleasure working with you," Sam said and broke the connection. He put the phone in its cradle and turned off the power. He walked over to the remaining rubble, scooped it up, and carried it to the fire. Carefully, piece by piece, he placed it in the flames, then stepped back. "Well, world, that is Sam Wong's last hurrah to humanity. A smoky fire made from car tires." He then sat back down beside Jack. "If we hadn't burned the sterno fuel," Sam said, "I'd fix us a last meal, but all we can do is wait."

He stared at the fire. "I wonder," he said slowly, "if we'll see the light or just hear the missile."

The fire burned and began to die. Flames flared briefly and then flattened into the sand. The coals glowed a heated red, still holding back the virus. Sam pulled his knees to his chest and watched the flames begin to flicker. In the distance, he heard the sound of aircraft. He doubted if it was a commercial airline. They would have all been diverted. He studied the sky. The smoke from the fire wasn't as bad and he could see the stars. These were stars in the Southern Hemisphere and he'd never really studied them before. The night was clear. He tried to see the reflected light of the satellite that would be passing overhead, the eyes that watched him before being passed off to the next satellite in the line.

Against the background of the night's noise, Sam heard the sound of the jet grow louder. The pilots, he knew, had to get close enough to mark the target, make sure ground zero would be taken out. He wondered how many nukes they planned to use. For a few seconds he tried to compute the square miles that would be turned into a radiation wasteland. And then, out of the African darkness, Moses's face appeared in the firelight. The bushman was back.

"Sorry I took so long," Moses said. "The San people are very good at hiding. They had to be to stay alive, avoid the hunting parties."

While Moses spoke, a progression of San men, women, and children walked into the circle of stones, dropped their precious collection of firewood, and moved on. Sam listened to the clicking sound of their strange language.

"Moses! Put the wood on the fire! Quick, build it up!" Sam said. He ran to the phone and turned on the power. As soon as the power was up, he activated it and waited for the connection to Washington to be established. When he heard Krauss's voice, Sam shouted, "Do you see them on your monitors?"

"Yes, we see them, Sam."

"They're bringing wood. I don't know where they're getting it in this Godforsaken desert, but they're bringing wood!"

"The fire is growing on our monitors."

"You bet it's growing, sir! They're feeding the fire!"

"Keep it going, Sam."

"Yes, sir!" Sam shouted then broke the connection and began helping Moses. They broke up the pieces of dry wood. "How much do they have?"

"They're bringing all they have," Moses said. "For as long as the stories of my people have been told, they have always saved the wood. To be sure they have a supply, they've learned to bury it in the sand, dig it up when they return to a place so they will have wood when they come back to it."

"You mean there is wood around here?"

"Yes," Moses said. "There is wood around us, but only the San who buried the wood will know where it is. Each San must get their supply and bring it."

The parade of San continued, most of them wearing a strange combination of cast-off Western clothes that had been shipped to Africa by missionaries or sold as rags. A few of the San wore more traditional clothes, hides that had been cured and softened and worn as clothes. Sam watched as the little people filed past, minute after minute. They brought small bundles of wood and dropped them at Moses's feet, then went back to the darkness. The pile of wood had grown substantially and Moses fed the sticks to the fire, circling it to make sure the coals and blazing wood from the bush covered all of the sand. Sam went back to Jack and sat down beside him.

"I told you," Jack whispered, "to trust the bushman."

Sam smiled at Jack. "Glad you can talk again. You sure that's what you said?"

Jack whispered, "Yes." He tried to smile but the effort to speak tired him and the muscles in his face went slack.

Sam helped Moses keep the fire going. Gradually the number of San people who came into the circle to drop their hoard of firewood slowed, then stopped. They now had an ample supply to burn. The men worked together, keeping the fire burning. Once, Sam looked to the horizon. The first light of dawn was breaking up the heavy darkness. Minutes later, he noticed the red light on the phone flashing. He scrambled to pick it up. Krauss's voice came over the line.

"You made it, Sam."

"Sir?"

"The experts here are saying you made it. For a while

there, we didn't think . . . but you did it. I suggest you keep the fire going until help arrives."

"Yes, sir," Sam said. Then, curious, he said, "Just how close did we come, sir?"

"The launch sequence had started when Moses and his people reappeared on our screens. We still weren't sure until we picked up the fire's temperature so we were on hold but locked on target."

"Yes, sir," Sam said. "What help is coming?"

"South African and Namibian hazardous waste units are en route to your position. No helicopters, we don't want to scatter any sand. We're still going to contain it."

"Transport for us as well?"

"You and Captain DuBois are going to have to live in a bubble for a few days until we are absolutely sure there is no contamination."

"What about the San?"

"The local government will keep them in the area until there is no chance of a break out. We couldn't find them if we wanted to."

"What do you mean, sir?"

"All those people who brought you wood?"

"Yes, sir."

"We can't find a one on an IR scanner. They walked out of our image area and disappeared."

Sam thought about the San disappearing for a few seconds then realized it was the best thing for them to do. "Yes, sir." He tried to think of something witty to say. Instead he said, "Out," and placed the phone in the cradle and went to stand beside Moses until the morning was full light. In the distance he heard the sound of approaching vehicles.

"It is time for me to go," Moses said. "I am sure the officials would like to talk with me. I don't trust them either."

"Do you trust me?" Sam asked.

"No," Moses said. "I don't, but you are the most trust

worthy of them, but he"—Moses pointed to Jack—"is the only one who really knows."

"Knows what?"

Benjamin Moses didn't answer but walked out of the clearing. Sam followed him, tried to see him, but Moses was already gone into the desert. Sam returned to Jack, who could now talk and move his arms.

"You did a good job," Jack said with effort.

"Thanks."

A few minutes later a convoy of a half-dozen vehicles stopped near the circle of boulders. Soldiers, fully dressed in chemical/biological suits, climbed from the vehicles. A few had guns and they set up a secure perimeter around the circle of boulders. Others came into the clearing and began their pre-assigned tasks. Two men walked over to Sam and Jack. Through the faceplate Sam recognized Major Sheidley.

"You had a rough night there for a bit but it's over now," he said. His voice was muffled by the faceplate. "Captain, we're going to place you in a plastic bubble and get you into the containment vehicle."

Jack nodded and waved Sam closer.

Sheidley was still talking. "We were all watching monitors, waiting to see if you could pull it off."

"It was the San people," Sam said. "They brought their wood to burn."

Sheidley nodded. "Can't understand those people sometimes." Then he looked around. "We're going to use those biohazard containers for the sand and coals of the fire. We've got another truck coming. We will sterilize this entire area, just in case." He put his hands on his hips and studied the boulders around them. "Wonder who in bloody hell rolled these boulders into this circle?" He turned around and signaled for the crew with the biological containment suits for Jack and Sam to hurry. The two men assigned to the fire let it burn down.

Sam watched the operation, impressed with the efficiency of the South African and Namibian soldiers. He felt Jack tug on his pant leg and bent over to hear what he wanted to tell him.

Jack held up a folded piece of yellowed paper. "Burn this," he mumbled.

Without moving toward the fire Sam unfolded the paper and looked at it. Jack had stolen the permit to hunt bushmen that had been in Humes's lodge. "This is a historical document," Sam said.

"Burn it . . . the fire," Jack said.

Without responding, Sam walked to the fire, wadded up the paper and dropped it on the hot coals. The paper unfolded slightly, browning at the edges, and then it turned black. It flattened completely, burning to ashes. Before it disintegrated, Sam read the fine type. He watched it burn. When it turned to blackened flakes, he turned back to Jack.

"What was that you burned?" Sheidley asked. "We need to decontaminate everything. What was that?"

Jack struggled, managing to raise himself slightly. He studied Major Sheidley in his containment suit. "It was just another virus, Major. We're still trying to kill it."

Sheidley looked from Jack to the fire.

Somehow, Sam thought, the major knew what had happened because without answering, he turned and walked to the edge of the circle and looked out over the desert, as if he were watching someone in the distance. He raised his arm in a salute.

Epilogue

Less than a month after they were released from the containment ward in Atlanta, Georgia, Sam and Jack went fishing. They were off the coast of Mazatlán, Mexico, on a boat, one of the several belonging to the Star Fishing Fleet. This was their fifth straight day of fishing and Jack sat in the fighting chair, holding a deeply bent rod against a fighting marlin.

They had spent most of the night discussing their future and the future of TALON Force. Jack didn't know if he wanted to stay a part of the unit. Sam wanted him to stay with the team. The mistakes in Operation Bovine had been analyzed, studied, and plans were made to insure they never happened again. But, Jack had still refused to commit. When the satellite phone buzzed, Sam hesitated before picking it up. He watched Jack fight the trophy fish, the kind of fish Jack said that he'd wanted to catch all of his life. The marlin struggled, now only a few yards behind the boat. Jack could finish the fight and tag the fish before letting it go if he would give it another ten minutes to tire.

"What do I tell them?" Sam asked.

Jack didn't answer.

Sam asked again.

Jack ignored him.

"They'll need an answer, Jack."

"That's a good fish out there," Jack said.

"It's a hell of a fish," Sam said.

"It sure is," Jack said, then he reached into the deck hand's bait bucket and picked up the bait knife. With deliberation, he cut the line. "You know what Von Heich told me, Sam?" Jack's voice took on a faraway quality. Without waiting for Sam to answer, he continued, "He said that he had furniture covered with the skin of my people—his favorite piece was a footstool." Sam's jaw dropped. He felt like he was going to be sick.

The marlin came out of the water and shook his head. Sam saw the lure spin from the marlin's mouth, the pressure that had been holding it there finally gone.

"Tell them," Jack said, smiling at Sam, "that Marine Captain Jack DuBois is ready to report for duty."

Sam nodded and picked up the handset, hearing the familiar electronic clicking as the connection was made. The clicking noise, so similar to the clicks made by the San in their strange language, reminded him of Benjamin Moses. No one had been able to find him in the vast desert of Namibia. As one American officer said, "His people have always been there. It's their desert."

Into the telephone, Sam said, "Captain DuBois is ready for duty, sir." He replaced the handset.

The boat turned toward the harbor and Sam knew the airline tickets would be waiting at the counter. *It is time* he thought, *to go back to work.*